The Day My
Husband
Left

BOOKS BY AMY MILLER

WARTIME BAKERY SERIES
Heartaches and Christmas Cakes
Wartime Brides and Wedding Cakes
Telegrams and Teacakes

They Call Me the Cat Lady

WRITING AS AMY BRATLEY
The Girls' Guide to Homemaking
The Saturday Supper Club
The Antenatal Group

The Day My Husband Left

AMY MILLER

bookouture

Published by Bookouture in 2021

An imprint of Storyfire Ltd.
Carmelite House
50 Victoria Embankment
London EC4Y 0DZ

www.bookouture.com

ISBN: 978-1-80019-073-3
eBook ISBN: 978-1-80019-072-6

For my mum, Anne Cook

The Bournemouth *Gazette*
Death Notice

EAGLE, Johnny, 54, of Southbourne-on-Sea, Bournemouth died suddenly on 12 April. Wonderful husband to Heidi and fantastic father of Scarlet and Zoe, Johnny will be desperately missed. A private cremation will be held and his life celebrated, always.

Chapter One

A week earlier

When Heidi Eagle felt worried, she hummed the theme tune to the TV show *Dallas*. In the year since her husband Johnny's heart attack, she had hummed the tune over and over again. And, that day in April, when Johnny had gone out without her, she was humming it again. The best thing she could do to stop worrying was shift her focus and work hard in the workshop, until her back ached and her fingers were sore. Dressed in her white upholstery apron and elbow-deep in fabric, twine and tacks, she was doing just that.

Immersed in stripping a wingback chair back to its wooden frame, Heidi distracted herself by thinking about what life would be like when her daughters, Scarlet and Zoe, left home. It wouldn't be long now before she and Johnny would be alone together, rattling around the house like marbles in a biscuit tin. A prospect that, a year ago, she thought might never happen.

She paused to take a deep breath, pushing away an ever-present bubble of anxiety, and was grateful for the arrival of a client, Annie Young, carrying a pink vintage cocktail chair that she'd booked in to be reupholstered.

'Let me help you carry that,' Heidi said, dusting off her hands. 'We could have collected this in our van.'

Together, they placed the chair down and Heidi ran a hand appreciatively over the chair's elegant fantailed back. She could see that the webbing had snapped, and the springs had fallen out of the bottom. Rather than having a plump seat, it was pancake flat.

'I thought I'd save you the bother,' Annie smiled, before turning her attention to the chair. 'It's lovely, isn't it? My husband bought it from a second-hand shop when we were furnishing our first ever apartment, years ago. We lived in London, and the singer Barry Manilow was staying in the property next door. One evening he popped by to borrow something and he sat on this chair. We've called it the "Barry Chair" ever since.'

Be it an Ercol armchair found in a vintage shop, a Victorian nursery chair passed down the generations of a family, or a set of mid-century dining-room chairs, Heidi loved the variety of furniture that came into the workshop. Things people loved and couldn't part with. Heidi knew, without hesitation, what item she couldn't part with: the brightly painted dancing-clown musical trinket box given to her on her seventeenth birthday. Wrapped in tissue paper, tied with string and locked in a rusty old money tin, it was hidden on top of the haberdashery unit in the corner of the workshop. Inside it was her heart's deepest secret.

'It'll be a pleasure to work on this,' said Heidi, locating a label, writing on Annie's name and the date before tying it onto one of the chair's legs.

'Thank you,' Annie said, peering over Heidi's shoulder, deeper into the workshop. 'What a great studio.'

Heidi smiled as she followed Annie's gaze to the rolls of upholstery fabric, in colours from eggshell to garnet, the tools on the fabric cutting table and the wingback chair stripped to its bones. Eagles Workshop was housed in a large outbuilding situated down one side of Johnny and Heidi's garden in Southbourne-on-Sea, a suburb of Bournemouth on Britain's south coast. The outbuilding, once a two-storey, old-fashioned garage, had been converted and extended for their small, family upholstery business. An open-plan space and with large windows, it was flooded with natural light.

Offering modern and traditional upholstery, Eagles worked with both domestic clients and on contracts with interior designers and joiners. The grand plan was to offer upholstery courses one day too, but until Johnny was one hundred per cent better, that was on hold.

'I'm not sure where I'd find another chair like this. We bought it forty-odd years ago,' Annie said. 'Makes me realise that we've been together *forever.*'

Heidi laughed gently and tucked her grey wavy hair behind her ears which were studded with blue button-shaped earrings – a gift from Johnny. They matched her signature blue denim work dungarees, which she wore with a grey jumper and black Dr Martens boots.

'You're lucky, really,' she said quietly, with a small smile. She and Johnny had been married for twenty-five years but together for a dozen more. Over the years they'd shared some highs and, also, some gut-wrenching lows. Johnny's heart attack a year ago had come like a bolt out of the blue, stopping them both in their tracks, and now, nothing felt certain.

'I suppose I am,' said Annie, as if she wasn't so sure. And Heidi had to remind herself that not everyone had been through what she and Johnny had been through. Not everyone felt a huge sense of relief every time their husband opened his eyes in the morning.

'It's still beating,' Johnny would say patiently, hand on his chest, smiling, when she asked after his heart.

'I better make a dash for it,' said Annie, glancing out the window at the rainclouds gathering overhead. 'Thank you again.'

The bright workshop was plunged into sudden gloom, sending a shiver up Heidi's spine. She showed Annie out and checked her watch, wondering why Johnny wasn't yet home. Chewing the inside of her cheek, she tasted blood.

'Don't start worrying,' she instructed herself, resisting the urge to call him. Earlier, when Johnny had left to catch the train to Poole to view a potential job at a client's home, he could hardly contain his excitement. He'd smiled at her with bright eyes, a single dimple on his left cheek. Dressed in his uniform of desert boots, utility trousers and a vintage khaki army jacket, he was thrilled to be getting out on his own again after a long recuperation. The last year had been tough and Johnny had gone through spells of feeling low. He'd fall silent for long periods or sit staring glumly at his phone. She'd suspected he was anxiously googling his health condition, but when she'd once asked him what he was looking at, he'd mumbled something about a surprise birthday present – she was going to be fifty-four in June. Johnny knew better than anyone that she didn't like to celebrate her birthday, but this year he said he was doing something special and that she wasn't to ask questions, or she'd spoil the surprise.

I don't like surprises, Heidi thought now, checking her watch again – and again – when Simone English, a woman Heidi had met at one of Johnny's numerous hospital appointments, came in. Simone's husband, Richard, had suffered a heart attack at the same time as Johnny and the women had kept in touch to compare notes. In one hand, Simone held a footstool with a cloud of horsehair billowing out of it. In the other, she had her poodle, Roxy, on a lead. Heidi welcomed them both.

'I spoke to Johnny about this, on the phone,' Simone said. 'Richard stood on it thinking it would take his weight! Johnny said you might be able to squeeze it in?'

The footstool was a lovely old thing. Small and round, with a blue velvet cushion (covered with dog hair) and finished with brass tacks, she guessed it to be from the 1930s. She ran her hands over the gently curved wooden feet.

'Of course,' Heidi smiled. 'How's Richard doing? Still eating his greens?'

'He's fine, but we do worry about him, don't we, Roxy?' Simone sighed, patting Roxy's head. 'Where's Johnny today?'

Heidi swallowed and checked her watch for the fourth time.

'He'll be back shortly, expecting applause,' she said, forcing levity. In truth, he was late. 'He's out on his own viewing a job, so he's in his element.'

She rolled her eyes and smiled conspiratorially. But mid-smile, her stomach turned over and she had a strange sensation in her scalp. As if someone was yanking her hair. She fell silent. Sudden torrential rain beat against the workshop windows, and the hairs on the back of her neck stood up as a feeling of absolute dread washed over her.

Simone continued to talk, but her words seemed slow and strange. All-consuming darkness crept into Heidi's heart when, in her mind's eye, she saw an image of Johnny's lifeless body. In that instant, she knew that her worst fear had been realised. Her darling Johnny had gone.

Chapter Two

After Johnny's first heart attack, Heidi felt utterly helpless. She didn't know what to do with all her worries, so she obsessed about Johnny's diet. Ordered a weekly organic fruit and vegetable box. Banned biscuits, burgers and beer. Cooked healthy meals from scratch and monitored his every mouthful. Food was something to focus on because, in truth, Johnny's heart attack had stunned everyone. They were used to him hauling around armchairs and sofas without breaking a sweat, and for the first few weeks after it happened, Heidi, Zoe and Scarlet watched his every move. Despite the awful shock and realisation that life can change at any moment, in time they tried hard to look on the bright side. It was a one-off, they told themselves; a warning. They had been given a second chance. Johnny insisted that he had been lucky and that, with a few tweaks to his lifestyle, he would be back on track. But though Heidi tried to be brave, every day she worried terribly that it would happen again.

'Johnny suffered a cardiac arrest caused by a heart attack,' the doctor at the hospital had told her. Apparently, he said, Johnny had died on Main Street in Poole at approximately 2 p.m. He had been on his way home.

I knew it, she wanted to say. *I felt it.* But she'd listened in silence, tears sliding from her eyes.

Now, back at home with Scarlet and Zoe, she felt bewildered and guilty somehow. As if, by dreading this happening, she had caused it.

'He seemed so much better,' Scarlet, Heidi's eldest daughter, said now, her eyes red with bemused tears. Her make-up – black eyeliner that flicked up at the edges in wings – was smudged and her normally pink cheeks drained of colour.

'I know,' Heidi said, sniffing. 'But the doctor said that the statistics show there's an increased risk of a second episode up to five years after the first.'

'We've only had a year…' Zoe, their youngest daughter, said in a faint voice, twisting her long auburn hair in her fist.

The three of them huddled together on the old dark-green leather Chesterfield sofa in the living room. Reupholstering it had been one of the first projects Heidi and Johnny had worked on together. The curtains were pulled. Zoe had lit the wood burner and Heidi had found blankets for them to wrap up in. A plate of toast sat untouched on the coffee table – none of them could eat. A lamp was on. It stood on an old glass-fronted cocktail unit which housed a collection of blue vintage Milk of Magnesia advertising bottles, a jug in the shape of a peach and a bundle of old Penguin books tied with lace. 'Junk-shop chic' Johnny liked to call Heidi's curations.

'I should have gone with him today,' said Heidi, staring into the flames. 'If I'd been there, I could have done something.'

'It's not your fault, Mum,' said Zoe. 'He didn't want to be wrapped up in cotton wool. Don't blame yourself.'

'I bet he overexerted himself,' she said, feeling another wave of tears rush into her eyes. 'I should have gone with him. I knew this would happen!'

Zoe held Heidi's hand and squeezed. Since coming home from hospital, the three women had moved around the house together as if attached by string. It had felt safer that way. They held hands in the hospital too, like a family paper chain, when a bereavement counsellor had spoken to them in a soft, kind voice about bereavement services and death certificates and funeral directors. The words were so upsetting that Heidi had had to break the chain and go outside to breathe in the fresh air – and Scarlet stepped in.

'He was fine this morning, eating muesli, happily chatting away,' started Heidi, registering the sound of a mobile phone coming from her bag. It was Johnny's phone, beeping to indicate low battery – she had been given it at the hospital, along with his watch, wallet and keys.

Bleary-eyed, she lifted the phone from her bag and typed in Johnny's pin. It had fifteen per cent battery remaining. She opened his text messages. The first one that flashed up was addressed to her, but it was in italics – indicating that it was unsent. There was a photo attachment. She frowned and tapped the screen and stared at the photo. It was a slightly blurred image of a busy street. She looked at it for a moment and recognised it as Main Street in Poole. There were people on the pavement holding umbrellas; a row of shops and a café – called the Blackbird. She remembered going there once for carrot cake.

She sat up straight. The message didn't say what time it had been composed, but she opened the photo gallery and found the photo. It had been taken at 1.54 p.m. Heidi's stomach cramped.

'What is it?' said Zoe, moving closer to look over Heidi's shoulder at the screen. Heidi trembled.

'I think Dad tried to send me this photo,' she said, her voice cracking. 'It was taken just before he—'

'Can I see it?' said Scarlet, peering over her other shoulder.

Heidi held out the phone so Scarlet and Zoe could see the photo.

'It's Main Street in Poole,' Heidi said. 'He would have walked this way back to the train station. He was coming home. I don't know why he'd take a photo.'

'Perhaps he didn't mean to take it,' said Zoe quietly. 'You know when you accidentally take a photo? He might have been holding the phone, trying to ring… for help… or something… or call you to say—'

Goodbye.

Zoe burst into tears, and Heidi put the phone down on her lap, feeling sick. Had Johnny been trying to call for help? They did have an emergency procedure planned between them. Any shortness of breath or pain – even a twinge – and either one of them would ring 999 immediately. Had he got confused? Had he known he was going to die? She sat there in shocked silence, listening to the crackle of the fire.

'I think you should delete it,' said Scarlet, taking the phone from Heidi's lap. 'It's too horrible to think that this is his last moment on earth.'

'No,' said Heidi, quickly taking the phone back from Scarlet. 'No, don't delete it. Leave it for now.'

Heidi slipped the phone into her pocket and sat stiffly back in the Chesterfield, putting her hands over her lips. She had to physically hold in her grief, because if she started to cry, she thought she'd never stop.

'Mum, don't worry,' said Zoe. 'You're not on your own and I won't be a burden.'

Zoe's fear was written across her face. Heidi swallowed and put her arm across her daughter's shoulders and kissed the side of her head. Zoe's use of the word *burden* had not escaped her. She'd had this irrational sense of wrongdoing her whole life.

'You could never be a burden,' Heidi said. 'How could you ever even think that? And I'll be alright. I'm made of strong stuff.'

A memory from years ago, when she'd felt too weak to even get out of bed, flitted into her mind. In truth, she could only think of how horribly alone and frightened she felt. The one person she wanted to turn to – Johnny – was gone. But the sight of her daughters, pale and stricken with worry and shock, broke her heart.

'We will get through this,' she said. 'Your dad would want us to get on with our lives. The future doesn't end here, tonight, even if it feels like it.'

Zoe and Scarlet rested their heads on each of Heidi's shoulders. Despite her speech, she couldn't see a future without Johnny. Their lives together had been cut brutally short. Her stomach cramped again as her eyes scanned the walls where photographs of their lives together were displayed. Sadness weighted her gut like a bag of cement, and she felt compelled to get up and do something. Anything.

'I'm just going to charge up your dad's phone,' she said, getting up from the Chesterfield. 'His charger's in his drawer in the workshop. I'll need to go through his contacts and everything.'

With Johnny's phone in her pocket, she went into the kitchen and stared at the packet of muesli on the shelf which Johnny always had for breakfast. He always cheered when a banana chip dropped into his bowl.

'Mum?' Zoe said. 'Do you want me to come with you? It'll be weird without Dad out there.'

Zoe's eyes shone out of her face like two blue moons. Heidi's heart twisted in her chest. Zoe adored her dad. They were such similar people; gentle, sweet, big-hearted. What she said was true – the workshop was Johnny's favourite place in the whole world.

'No,' Heidi said. 'Why don't you put more wood on the fire? I just want to sort a few things out. I need to find some paperwork. Our life insurance documents. There's Simone's footstool I need to work on.'

Zoe glanced at the wall clock. It was 9 p.m.

'Footstool?' she said worriedly.

She looked at her mother with big eyes, but Heidi gave her a small smile, pushed her feet into Johnny's trainers and opened the back door, treading a path of size-eleven footprints through pouring rain to the workshop.

Heidi opened the workshop door and turned on the light. Rain hammered noisily on the roof and windows. Despite the bright start to the day it had rained all afternoon, as if the clouds were mourning Johnny too. Heidi stared at Johnny's leather work apron hanging on a hook near her sewing machine, before stepping over Simone's blue velvet footstool that she'd abandoned in a panic. Poor Simone had wondered what on earth was going on when Heidi had hurried her out of the workshop earlier, with no explanation. She and Richard would be devastated by this news. She sighed, wondering if she'd ever be able to work again; continuing the business without Johnny seemed impossible. *Was* impossible. When he'd been ill before, she'd been unable to care for him *and* work. They'd had to close up for weeks until their friend Max came on board. Max would be heartbroken by Johnny's death. The thought of telling Johnny's friends and family, making the awful phone calls, made her feel utterly sick.

Locating his charger, Heidi plugged in Johnny's phone and had another look at the picture he'd taken, pinching the image to zoom in. Strangers on the pavement carried bags and umbrellas; there was a street lamp, a tree, bunting strung across the street, shops – including a shoe shop, an estate agent, an optician and a betting shop – and the Blackbird Café on the corner. A busker playing the guitar. She wondered if Johnny had been trying to call for help or had sent the image to her for a reason, or, knowing he was about to die, as a sort of goodbye. The thought made her cry in wretched, shuddering sobs.

'Oh, Johnny,' she mumbled tearfully. She was going to miss him so very much – there were things he knew, things they shared, that nobody else knew about. Her eyes travelled to the haberdashery unit where the musical trinket box he'd given her all those years ago was hidden, on a day when her life changed beyond measure.

'I can't do this without you,' she said to the empty room. Thoughts of what she had to do snowballed in her mind. The funeral, the death notice, the life insurance – all that paperwork. The upholstery jobs booked in for the coming months. She felt so tired, she wanted to lie down and never get up. But she couldn't because she had to be strong for the girls – they were her priority. In fact, she thought, glancing towards the house, she should go back inside to be with them, not leave them alone with their sorrow and fear.

Taking a deep breath, she turned out the light, left the workshop and headed towards the house. Johnny's phone glowed from the corner of the workshop – a light in all the darkness.

Chapter Three

'We could send him up in a firework?' said Scarlet, with a sad smile. 'Or we could get his ashes made into a record, with his favourite song or a recording of his voice. I read about it on the Internet.'

It was a month after Johnny's death and Heidi, Scarlet, Zoe and Heidi's mother, Rosalind, were at Rosalind's beach hut on Southbourne beach. The hut had been in the family for decades and last year Johnny had painted it pale pink – a giant sugared almond. It was surprisingly warm, and they sat outside the hut on rainbow-striped deckchairs, a small round table between them with a pitcher of lemonade and a packet of shortbread on the top.

'I like the idea of the firework,' said Heidi.

Scarlet sat on her hands, lifting her shoulders to her ears before dropping them down again. Dressed in a short green dress, with kitten-heel boots, she'd recently coloured her dark brown hair a shade of aubergine and cut a heavy fringe that hung just above her hazel eyes, outlined with her characteristic dramatic eye make-up. She looked every bit the arty university student she was – and Heidi had repeatedly told her she didn't need to come home every weekend. Scarlet had her own life at college in Southampton. A graphic-design course she loved; a boyfriend, Charlie, who she was mad about; and a small business selling illustrated cards on Etsy.

'I thought he said he wanted to be scattered here, into the sea?' said Rosalind, lowering her sunglasses so that Heidi could see her pale-grey eyes. It was a habit of hers – she insisted she couldn't hear properly with her sunglasses on. She was seventy-nine, after all.

Heidi nodded in agreement. This was Johnny's favourite beach. Sandy and unspoiled, it was nestled at the bottom of the cliff where a herd of wild goats chewed on shrubs – they'd been introduced to keep the shrubs down and therefore stop the cliff collapsing. Heidi glanced up at them now, happily chomping away, as if life hadn't irrevocably changed.

'Maybe we could scatter the ashes next month?' said Heidi, wanting to keep hold of him for a bit longer.

The day after Johnny's private cremation, which Heidi couldn't remember in any real detail (thanks to the sedative the doctor had prescribed) apart from the anonymous bouquet of white lilies that had turned up with 'thank you' written on the label, she had collected his ashes in the standard metal urn – like a trophy she'd won at school. At home, she'd transferred them into a stoneware glazed green pot with a frog painted on the side. He was currently on the shelf in the workshop, keeping her company. She'd found herself talking to him on more than one occasion and didn't want to part with them.

'I'll be doing my exams then,' said Zoe, tucking her hair behind her ears and pulling a frightened expression.

Heidi leaned forward in her chair to squeeze Zoe's hand. In her 'boyfriend' jeans and oversized jumper, she seemed tiny. She was studying A levels in Human Biology, Psychology and Health and Social Care, aiming to take up her conditional offer of a place at Plymouth University to study Paediatric Nursing the following year. Since Johnny's death, Heidi had been giving Zoe motivational talks, making sure she knew how important it was that she stayed focused – even while she was grieving.

'You'll be fine,' said Heidi. 'Just keep on studying hard. Nothing's going to get in the way.'

'Mmm,' said Zoe, helping herself to a piece of shortbread.

Scarlet's phone rang, and after checking the number, she turned it to silent, sighed and put the phone into her bag. Heidi looked at her questioningly but was ignored.

'We could have a picnic or something and play that game Dad liked,' Zoe said. 'What's it called?'

'Boules,' said Heidi, remembering Johnny's excitement when she'd bought him a set for his birthday to encourage 'gentle' exercise during his cardiac rehab programme. 'It's French.'

'And Grandma could make one of her famous pavlovas,' Zoe said.

'I hope it's famous for the right reasons,' said Rosalind, with a small laugh, pulling her floaty jacket tighter over her shoulders.

Always well dressed, Rosalind put Heidi to shame. Glancing at her work dungarees, which she'd worn almost every day since Johnny died, she sighed and closed her eyes. With the sun warming her face, she felt absolutely exhausted. She'd found it hard to sleep these last few weeks, without Johnny in the bed, but also because she couldn't forget about the photograph Johnny had taken before he died. When she closed her eyes at night, it was glued to the back of her eyelids in little rectangles, like postcards from beyond the grave.

'Zoe, shall we go for a walk?' asked Scarlet, grabbing her sister's hand and pulling her up out of the deckchair. There was only two years between them, and with their willowy, slim frames, they were definitely cut from the same family cloth. Zoe grabbed another piece of shortbread and they walked to the water's edge arm in arm, locked in deep conversation. They both had boyfriends, each other and close friends, but Heidi worried she wasn't supporting them enough.

'I think I'll go in for a quick dip,' she told Rosalind. 'I'll just get changed.'

She went inside the beach hut, pulled the curtain across the door and changed into her swimsuit. Fishing her neoprene socks, swimming hat, goggles and earplugs from her bag, she pulled on her swimming robe and went back outside to join Rosalind, who shook her head and raised her eyebrows.

'I don't know how you can go in at this time of year in just your swimsuit!' Rosalind said. 'You've a screw loose.'

Heidi smiled at her mother. She'd been going into the sea all year round, at least twice a week – even on Christmas Day. The cold water was a tonic against the anxiety she felt about Johnny's health. He had thought she was crazy too, but often came down and sat on the beach to watch her, giving her a clap when she came out. Her eyes pricked with tears at the memory.

'It's good for me,' she said to Rosalind. 'There's nothing like it.'

While Heidi put on her swimming cap and goggles, Rosalind nodded.

'How's the workshop?' she asked, pulling down her sunglasses to the tip of her nose again. 'Are you managing okay without Johnny?'

Heidi's stomach plummeted. She'd had to put some bigger projects on hold for the time being and thoughts of Annie's 'Barry' chair, Simone's footstool and a vintage tub chair waiting for attention spun through her head. Though she spent hours in the workshop, knowing that she needed to be busy to stay sane, she achieved comparatively little. The work felt overwhelming, suffocating and exhausting when she felt so utterly broken herself.

'I'm behind, but Max is helping,' she said. 'The life insurance will help and I'm going to look into taking on an apprentice eventually. I'll get there.'

'You will,' said Rosalind encouragingly. 'When the going gets tough, the tough get going. You always get there in the end. Even in difficult times.'

Heidi knew what Rosalind was referring to, but some subjects were locked away and buried in the past, never to be dragged up through the decades and forced under the spotlight.

'I can't stop thinking about that photograph Johnny sent me though,' said Heidi, her eyes pinned to Scarlet and Zoe as she pulled on her swimming socks. 'What if it means something? And what about those flowers? Isn't that weird that they didn't have a name on them?'

Rosalind pulled her glasses right off and put them on the table by the lemonade.

'Those flowers could have been from one of the customers who simply forgot to add their name,' said Rosalind in a firm voice. 'And the photo was probably just a mistake. I often ring the wrong person because I accidentally press a button on my phone. They're so fiddly! Put it out of your mind now, Heidi, or you'll drive yourself mad. You have to be strong.'

Heidi closed her eyes for a moment. The postcards immediately appeared on the back of her eyelids again, like a filmstrip. She had a thought: *I can't put it out of my mind. I just can't.*

'Okay, I'm going in,' she said. 'I won't be long. I'll swim to the buoy and back.'

'All the way out there?' said Rosalind, peering out to sea. 'I'll be here watching. Ready to call the coastguard.'

Heidi grinned at Rosalind before crossing the sand to the sea. Wading into the water, pausing to acclimatise to the cold, she splashed her face and arms and gradually entered the sea until her shoulders were submerged. Skin tingling, she pulled down her goggles, lifted her feet from the seabed and started to swim, front crawl, towards the yellow buoy in the distance.

Keeping her eyes open underwater, she was acutely aware of the sound of her heartbeat, still drumming its regular rhythm, while Johnny's had fallen silent. She forced her mind to empty and swam.

Chapter Four

'I just *know* your photo means something,' Heidi whispered to nobody as she stood on Main Street in Poole. The thought of Johnny dying there was so awful, Heidi wanted to scream. She couldn't bear it. But she tried her hardest to focus on the reason she'd come. Convinced that Johnny had tried to send her the photo for a reason, that it was a key to something, she planned to go into all the shops and wait for something significant to present itself to her.

One idea she'd had was that perhaps Johnny had been into the travel agency to book something for her birthday and that he was trying to tell her about it with the photo. So, with a sigh, she decided to go there first. Trembling, she pushed open the door and went inside, waiting awkwardly for an assistant to acknowledge her.

'Can I help you?' a young woman dressed in a blue-and-red uniform finally asked. Her name label told Heidi that she was called Carolyn.

'I've got a bit of a strange request about my late husband,' said Heidi quickly, taking a seat opposite Carolyn. Every other travel agent in the shop stopped what they were doing and listened in while Heidi explained that she had reason to believe he might have booked a surprise holiday for her birthday, but that he'd sadly died and there was no way of telling if he had or hadn't. When she finished talking Heidi congratulated herself for not crying – a struggle with her throat threatening to close at any moment.

Carolyn checked the records – clearly thrilled to be part of the mystery – but after a few minutes, she sighed and shook her head.

'There's no record of any booking under either of your names,' she said. 'I'm so sorry, Mrs Eagle. I'm sorry for your loss.'

Heidi felt winded. She sat for a moment, then gathered up her bag and coat, thanked Carolyn and headed out into the street. Moving next door to the optician, she stared through the window. It was completely empty apart from one member of staff who was trying on sunglasses in front of a mirror. How could the optician be relevant in any way? It couldn't be.

The betting shop was next. She poked her head into the dingy premises and blinked at the numerous screens on one side of the wall. A man wearing a cap turned to look at her, didn't smile, then returned his gaze to the screens. She left the shop and moved to the shoe shop, staring blankly at the rows of shoes on display in the window. There was a pair of desert boots, a bit like the ones Johnny wore – but besides that, there was absolutely no connection.

'This is silly,' she said, feeling despondent. She thought about the times she and Johnny had been to this street before, to go shopping. They hadn't bought anything unusual; sportswear, medicines from Boots, nothing much else. Standing still for a moment, crushing disappointment washed over her. Rosalind was right – the photograph meant nothing. Poor Johnny had simply pressed the wrong buttons when trying to call for help. Her throat ached.

'A complete waste of time,' she said in her head. 'Stupid woman.'

Feeling hollow and lost, she wondered if she should somehow mark the spot where Johnny had spent his final moments. But tying a bunch of flowers to the railings wouldn't do – they would be brown and wilted in a couple of days. It always made her feel sad to see dried-up, dead flowers on the road where people had died, or tied to the back of benches, wishing they could remain fresh – alive. She remembered once being frozen to the spot when she saw a young woman – possibly a mother – furiously wrenching dead flowers and a soggy teddy bear from railings on a road near a school and hurling them into a bin bag. Heidi wished that someone else had got there first.

'I need to sit down,' she said, glancing over at the Blackbird Café – the café in the photograph. She'd been there once before with Johnny.

Feeling dazed, she took a few steps forward and tripped over the kerb, falling forward and landing heavily on her hands, grazing her palms.

'Careful now,' she thought she heard Johnny say.

Standing up, blinking, she picked gravel from her palms and suppressed the urge to cry. She'd heard Johnny's voice a few times lately; during the night when she couldn't sleep and once in the workshop, when she'd been concentrating on sanding down a chair frame. Simone, who had called her regularly since Johnny died, had told her it was normal to hear voices after suffering a bereavement – but it made her feel like she was losing her mind.

She made her way to the Blackbird Café – passing a busker playing the guitar – and pushed open the door. The inside was rustic in style, with sanded floorboards, wooden tables and chairs, and industrial lights hanging from lengths of exposed cord. The café's logo of a blackbird had been stencilled on the wall and was surrounded by old-fashioned maps of the surrounding area and large vintage mirrors that made it seem bigger.

She chose a table near the window and tried to calm down. Breathing deeply, she made circles with her neck, which made faint clicking noises on every rotation. Catching sight of herself in one of the mirrors, she sighed. Weeks of not being able to sleep properly had caught up with her.

'What can I get you?' a young waitress asked. 'Coffee? Anything to eat?'

'Just a coffee thanks,' Heidi said, fumbling for her purse in her bag, her fingers resting on the tape measure that Johnny used to carry around, ready for measuring up jobs. Just the feel of it made her miss him terribly.

The waitress put down the coffee and Heidi thanked her. Sipping the warm liquid, her lips quivered. It was time to accept that Johnny's photograph was meaningless. It was time to do the inevitable; accept he had gone.

'Oh, Johnny,' she said out loud, blinking away the tears threatening her eyes. The man on the table next to her glanced up and gave her a quizzical look.

'I've just lost my husband,' she burst out.

'Oh,' the man said jovially, misunderstanding her. 'I hope you find him again soon. He's probably in the bookies!'

Heidi forced a smile, but Johnny never went anywhere near the bookies – and she hated the man for even suggesting it. She didn't know what she was doing in the café and chastised herself for coming.

With a sigh, Heidi finished her coffee and placed three pound coins on the table. She thought of the busker outside; he might well have been one of the last people to see Johnny. Had he seen him fall to the ground? She wondered if she should ask if he remembered.

'Stop… just stop this,' she muttered to herself, lifting her hands to either side of her head, trying to still the thoughts spinning out of control in her mind.

She tucked her chair under the table and turned to thank the waitress. The café had filled up – and waiting staff were serving hot food and drinks to customers.

She opened the door to a blast of cool air that made her eyes water. At the same time as she was leaving, a couple were coming in. She moved aside to give them space, still holding the door open, and caught sight of the profile of a man in the opposite corner of the café. A waiter, he was placing cups of coffee onto a table for two women.

Heidi gasped and froze. Other customers glared at her, wishing that she would hurry up and close the door. But she couldn't move. She knew that nose and that chin better than any other. Those broad, strong shoulders.

'Johnny?' she whispered, incredulous, as the waiter returned to the kitchen with an empty tray, oblivious to her stare. Staggering outside, her heart threatened to burst from her chest. Either she'd found a key, or she really had lost her mind.

Chapter Five

One Saturday morning, when Heidi was sixteen years old, a door-knob changed her life. Rosalind had sent Heidi to Johnny's family's ironmongery to source the right size screws for a brass doorknob and backplate that had come loose on the bathroom door. Heidi was pleased to take a break from her O level revision and knew that Johnny, a boy from school that she secretly liked, worked there. He was alone in the shop that day, and when Heidi walked in, carefully dressed in a striped dress and cropped denim jacket, and placed the brass doorknob down, he flamed every shade of red.

'I need to get a screw for…' Heidi said, blushing madly at the connotation.

'For the doorkn—' continued Johnny, letting the end of the word hang suspended in mid-air.

'Yes,' she said, stifling laughter. They had clocked each other at school – and blushed when they bumped into one another – but were not in the same classes and had never said more than two words to each other.

She watched as he turned away and searched through the incredible drawer unit behind the counter. Whatever was inside each drawer (keys, screws, nails, hinges) had been handwritten on the front – it was a spectacle. The whole place, in fact, was a treasure trove. Above her head, wicker baskets, buckets, ropes and doormats hung. There were stainless-steel tubs, fire pokers and sweeping brushes, keys and bicycle wheels, spades and bread bins. The air smelled of boot polish and sawdust – and something else. Right Guard body spray.

'This is what you need,' he said, putting a box of screws down in front of her. They both noticed his hands were trembling.

'Is this your dad's place?' Heidi asked, not wanting to leave.

'Yeah,' he said. 'It was his grandfather's, then his dad's and one day I guess it'll be mine. If it wasn't for my O levels I'd work here full-time. How are you getting on with the revision? You're alright, you're clever. School's not my thing, but I'm good with my hands.'

They both blushed again, interrupted now by another customer clearing his throat. Heidi was desperate to keep the conversation alive.

'I could help you revise?' she said. 'If you'd like? I mean, if you needed help?'

'Alright then, yes,' he said. 'I'd like that. Thanks.'

So, one evening a week, Heidi would go over to Johnny's house to study, but though he'd initially make an effort with revision, he would spend more time taking photos of her with his dad's old camera than revising. She tried to ignore the camera, focusing on trying to explain the themes in a text, but secretly she was flattered by the attention. He wasn't like other boys she knew. He actually admired her brains and ambition. He listened, rapt, when she told him she wanted to be the first person in her family to go to university. 'I want to get away from this place and do something with my life,' she said earnestly, before apologising for offending him.

'Don't worry,' Johnny said, grinning. 'I *want* to stay here. This is my home.'

They studied in Johnny's small bedroom, and one evening, when the rest of his family were out, Heidi felt acutely aware of how attractive Johnny was and how much she wanted to kiss him. Suddenly brave, she leaned over to him and pecked him on the cheek, watching his face turn from pink to flaming red – and his expression of nonchalance turn to sheer delight. She grinned.

'You're spending a lot of time with this boy; don't let him take advantage of you,' Rosalind warned when Heidi talked about how much she liked Johnny, to which Heidi would think but not say: *He's mad about me. We're mad about each other. Nobody's taking advantage of anyone.*

Feeling more daring the next time they met, Heidi reached for Johnny's hands and pulled him close in his cramped bedroom. This time she kissed him on the lips. They clashed teeth. Neither of them closed their eyes, which made both of them laugh. They were unsure and tentative but enthusiastic learners.

During the summer holiday after O levels, Heidi and Johnny became inseparable. They went on adventures together, catching the public ferry from Poole Harbour to Brownsea Island – an island owned by the National Trust – and wiled away the hours sunbathing on the secluded beaches, arms and legs draped over each other, feasting on doorstep cheese-and-salad-cream sandwiches. They didn't talk much about what was happening in the wider world at the time; they were too focused on each other.

When Johnny worked in his parents' shop – which he'd confided was hanging on by a thread since the opening of DIY superstores – she would sit and watch him play the piano that they randomly kept downstairs in the cramped shop basement, with a selection of odd pieces of furniture.

She loved the way he was in the shop and admired the way he dealt with customers, winning over the older generation with his gentle charm. Her feelings for Johnny grew stronger. Love was mentioned. As soon as it had been said once, it was said daily, twice, three times, more. When they started a sexual relationship, they were sensible, but one day, an accident happened. When, after Christmas, Heidi dared to tell Rosalind she was pregnant, her mother's reaction shocked Heidi to the core. Normally kind and loving, Rosalind seemed to turn to stone.

'How could you let this happen?' Rosalind said, all the colour draining from her face. 'Oh, Heidi, I had such high hopes for you. University. A career. But you're just as bad as one of the silly young trollops you see pushing a pram around the town! I brought you up to be better than that! I'm so disappointed.'

Her mother's disappointment was a slap in the face. She knew she wouldn't be happy, but she had expected and hoped for support and comfort. Her father, Alan, seemed bewildered and immediately took a back seat, deferring to Rosalind. He gently explained that her mother was just worried – and couldn't express how she felt. But Heidi's world collapsed. She felt alone, frightened and stupid – but she also felt furious with herself and Johnny. Heidi had high hopes for her own future. Were those hopes now dashed because she'd made a mistake?

Arrangements for an adoption were made, and Heidi was forced to temporarily drop out of school, to study for her A levels at home with a private tutor. She was not permitted to see Johnny, but he wrote to her instead.

'We could live together at my house,' he wrote in one letter. He drew a diagram of his bedroom – and how they could move it around to fit in a double bed and a cot. 'I can look after us. You, me and the baby. I love you and always will.'

Rosalind found one of his notes, threw it away and phoned Johnny's mother to tell her to keep Johnny away from Heidi because Heidi had a bright future ahead of her. The letters then changed in tone. 'Maybe this is for the best,' he wrote dully. 'I'm sorry.'

Heidi didn't want to live in Johnny's bedroom. That seemed laughable. But she also didn't want him to have given up so easily. A few cross words from her mother and he'd backed down – what did that say about him? Was he really that spineless? If he really wanted the baby, he would have fought a bit harder, wouldn't he? Heidi didn't know what she wanted. She only knew that she felt a combination of terror and instinctive protectiveness over her body and a sense of bewildered awe about what was happening.

Close to her due date, Rosalind decided it would be best for everyone if Heidi went to stay with her great-aunt Joanna who lived a few miles away on the Dorset coast. Heidi had stayed with her when she was a small child and loved her house overlooking the sea. When Heidi arrived, Joanna showed her upstairs to the spare room, which was small, simple and flooded with sunlight. There was a single bed with a padded headboard, a dark wood bedside table and matching set of drawers. And in front of the window was a beautiful spoon-backed chair with an embroidered seat of bright red and pink roses on a background of black and with gold braided trimming. She lowered herself into the chair and it seemed to hold her up, like a strong, warm hand. Staring out of the window, she could see the glimmer of the sea in the distance – and she longed to be in it, floating on her back, staring up at the bright blue sky.

'How are you feeling?' Joanna said, coming into the room and setting down a tray of apple pie and milk. She hugged Heidi and explained that, when the baby was born, she could spend a few days with him or her if she'd like to before it went to the adoption agency and new parents.

'Yes, please,' Heidi managed to say, her heart constricting.

'You'll be alright, my love,' Joanna said gently before leaving Heidi alone in the room. 'You'll be home soon.'

But Heidi didn't know what home was anymore. If home was where the heart is, the only heart that mattered was the tiny heart beating inside her womb. Without it in her life, would she ever have a home?

When she wasn't sitting in the rose chair, reading, she walked deserted stretches of the south-west coastal path. Parts of the route, after a night of rain, were treacherous. With her pregnant belly making it difficult to manoeuvre along the narrow, cliff-edge routes as waves crashed against the cliffs hundreds of feet below, she felt as if she was all alone in the world. She saw dolphins leap in and out of the water, travelling in the same direction as she was. It had felt like a gift – as if nature was looking out for her or saying: *this way; come this way.*

On the route she walked, there was a small bay, with a deserted sandy beach, and she carefully climbed down the rocks to the water's edge, where the sea lapped at her toes. One morning, Heidi decided to go into the water. There was nobody around, so she took off her dress and walked into the sea in her underwear, gasping as the cool water tickled her skin.

'That's not too cold for you, is it?' she asked her belly when the baby did a somersault. Inching into the water, bending her knees and enjoying her weightlessness, she went deeper – and deeper still until she was swimming. Being in the water was a great relief, and she sensed the baby enjoyed it too. It was their private time together – a beautiful shared secret.

Clambering out inelegantly, she pulled on her clothes and walked back to Joanna's house, hanging her underwear out to dry from her window.

Did you really want this baby? she asked Johnny in her thoughts, perched on the rose chair, stroking her vast belly. She tried to imagine them, as a couple, raising a baby, but a clear image would never take shape.

She ricocheted between hating Johnny for not having to deal with any of this, to physically longing for him. Sometimes, she would pick up Joanna's phone and start dialling his number, but she would hold the receiver to her ear and listen to the dialling tone, before placing it back down in its cradle. She knew she was on her own in this; a lone sailor navigating the world's oceans, with only a dolphin to guide her.

'The baby will be well looked after,' Joanna assured her. 'Try not to worry.'

Try not to worry. She repeated this to herself in the hours when she couldn't sleep at night. Her pregnant belly too stretched, her heart rate too fast, it was impossible to get comfortable. At 5 a.m. on

24 June 1983, her seventeenth birthday, she went into labour, with Joanna by her side, holding her hand. Joanna called Heidi's parents to let them know and they sent a message to her to 'be brave'.

'Oh!' Heidi gasped, when the baby was placed into her arms and she was shown how to feed him. 'He's perfect.'

'He is,' said Joanna, beaming. 'What will you call him?'

'William,' said Heidi, enjoying the softness of what was her late great-uncle's name, which brought a tear to Joanna's eye.

Immediately, Heidi loved the baby. He looked like a minute, wrinkled-up version of Johnny, like a photograph of him screwed into a tiny ball. He had tufts of black hair the same colour as Johnny's. Full lips. Round eyes. Thick eyelashes. Long piano-playing fingers. He was utterly perfect, and he was hers, for a few days.

Her aunt had a Polaroid camera and took all eight pictures in the film; including one of Heidi in her nightdress sitting on the rose chair holding William in her arms and another of William carefully propped up on a cushion on the chair, swaddled in a cream blanket. There was one of the chair, with a Babygro folded up on it, and the others were close-ups of William. Joanna gave Heidi two pictures; the one of her holding William and one of him on the chair. The others would go to his new parents.

Later that day Joanna gave her a parcel that had come for her in the post. She didn't open it straight away. She waited until William had fallen asleep, his tiny fingers curled into fists, his head to one side. Then, taking off the brown paper and opening a box, she lifted out a gift from Johnny. It was a musical trinket box, of a dancing clown, with a small drawer at the bottom. The clown was behind a layer of glass, and when you opened the drawer, gentle, tinkly music played, and the clown danced. He'd written a note with 'love from J' on it.

Heidi sat in the rose chair, with William by her side in a Moses basket, and opened and closed the drawer over and over, watching the little clown dance, listening to the happy tune. The drawer was small, but she rolled the Polaroids slightly and put an elastic band around them, then placed them safely inside. She knew she would keep it until the day she died.

And then came the day she had to say goodbye. Heidi tried to tell herself that she was doing the right thing. Before she handed him over, Heidi breathed in the scent of baby William and locked it into her heart. After he'd gone, she couldn't get the sound of his cry out of her head, nor how warm he felt in her arms.

'It will get easier,' Joanna consoled her. 'Be brave.'

Heidi nodded and tried to be brave. And although she could still hear William's cry in her ears, she tried with all her might to imagine him sleeping soundly under the loving gaze of his new parents. It was all she could do.

A few days later she returned home to continue studying for her A levels. Rosalind had thawed and was more loving again and told Heidi to think only of the future and not of the past. Alan was quiet but kind, encouraging her to rest and relax, as if she was getting over a bug. Heidi hid the trinket box under a jumper in her wardrobe, sometimes pulling it out to listen to its tune and remember sitting on that rose chair, the sun fading, baby William sleeping calmly. She didn't see Johnny at all, and as the weeks became months, she knew she had to move on. She had no choice. But every day, many times a day, she was struck by the same, overwhelming and paralysing thought: *Somewhere out there, I have a son.*

Chapter Six

When Heidi finished her A levels, she got a place at Nottingham University to study English Literature, and for a while, she relished living on the university park campus, attending lectures and trying out being a different, more confident version of her old self. She got a tattoo at the base of her spine. A rose. She concentrated on not looking back. She worked as a waitress in Joe's, an American-style diner. It was very popular for its cheap, mountainous portions – and the plates were piled so high it was almost impossible not to shed fries or onion rings as she moved from kitchen to table. The staff were friendly and the tips good. For a while, she convinced herself that she was okay.

But on her nineteenth birthday, she couldn't pretend anymore. She hadn't told anyone it was her birthday, because it was also William's birthday, but a friend found out and insisted that she celebrate, literally dragging her to the pub. But the more beer she consumed, the louder she heard the sound of a baby crying in her ears and the more she felt herself sliding down into a pit. At the end of the evening, drunk and melancholic, she refused to go clubbing with her friends, saying she felt unwell, and walked home alone.

It was past midnight when she made her way to Trent Bridge and climbed up onto the barrier, staring down at the vast expanse of black water below. She had the strangest sensation, like a vision of the immediate future, that she'd jumped and was already in the water, struggling to breathe, the current pulling her under, a knowledge that she was going to die. A stranger passing by grabbed her hand, persuaded her to get down and called her a taxi. Back at home, trembling, cold and tearful, she realised she would never know who that stranger was, yet he had saved her life. What if he hadn't been walking by?

After that she couldn't concentrate on her studies. The words swam across the page; meaningless squiggles. She felt tired all the time, too tired to work at Joe's or see her friends. She no longer felt in control. She missed lecture after lecture, didn't hand in her assignments and was eventually thrown off the course. All the time she thought of William and was haunted by the sound of his cry and the warmth of his body.

Though she was clearly disappointed in Heidi, Rosalind tried her best to be sympathetic and encourage her to keep on reading and studying, but Heidi felt too blank for books. It was furniture that helped. Her father Alan taught her everything he knew about upholstery, and working with her hands and seeing the results of hard physical work felt good. Furniture was tactile and practical and beautiful. Though Alan mostly worked with heritage organisations, maintaining fine furniture in historic buildings and houses, he also enjoyed dragging an old chair from a skip and bringing it back to life in wild and wonderful ways. He encouraged Heidi to be imaginative, to express herself in the fabrics she chose to reupholster with, to enjoy herself making a wreck splendid again. She thought of the rose chair at Joanna's house – and how sitting in it, feeding William, had felt like someone was holding her.

Over time, her ambitions changed. She wanted to rescue things. Give furniture a new life. A second chance. Heidi became immersed in her father's world, and though she didn't have his formal training, she was resolute that she wanted to follow in Alan's footsteps. She wanted to make tired, sad things beautiful again.

Hearing from a friend that because the ironmongery was suffering, Johnny had gone to Manchester to take up an apprenticeship in carpentry, she knew he was consigned to the past. She dated one of Johnny's old school friends, Max Hartley. Max had been sporty at school – a windsurfer – who wasn't really in her social circle. He worked part-time as a lifeguard in the swimming baths and swam for Dorset. Swimming and surfing were his passions, but he was studying for a diploma in carpentry and construction too, so he had options. They went swimming together in the sea, gradually increasing their distance until they could swim side by side from one pier to another, occasionally pausing to appreciate the sun sinking into the water, like a giant peach on the horizon. Heidi fell in love with swimming in the sea and it lifted her mood better than any drug ever could.

They dated for a year and Max talked constantly about them both going to California for a year, to work and surf. Heidi went along with it but couldn't quite imagine herself on the other side of the world. Then, a group from their school year organised a reunion and because Heidi didn't want to go – couldn't face the questions about why she had dropped out of university – Max went alone. After the event, he was forlorn and moody. He told her that Johnny had turned up, and that Johnny, not knowing Max and Heidi were dating, had had too much to drink and confided in Max about the baby being the reason their relationship had ended.

'He basically told me he's still in love with you,' said Max. 'He said that to my face! He was literally in tears. Said he'd let you go because of pressure from your mum telling him to stay away from you. I couldn't tell him we're an item. How could I? You had a baby with him, for God's sake! He said he wanted you to keep it! That kind of takes me out of the equation! Did you not think to tell me about that? It's unfinished business!'

'It was an accident,' said Heidi, trying not to react to the news that Johnny still had feelings for her. That was too confusing. 'I don't talk about it. He was drunk, Max; ignore it.'

A week later Max gave her an ultimatum. She travelled to California with him or they broke up. Her passport stayed in her drawer.

Though she tried to resist, Heidi decided to ask Johnny to meet her. They should at least talk. In fact they had an epic argument;

Heidi shouted and screamed at Johnny, releasing the fury and sorrow she'd carried in her heart since the day she'd given birth to William. Johnny shouted and screamed too, arguing that he'd felt rejected and not listened to. She didn't tell him about Max. By the end of the evening, they were in each other's arms. The next month Max left the country and very gradually, Johnny and Heidi re-established their relationship.

Heidi hadn't expected they would get back together – it somehow made relinquishing William feel even worse, so they agreed early on it would be less painful to not talk about him. That he would be living happily with his adopted family. He would be loved and cherished.

Heidi and Johnny were together eight years before they got married and another five before having Scarlet. And, besides wordlessly marking his birthday each year, when it was also Heidi's birthday, they carried on with life and didn't speak about William again.

Chapter Seven

'I must have been hallucinating,' Heidi said to herself, parking outside her house. 'That's what it was. Some kind of anxiety issue.'

She couldn't remember a single thing about the journey home from Poole – only that a high-pitched whine had sounded in her head the whole way, like a washing machine on a high spin. She sat for a moment in the car – Johnny's 1968 forest-green Morris van – her heart racing, humming the theme tune to *Dallas*, trying to regain composure.

You imagined the whole thing, she thought, as an image of the man in the café flashed into her head. *It wasn't real.*

Zoe was at home – and she couldn't possibly find the words to tell her what had just happened or what she imagined had happened. She swallowed and closed her eyes for a moment, but her mind immediately returned to the café, where she had seen... what had she seen exactly? Was she seeing things? Grief could do that to a person; she knew that. Take your mind as if it was paper and rip it into shreds, before throwing in a match and watching the flames burn. Grief could make you lose your mind completely, couldn't it? Perhaps she was now seeing things in the same way she was already hearing Johnny's voice. Her own mind was not to be trusted. She felt strangely light-headed and faint.

She went into the house and straight to the kitchen, where she poured herself a glass of cold water.

'Hi, Mum,' said Zoe, appearing in the kitchen with Leo just behind her. 'Mum, Leo and I would like to talk to you, if you have a minute?'

Heidi's mind was still in the café. She looked at Zoe and tried to smile.

'Yes?' she said.

'Are you alright?' Zoe said. 'You seem a bit dazed.'

'I'm fine,' said Heidi, taking another gulp of water. 'I just need some food. I had a strong coffee and forgot to buy some lunch. The caffeine has made me jittery. I shouldn't drink the stuff; it's no good for me. Hello, Leo, by the way. How are you? Still at the guitar shop?'

'Alright,' mumbled Leo, not meeting Heidi's eye. 'Yeah. Still there. It's good. Yeah.'

Heidi sighed silently. Leo wasn't the best communicator in the world, unless he was talking about ukuleles. Zoe had fallen for him when she'd seen him perform as part of a local ukulele group.

'So,' said Zoe. 'We want to ask you something. Would it be alright if we go up to Scotland this weekend? I just don't want to leave you on your own, if you'll be too lonely.'

'What?' said Heidi, completely distracted.

'Will you be okay if Leo and I go up to Scotland?' Zoe asked again. 'He has a cousin up there, don't you, Leo?'

'I do,' he said. 'His name is Angus.'

Zoe glared at him and shook her head slightly.

'That okay, Mum?' said Zoe. 'Will you be too lonely?'

Heidi blinked. She was more worried about her mind than her loneliness. It had just played a trick on her that had completely floored her. It had to be a trick – the alternative was too much to comprehend.

'Well yes,' she said. 'I suppose so. Maybe it'll do you good to get away. I'm going out to the workshop, okay? I'm knee-deep in work I haven't done.'

'Thanks, Mum,' said Zoe, kissing Heidi on the cheek. 'I'm going upstairs to pack.'

Heidi waited until Zoe and Leo had gone upstairs and then she went out to the workshop. She had one thing on her mind.

Stepping over Simone's footstool, she dragged the stepladder over to the haberdashery unit stashed with fabrics and trimmings, then reached on top of the unit and felt around for the rusty old money tin that held her dancing-clown trinket box – out of sight and reach of anyone but her.

'Where is it?' she muttered, sweeping her hand left and right but finding nothing. Sweat prickled her forehead. The box wasn't there. Panic engulfed her.

'Where the hell is it?' she muttered, turning to scan the workshop.

Climbing back down the stepladder, she sat down and put her head in her hands. Either she really was completely and utterly losing her mind, or Johnny had moved the money tin.

'What did you do with it?' she asked the frog pot.

Feeling suddenly frantic, she moved over to the drawers, yanking open each one to reveal screws, door pulls, wires and nails. Finally, when she tried the last one, there it was. Relief flooded through her, but she was confused – she couldn't remember putting it there. She hadn't put it there! Had Johnny done it in a hurry one day?

The keys to the tin, she knew, were in a drawer in her bedroom, but the tin was already open. Johnny must have opened it.

Carefully, she unwrapped the trinket box. Just holding it in her hands brought tears to her eyes. The red, blue and white casing, the Dancing Clown label and the colourful clown with pom-poms on his shoes took her straight back to the day that William was born.

She opened the drawer to find not the two Polaroids she'd been expecting to see, held by an elastic band, but only one. She swallowed. With trembling hands, she held the remaining photograph, which curled at the edges, to the light; it was of William laid carefully on the rose chair she'd so loved. Heidi's nose filled with the scent of his skin, the warmth of that June day, the sunshine that had poured through the window of Joanna's spare bedroom, warming the floorboards, the grandfather clock chiming downstairs.

The beautiful rose chair, where she placed his tiny folded white jumpsuits. She thought of the man in the Blackbird Café and a hot rush of liquid flooded her throat. She closed her eyes.

'Hello!' said a voice from the workshop door, making Heidi jump. She knocked the tin off her lap, and it clanked noisily on the floor. A young woman came inside with her mobile in her hand. She introduced herself as Karen and showed Heidi a photograph of an elegant mahogany tête-à-tête or kissing chair, upholstered in gold fabric which was, by the look of the fabric, covered in damp and mould.

'This has been in my parents' garage for years,' Karen said. 'They're moving house in a couple of months – downsizing – so we're having a big clear-out, but my mum doesn't want to let this go. It was her mother's and she's very attached to it. I thought, as a welcome-to-your-new-home gift, I could get it reupholstered for her in a cheerful, bright fabric.'

She gave Heidi a small, hopeful smile.

'It's a beautiful chair,' Heidi said. 'I can understand why she loves it.'

'She's been meaning to get it reupholstered for years but never got around to it,' Karen said. 'I just want to do something nice for her. She's desperately nervous about the move, and I want her to walk into that new house and feel instantly at home.'

She raised her hands in the air and dropped them by her sides.

'I'd love to do it,' said Heidi.

'Are you sure?' Karen said. 'You look pretty busy.'

'I'm sure,' said Heidi firmly. She really would love to and wanted Karen's mother to enjoy her new home.

Forcing herself to concentrate, she and Karen discussed the details: a vivid floral fabric, dates, delivery and price. She also made a mental note to ask Max if he could work more hours. But as soon as Karen left, Heidi's thoughts flew back to the missing Polaroid.

Leaving the workshop, she went back into the house, upstairs and into the bedroom. Flinging open the wardrobe doors, she stared at Johnny's clothes, hanging in a neat line. Across the landing, she heard the sound of Zoe and Leo's laughter coming from her bedroom and the cheerful sound of ukulele music. Quietly, she closed the door and started to go through Johnny's things to see if she could find the missing Polaroid.

Opening the drawers of his bedside table first, she carefully lifted out his favourite book – *A History of Furniture* – and flicked open the pages. Nothing. A copy of *Uncut* magazine and some sheet music. She fanned them out on the carpet. Nothing. She pulled a shoebox from the bottom of the wardrobe and looked through birthday cards and drawings from the children that Johnny had kept. No sign of the photograph. She moved it aside and pulled out a rucksack. Digging in her hands, she found Johnny's swimming shorts and a pair of goggles. Nothing more. Pulling off shirts and jumpers from their hangers in the wardrobe, she threw his clothes into a pile on the bed, checking each and every pocket in every pair of trousers.

Halfway through the pile, she was interrupted by Zoe.

'Do you know where that travel bag is?' she said, bursting into the room. 'Wasn't it under your bed before?'

'Travel bag?' said Heidi.

'Yes,' Zoe said, looking at her as if she was mad. 'I'm packing for Scotland, remember? What are you doing? You're not throwing out Dad's stuff, are you?'

Zoe picked up one of Johnny's jumpers – a thick cream fisherman's sweater and hugged it. They smiled sadly at one another.

'Can I have this?' Zoe said. She lived in huge jumpers these days.

'Of course you can. I'm not throwing anything out,' Heidi said. 'I was just looking through… and I think the bag is under the bed.'

Zoe dropped to the floor and pulled out the travel bag, unzipping it and finding a pair of new shoes – a pair of black-and-white checked Vans.

'I don't think I ever saw him in those,' she said. 'Not very Dad.'

Heidi shook her head, and, picking up one of the shoes he'd never worn, she pushed her hand inside. Her fingers landed on something. A sock with something inside. Her heart raced. Instinctively she knew she'd found what she was looking for. She tried not to show any emotion on her face.

'Mum,' Zoe said, 'have you spoken to Scarlet recently?'

Heidi blinked. 'I speak to her a lot. Most days.'

'I mean, have you really spoken to her,' she said. 'About her life? It's just that she's finished with Charlie. She'll kill me for telling you. She says you have enough on your plate, but she's told Charlie he has to move out. He's not taking it well. He's really punishing her.'

'Oh, poor Scarlet!' said Heidi, feeling horribly guilty that she had missed such a massive event. 'I'll call her. And are you and Leo okay? Are you sure you want to go to Scotland? I haven't been there for you or Scarlet, have I? Too wrapped up in the shock of your dad and...'

The news of what she'd seen at the Blackbird Café was on the tip of Heidi's tongue, but she swallowed the urge to tell Zoe everything.

'I'm fine, Mum,' Zoe said quickly, not meeting Heidi's gaze. 'We're going for a walk on the beach, okay? I'll be back in an hour.'

Heidi smiled. 'See you later,' she said, waiting until Zoe had left the house before she pulled out the missing Polaroid from the sock. There was a roll of money too, which she counted out as £300, held together with an elastic band. And a small piece of paper, torn from a magazine. She frowned, confused, and her entire body shook as she unfolded a piece of paper. In Johnny's handwriting it said: William, 24 June 1983. Blackbird Café.

Stars fizzed in front of Heidi's eyes. Her head swarmed. William. His adopted parents had kept his name. She thought of the photograph of the street on Johnny's phone, that he'd taken just before he died. The man in the café. A shiver ran up her spine. She hadn't been seeing things. It wasn't a hallucination. Johnny had deliberately taken that photograph. He had known he was going to die and was trying to send her a message. He wanted to leave her a gift. His last photograph told her something Johnny hadn't been able to voice. He had done the unthinkable, the unmentionable. He had done what they'd promised they would not. Johnny had found their son.

Chapter Eight

Throughout their marriage, Heidi and Johnny didn't discuss William. It was an unwritten rule between them that they would keep his existence buried deep in their past, never to be exhumed. Some people might think this was strange. But locking the secret in a metaphorical box was the way they coped with the enormity of it. Of course, Heidi thought about William all the time, especially on his birthday. She'd imagine him surrounded by family and friends, blowing out candles on the top of a chocolate cake. She'd wonder if, when he smiled, he had Johnny's signature dimple. She thought about her great-aunt Joanna, who had since died, but who had shared the joy of holding William on the day he was born. Sometimes, when she was alone, she'd pull the photographs out of the musical trinket box and tell baby William that she loved him. But otherwise, she kept William's existence in the dark recesses of her mind.

Until now, she thought. Johnny had changed everything, and she didn't know how she felt about that: furious or thrilled?

Feeling light-headed, she took the piece of paper and the Polaroid of her holding William while sitting on the rose chair downstairs. Leaning it up against the computer, she googled the Blackbird Café. An idea flashed into her head. Perhaps she would ring the café to find out if they had a William working there. Just to confirm things to herself. It was the sort of thing Scarlet would do; go directly to the heart of the storm.

Before she had time to change her mind, she called the café, breathless with panic.

'Hello, Blackbird Café. How can I help?' said a female voice after one ring. Heidi's heart thumped in her ears.

'Hello, I wondered if you have a William working there please?' she asked.

There was a noise as the person on the other end held the phone against their chest and called the name 'William'. A few more seconds passed, before more rustling, and a cough, then:

'Hello, this is William,' a deep male voice said.

His voice sounded like Johnny's! Heidi's legs gave way and she slumped down into the Chesterfield sofa, still clutching the phone. She wasn't expecting his voice. Heidi could see him, vividly, standing there in the café, holding the phone, dressed in black T-shirt and black jeans, blinking and waiting for a conversation to start. She opened her mouth to speak but couldn't find a single word. What could she say anyway? She didn't even know if he knew about her existence. Had he ever actually met Johnny? She didn't know that either.

Without making a sound she finished the call, pressing the 'End' button with trembling fingers, then closed her eyes.

'Shit, shit, shit,' she said to the empty room. 'I shouldn't have done that. God, what am I doing? Stupid, stupid, stupid!'

Throwing down the phone, she moved into the kitchen and leaned up against the kitchen counter, humming her go-to tune until she felt calmer. She needed to think carefully. If she did want to contact William, she had to make the decision with a clear mind. People spent months or even years trying to track down their adopted or adoptive families; finding William like this had happened too quickly. If Johnny had talked about this to her, if he had shared what he was doing and not kept it secret – maybe she would be able to get her head around the conflicting, confusing emotions rinsing through her.

You can't just phone someone up and tell them you're their mother, she chastised herself.

No, if she went ahead with this at all, she would have to go through the formal process of searching through the contact register for adoptees and birth parents and see if William had tried to make contact. Or do it her own way, start a campaign on social media or something. She'd heard about someone else doing that – holding up a board with their baby's birth date and birth name on it, asking for it to be shared on Facebook. Within days she had found her child. But she already had a phone number to call and a place to find William. Had Johnny already met him? If he had – and had suddenly disappeared – how did William feel now? Had William been there that day when Johnny died? Her head pounded with questions.

'Argh!' she said, lifting her hands to her head.

At that moment, Heidi's mobile rang, making her jump. Physically shaking, she thought for one terrifying moment that William was calling her back. She located her phone and checked the number. Scarlet. Her heart continued to pound.

'Mum, it's me,' said Scarlet. 'I've got classes soon, but can we talk? I didn't want to bother you with all of this, but I need your advice. I'm having a bit of a nightmare.'

Heidi swallowed, recalling what Zoe had told her. Scarlet rarely showed vulnerability. Even as a child, when she fell over and took the skin off her hands and knees, she refused to show that she was suffering. Heidi knew she mustn't overreact.

'Of course, Scarlet,' she said, hearing Scarlet sigh with relief.

'Can we go to Jack's? said Scarlet. 'On Saturday?'

'I'd love that,' Heidi said, blinking away the sudden tears that had hit her eyes. Jack's was a reclamation yard near Scarlet's university – Johnny had loved it there and could spend literally hours wandering around the yard or talking to Jack, who was full of stories.

After ringing off, Heidi clutched her phone and stood frozen to the spot, but the sound of Zoe's key in the door prompted her into action.

'Hi, Mum,' Zoe called through the door. 'I'm back. Leo's gone home.'

Heidi followed her into the living room and watched her throw her coat onto the Chesterfield before heading towards the computer. Heidi swallowed. She had stupidly left the photograph leaning against the computer and the Blackbird Café website up on the screen. Her legs turned to water.

'Zoe!' Heidi shouted.

'What?' Zoe said, spinning around to face her.

Heidi could see from Zoe's eyes that she'd been crying. Heidi frowned.

'Are you okay?' she started, but Zoe changed the subject.

'Who's this?' said Zoe, picking up the photograph.

Heidi's ears hummed with panic as she struggled to find an explanation.

'Is it you?' Zoe said, looking more closely. 'When you were really young?'

'It's me, yes, years ago,' said Heidi, her voice cracking. 'Holding my aunt's friend's baby when I visited once I think.'

'Why do you have a nightie on?' said Zoe, frowning. 'You look so eighties!'

'It was the eighties!' said Heidi, trying to sound vague and disinterested. 'I'd probably just got up. I have no recollection. It was a lifetime ago.'

Zoe dropped the picture down by the keyboard without giving it more consideration and climbed the stairs to her room, giving Heidi the chance to close down the computer and tuck the photograph between the pages of a book. She exhaled. 'Out of sight, but never out of mind,' she muttered.

Physically shaking, she felt as if the walls were closing in on her. She needed to calm down.

Changing into her swimsuit and pulling on her clothes over the top, quickly gathering together her swimming bag, she called up to Zoe before she left.

'I'm going for a swim,' she said, waiting for the muted 'okay' from Zoe's bedroom.

Closing the front door, she headed to the beach, where the water was choppy and the waves messy. She quickly undressed, leaving her things in a pile on the beach, and ran into the water, thinking only of the man in the café. William.

Chapter Nine

'I think I've changed since Dad died,' said Scarlet as they wandered through Jack's Yard, past reclaimed chimney pots, sinks, stained-glass windows, a phone box, garden statues and a huge enamel advertising sign for Coleman's mustard. She paused to stroke a black-and-white cat curled up in a stone garden planter.

'What makes you say that?' said Heidi.

'I think I've realised that you only get one shot at life,' she said. 'I'm more honest with myself now and have started questioning what I'm doing and asking myself if I'm really enjoying it, rather than just going along with things.'

Heidi nodded.

'You should get some of those for Grandma and use them as planters,' said Scarlet, pointing to a collection of galvanised metal buckets. 'She'll be planting her dahlias now.'

'Good idea,' Heidi said, picking up a couple of buckets and checking the price. 'So, you were saying you feel like you're being more honest with yourself. That's a good thing, isn't it?'

Scarlet murmured her agreement but didn't divulge anything further. On the way to Jack's, Heidi hadn't asked any questions because Scarlet was very much like Johnny. When she was ready to talk, she would, not before. And besides, Heidi wanted to make this last as long as possible. Being with Scarlet helped her stop thinking about William and that mad, wild phone call she'd made. Knowing that he was close by was a wonderful, yet terrifying, secret.

'Shall we get coffee and cake?' she said to Scarlet.

They went inside Jack's warehouse, which was full to the rafters of yet more lovely old things, from vintage mirrors and wardrobes, to crockery and jewellery. Heidi lugged the buckets to the till and paid, while Scarlet ordered coffee and carrot cake and found them somewhere to sit down. When Heidi joined her, Scarlet yawned.

'I've not been able to sleep, so I'm binge-watching *Killing Eve* on Netflix,' said Scarlet. This morning, with her hair gathered on top of her head, she reminded Heidi of Johnny. William had looked so much like Johnny. Would Scarlet, Heidi wondered, recognise herself in William, should they ever meet? *Stop*, she told herself, taking a gulp of the scalding coffee. *Stop*.

'You and me both,' said Heidi. 'I don't mean the *Killing Eve* bit, but I couldn't sleep either. I haven't slept well since your dad died. I feel like I did when you were born. You wanted feeding every forty-five minutes, so I didn't sleep for months.'

Scarlet rolled her eyes.

'I thought you'd blame me!' said Scarlet. 'But apparently breast is best, so you did the right thing. I heard a radio show about it. Babies are less likely to have allergies or get ill, infant mortality rates go down, new mums are less likely to develop ovarian cancer. The list goes on. I suppose there's no reason why any good mother who was physically able wouldn't breastfeed.'

Heidi suffered a blast of guilt, thinking of William.

'Each to their own,' she said. 'Some women have all sorts of reasons for not breastfeeding. You mustn't be all almighty about it. You can't really judge a situation until you've lived it.'

Scarlet rolled her eyes again. She was the queen of eye-rolling.

'You would say that,' she said. 'You're always looking out for the underdog, forgiving everyone for everything.'

'Course I am,' said Heidi, with a smile.

'And I wouldn't have you any other way,' said Scarlet, gently squeezing Heidi's arm. 'Imagine if you were one of those strict mums who disapproved of everything?'

Heidi thought of Rosalind, who had disapproved so strongly when Heidi fell pregnant. The disapproval had been so painful she had striven to make Zoe and Scarlet feel they could tell her and Johnny anything, however terrible. 'Even if you accidentally kill someone or get involved in some hideous crime,' she once told them when they were wide-eyed youngsters, tucking into fishfingers and beans, 'I'll be here for you. Always.'

Scarlet had immediately taken her to task, quizzing her over various awful scenarios. 'So, if I suddenly murdered six innocent people,' she said, 'you'd support me? You'd actually stick by me and visit me in jail? Even if all those people's families sent you hate mail or spat at you?'

'I would,' was Heidi's reply.

'If I ever kill someone,' Zoe had said, after thinking it over, 'I wouldn't want you to visit me. I wouldn't want anyone to visit me.'

'So,' ventured Heidi now, 'why aren't you sleeping?'

Scarlet sipped her coffee and stared into the distance.

'When Dad died, I started thinking about relationships – how you and him have been together forever,' she said. 'It just hit me when I was at a Mexican restaurant one night that I didn't love Charlie in that way. I had stronger feelings for someone else. Romantic feelings. Whatever you want to call it.'

Heidi nodded, desperate for Scarlet to feel relaxed enough to get everything off her chest.

'And does this someone else feel the same about you?' Heidi asked. Scarlet nodded and sighed.

'Charlie isn't taking it very well,' Scarlet said. 'I've asked him to move out of my room, and at first, he refused, until I put all his belongings on the street outside. Then he got furious, said I was a heartless, selfish bitch and that I was doing all of this because I hadn't dealt with Dad's death properly. Apparently, I'm in denial. When I told him that wasn't true and that actually I'd fallen for someone else, he went mad. He punched the wall and cut his knuckles! I didn't know what to do. I handled it all wrongly. Shouted a lot. But now, he won't leave me alone. He goes to the places he knows I go to, you know, the bars, and waits outside. He emails me all the time. I feel this kind of dread whenever I see him.'

Heidi nodded, her heart aching at the tremble in Scarlet's voice.

'There's no excuse for him to lash out at you or follow you around,' Heidi said. 'You've broken up with him. He has to accept it. Are you frightened of him?'

Scarlet shook her head. 'No,' she said. 'I'm just sick of him.'

'And who have you fallen for?' Heidi said.

'I've fallen for a woman called Frankie,' said Scarlet. 'You have to understand that everyone is much more open to experimentation these days and to allowing themselves to be attracted to the person rather than a gender. It's not that I don't still like men, I do, but I also like Frankie. She's on my course.'

'Okay,' said Heidi, 'and what's Frankie like? Is she clever and ambitious like you? Is she the first woman you've had a relationship with?'

Scarlet smiled.

'You and Dad are so normal,' she said, emphasising the word normal as though it were an insult. 'You're so conventional and straight down the line and black and white.'

'We are not!' Heidi said, aware that they were both referring to Johnny as if he was still alive. She grinned at Scarlet, trying to lighten the mood. 'I've got earrings and a tattoo. Your dad played in a band and smoked a joint on his thirtieth birthday!'

We've got a long-lost son who your dad found before he died. That photograph he took, it wasn't an accident; it was a message. A gift.

'Joint! That's not even a word now, Mum. Oh, you know what I mean,' Scarlet said. 'Anyway, my point is that I don't want to be pigeonholed as gay or straight.'

'I wouldn't pigeonhole you, Scarlet,' Heidi started, 'I'm totally supportive of whatever makes you hap—'

'So basically,' interrupted Scarlet, 'what I'm trying to tell you is that I'm flexisexual. It basically means my sexual attraction is flexible; it changes.'

Heidi had never heard the term before, but she grinned and hit the table with the side of her fist to demonstrate her enthusiasm and encouragement.

'Well that's brilliant,' said Heidi. 'I'm glad.'

'Don't be all weird,' sighed Scarlet. 'I knew you'd be weird.'

To be truthful, Heidi didn't give a damn whether her daughter was in a relationship with a man or a woman – what she did care about was whether that man or woman made her happy. She felt suddenly silently furious with Johnny. Him dying meant she was left to bring their daughters up alone. Make the right decisions. Point them in the right direction. Be a father and a mother. What if she got it all wrong? Suddenly she felt the choking weight of Johnny's absence bear down on her chest. She breathed deeply and reached across the table to hold Scarlet's hand.

'Darling girl,' she said. 'I love you, and no doubt Frankie loves you, and Charlie still loves you because you're an incredible young woman. Clever, funny, determined, strong and beautiful. Whoever you fall in love with and have a relationship with is lucky. I'm supportive of you in every single way. I might have been a bit… absent… since Dad died and not as good a mum as I should be, but I love you and Zoe so much. I hope you know that.'

Scarlet blinked.

'You're always a good mum,' she said in a wobbly voice. 'I love you too. It's been really hard breaking up with Charlie. He's made such a performance out of it. I think he's one of those people who will hold a lifelong grudge. When I see him randomly in thirty years' time, he'll probably ignore me or tell me that I ruined his life. Hold me personally responsible for all of his life's failings.'

Heidi's face fell. 'Don't say that,' she replied, Scarlet's words hitting her raw nerve. Did William feel the same?

'Maybe he'll surprise you,' she added hopefully.

'I don't like surprises,' Scarlet said. 'They never end well.'

Heidi didn't like surprises either. She thought about the enormous surprise she might be about to unleash on her girls. Perhaps it was impossible. Perhaps, even if she did instigate contact with William, she would have to keep him at arm's length and his existence secret from the girls. Was that fair on anyone? No, it wasn't. Despite instructing herself to not breathe a word about William's existence to Scarlet, she felt a compulsion to confess everything. She needed an ally.

'I miss Dad so much,' Scarlet said suddenly. 'I can't get over the thought that we'll never see him again. He was always so gentle with us when we were kids. I can't ever remember him shouting. When he had his first heart attack, I was so shocked. I couldn't stand the thought of losing him, and now we have. There's nobody like him.'

Heidi swallowed. *There's nobody like him.* Was this the moment to tell Scarlet about William?

'Scarlet, I—' she started, her words instantly drying up.

'There's this massive void,' Scarlet went on, 'where he once was, isn't there? A Dad-shaped void. I suppose it will always be there. Nobody could fill it. I sort of wish Uncle Edward lived here, so at least we had someone similar around, but he'd never be as good. There could only ever be one Johnny.'

Heidi couldn't speak. All she could do was nod and reach over to Scarlet and pull her in for a hug, her heartfelt words ringing in her head. There could only ever be one Johnny.

Chapter Ten

Heidi inspected the rusting galvanised buckets in the passenger seat, hoping Rosalind would approve. Heidi loved the character in anything old, used and slightly battered – and knew they'd make fabulous planters. Parked up outside where Rosalind lived, she looked up at her mother's flat. With a view of Southbourne beach, it was on the third floor – the only one *without* net curtains – and had a glass-fronted balcony big enough for a sunlounger which she turned around during the day, depending on the position of the sun.

'You're like a sunflower,' Heidi had said when she first got the flat. 'Facing the sun at all times of the day.'

'Dandelion seed more like,' Rosalind had said, pointing at her silvery hair.

Rosalind had moved to the flat when Alan had died ten years ago and their three-bedroom semi-detached house became too big for her on her own. She hadn't been sentimental about their family home. While Heidi had wandered through the rooms, asking Johnny to take photos to remember it, Rosalind had seemed relieved to be packing up and moving out. That was her approach to life in general: don't dwell; don't look back.

She had been remarkably stoic about Alan's death too – of the stiff-upper-lip generation, she very rarely showed any vulnerability, although Heidi knew it was there, like a deep concealed well at the bottom of a garden. Rosalind had thrown her energy into making a new life without Alan, nurturing her balcony flowers and sometimes helping out Walter, who lived in the flat below hers, in the communal gardens. Now, as Heidi approached the flats, she saw Rosalind deadheading flowers while Walter weeded the beds.

'Dressed for the job as usual,' said Heidi, raising her eyebrows at Rosalind's outfit: a long red skirt, purple jumper and floral jacket, with ballet pumps on her feet. Her hair, as always, was held up with tortoiseshell combs, and she wore her glasses around her neck on a chain. Her cheek was streaked with mud.

'I'm not one for trousers and wellies,' Rosalind said, pulling off her gardening gloves. 'What have you got for me there?'

'I bought you some buckets for your dahlias,' she said. 'Are they the right size?'

Rosalind took one and inspected it. 'Perfect,' she said. 'Thank you. Is everything else okay? You don't normally come bearing gifts.'

Heidi took a deep breath. *Don't say anything*, she told herself. *Just do not say anything. Not yet.* But another voice told her that Rosalind at least knew about William's existence, so she alone would understand the gravity of finding him after thirty-six years.

'Heidi?' Rosalind persisted. 'What is it?'

Heidi's mouth went dry and her heart raced. She glanced at the view: the sea was an inviting shade of matt silver, the sand a strip of gold and the sky above a mixture of blues, greys and pink, like the inside of a seashell. Against that beautiful backdrop, people walked their dogs, and from that vantage point they were small dots on the sand. There were couples walking arm in arm, people on their own and a mother with a young boy, perhaps her son, teaching him to fly a kite. An image of William burst into Heidi's mind – how she imagined him as a child. Though Heidi had instructed herself to say nothing, she knew she couldn't hold it in any longer.

'I've got some news,' she spat out. 'Something's happened.'

'Something else?' said Rosalind. 'What else could possibly happen?'

'You know on the day that Johnny died, he took a photo?' said Heidi.

'Yes,' Rosalind said slowly. 'You were talking about it the other day. You're not still thinking about that, are you?'

'In the photograph was a café called Blackbird,' Heidi repeated, ignoring her mother.

'I know, love,' said Rosalind with an exasperated sigh. 'You showed me.'

Heidi shook her head and opened her eyes wide.

'And it turns out that… he… he…' Heidi gulped, knowing that it was all going to come tumbling out, here, now. 'It turns out that Johnny had found William. Our son. He works in that café. The Blackbird. On the day he died I think he was on his way to see him or had seen him. He found him. Can you believe it? Without breathing a word to me, he found our son.'

The words were rushing from her lips. And it was such a relief, sweet relief, to tell someone. Rosalind's mouth fell open.

'He never did!' she whispered.

'He kept it all a secret from me,' said Heidi, nodding. 'I think he decided to find him and find out what sort of person he was before telling me about it. Or something like that. That's all I can think that he would be doing.'

'Good God,' said Rosalind, the colour draining from her cheeks. 'I'm speechless… I'm so shocked, Heidi… I thought that was all in the past. What was he thinking of, dredging that up, looking for him without your agreement, for heaven's sake? How could he do that?'

Rosalind's demeanour had completely changed. Something about it reminded Heidi of all those years ago, when she'd told Rosalind she was pregnant. Her mother seemed to turn to stone in front of her eyes.

'I think he wanted to leave me a gift,' said Heidi shakily. 'That's what I believe. I think it was a gift.'

'Well I think he was wrong to do that,' Rosalind said. 'Very wrong. Selfish. What a terrible thing to do. The arrogance of the man! What a dreadfully selfish thing to do.'

Heidi's eyes filled. Rosalind stared at her shoes, shaking her head in disbelief. Heidi longed for Rosalind to put her arms around her, comfort her, but she quickly deduced that that wasn't going to happen.

'For heaven's sake, please tell me you haven't contacted him,' said Rosalind, suddenly looking up and fixing Heidi with her pale eyes, 'or seen him? Does he know about Johnny? What have you done?'

Heidi looked away.

'I think Johnny may have met him, yes, but I don't know for sure,' Heidi replied, 'but William won't know about Johnny's death yet. How could he? And I haven't made contact.'

She studied her hands to cover the lie.

'I think I'm going to write to him at the café he works in,' she went on quickly, knowing she shouldn't. 'What do you think?'

Rosalind shook her head again, as if trying to rid her mind of a noise that wouldn't go away.

'I think you need to be bloody careful,' she said in a cold, steady tone. 'You need to leave well alone. You have your girls. Aren't they enough? You can't fill the hole in your life that Johnny has left with your long-lost son. It's not the movies, Heidi. This is real life. You gave up your right to him long ago, and Johnny was a stupid fool to do this and leave you with this… mess! I'm so cross with him. If he was here now, I'd throttle him.'

Heidi was trembling. She wrapped her coat tighter around her body and instructed herself not to cry.

'Of course the girls are enough!' Heidi said. 'It isn't about them being "enough". It's not about them at all. I'm not trying to fill a void either. This is Johnny's doing. He started this. He was trying to be kind and I can't just leave it hanging in the air.'

'Oh, but it is about the girls,' Rosalind snapped. 'How will they feel when you tell them you've deceived them their entire lives? That their own mother has lied to them every day of their lives?'

Heidi staggered backwards, aghast at the ferocity of Rosalind's reaction.

'I haven't deceived them or lied to them,' Heidi said quietly, 'and if I explain exactly what happened, maybe they would understand. I think my girls would understand that it's all very complicated, but at the end of the day, Johnny was trying to be kind and leave me a message, a gift, our…'

Her voice faded to nothing.

'Don't be naive,' said Rosalind. 'These things break families apart. You can't just expect him to slot into your life and your daughters' lives without all hell breaking loose. You're not thinking straight. It's because you're grieving. You've lost your mind. It happens. In days gone past, women were sent to the asylum for being hysterical after a bereavement!'

'What…?' Heidi said. 'I am not hysterical, but I do have emotions and I'm not afraid of them. Unlike you… you cold-blooded robot!'

The two women fell silent and stared at one another, their eyes conveying pain they couldn't express, just as they had done decades earlier. Each seemed on the verge of exploding further, but both knew how ugly that would be.

'Don't speak to me like that,' said Rosalind, her voice trembling. 'We made the right decision for you, Heidi. You were a child.'

'Sixteen actually,' Heidi said. 'Seventeen when he was born.'

'That is a child,' Rosalind said. 'For heaven's sake, you were unmarried and still at school. I wanted more for you.'

'It was the 1980s!' screamed Heidi. 'Not the 1950s!'

'We were trying to protect you!' shouted Rosalind. 'Give you the chance to have a decent future! We were protecting your reputation!'

'And look where that's got me,' Heidi snapped.

'Yes,' said Rosalind. 'Look where that's got you!'

Rosalind marched towards the block of flats, where a couple of white-haired old ladies were staring out of their open windows, intrigued by the raised voices outside.

'Where are you going?' Heidi demanded, but Rosalind dismissed her with a sharp wave of her hand.

'Don't bother following me inside,' she called over her shoulder. 'I've heard quite enough.'

Heidi stood alone in the garden, the breeze blowing her hair into her eyes, feeling as though she had been punched in the guts. Tears on her cheeks, she carefully picked up her gift of the buckets that Rosalind had left on the floor and carried them over to the front porch, where Walter was putting away his tools, his tanned, knobbly arms and legs like pretzels.

'Everything okay?' he said. 'Your mum's doing a great job helping me in the garden. Fit as a fiddle that one.'

Heidi nodded once before returning to the car on jellied legs. Her hands were shaking and her breathing ragged. Before pushing the key in the ignition, she glanced up to Rosalind's flat and saw her framed in the window, arms crossed defiantly, staring out at the horizon. Heidi raised a hand, waving a little white flag, but Rosalind ignored it and turned away, disappearing out of sight into the shadows. Nothing like a sunflower now.

Chapter Eleven

Heidi lined up her tools. Mallet. Tack remover. Pincers. Screwdriver. With her life in bits, she felt compelled to make something whole. She inspected the tête-à-tête chair that Max had collected, imagining the people who had sat on it and gossiped or stolen illicit kisses. It was looking rather sorry for itself, but Heidi was determined to bring it back to life. Preparing to carefully disassemble it, Heidi's head rattled with Rosalind's harsh words.

'My mother was furious,' Heidi told the green pot of Johnny's ashes. 'She said she wanted to throttle you.'

She couldn't understand why Rosalind had been so furious. It was thirty-six, nearly thirty-seven years since William had been born – yet it still provoked the same shock in her mother as it had back then. She'd expected apprehension but not fury. There was something odd about it that Heidi couldn't put her finger on.

'Anyone in?' came a voice at the door, along with a gentle knock. Max poked his head – scruffy sandy hair, a permanent tan and deep blue eyes – around the door and smiled, his gaze resting on the kissing chair. He wasn't due in to the workshop today, but Heidi was relieved to see him – she needed him to do more hours to clear the backlog.

'Hi, Max,' she said. 'Come in.'

Max smiled. Perhaps it was all the swimming he did now and in his youth – and the twenty years he had lived in California – but he radiated health. In his blue sailing jacket, he looked like he'd just stepped off a yacht. Indeed, since his wife Jane had died five years ago, he spent more time out on the sea than ever – on his kayak.

'Been out on my kayak fishing for mackerel,' he said. 'I've brought you some – here.'

He placed a paper parcel on the worktop. 'I've filleted them,' he said. 'They're beautiful cooked on a barbecue, or you could do them in a pan with a bit of butter and lemon.'

'Thank you, Max,' she said. 'That's so kind.'

'You should come with me sometime,' he said. 'It's the most peaceful way to spend an afternoon.'

He ran his hand over the back of the tête-à-tête chair. 'Isn't this great? Can I sit?'

He sat down in one of the seats and gestured that Heidi should sit on the other. The two of them twisted to face each other and smiled.

'How are things this week?' Max said. 'Are you swimming or sinking?'

'Sinking,' said Heidi, with a small sad laugh.

Max nodded and smiled kindly and knowingly. Ever since his return to the UK with his wife and son twenty years ago, Max had been in hers and Johnny's lives. Their past relationship was forgotten and the two families had become firm friends. Heidi trusted Max and didn't need to pretend she was coping when she wasn't.

'I'm drowning a bit with all the jobs even though I've postponed some projects,' she said. 'I could do with some more help.'

'That's why I'm here,' he said. 'I've got a proposition for you.'

'What?' she said, feeling suddenly nervous.

'A couple of people have asked if you'll close now that Johnny has gone,' he said.

'What?' Heidi said, leaping up from the seat. 'Why would anyone say that?'

The question didn't need an answer. She knew very well why people might wonder such a thing. With Johnny gone, she'd had to reduce her workload and was late with various projects. She lay in bed at night worrying that the business was spiralling out of control, but she felt this awful numbness where she felt powerless to take control.

'It's probably just because you've been closed more than normal,' Max started gently, but Heidi interrupted.

'Of course I've been closed more than normal!' she snapped. 'What do people expect? Their furniture can't always come first!'

'That's why I'm here,' said Max. 'Don't get upset, Heidi. I thought I could come in full time to help clear the decks. Free of charge. As a friend. It's the least I can do. I know how you're feeling right now. I've been through this too. Some days it's as if the world has totally collapsed, isn't it?'

Heidi folded her arms defiantly across her chest.

'And I thought, in the longer term, that maybe I could work here more,' he said. 'Become a bigger part of the business. I have some savings; I could contribute.'

'Oh, Max,' she said. 'I don't need bailing out.'

'I'm not trying to bail you out,' he said. 'This place is yours and Johnny's family business and always will be. It just struck me that the two of us could become more of a team. I'd love to be more of a part of Eagles. But you're the boss, obviously.'

Heidi gave him a gentle shove and swallowed. His kindness touched her but also made her miss Johnny dreadfully. They'd poured blood, sweat and tears into this business – it had been their dream.

'Sorry,' she said, wiping her eyes. 'I don't know what's wrong with me.'

Max gave her a smile that overflowed with understanding.

'You're under a lot of pressure and you're grieving,' he said. 'It's never pretty, grief. I found it so hard when Jane died. I was so lonely without her, yet I didn't want to mix with people. That's why I spent so much time in my kayak! The sadness never goes away, but I think you find a way to live alongside it. I'll make us a cup of tea, shall I? You'll have to put those fish in the fridge soon too.'

She watched him move over to the sink and fill up the kettle.

'You'll get there,' he added. 'You just need more time.'

Heidi was quiet for a long moment.

'There's something else,' she said quietly. Still holding the kettle, Max turned to face her.

'Remember that Johnny and I had a baby?' she said.

Max blanched.

'Of course you remember,' she said, blushing. 'Sorry, Max. Anyway, we had this silent pact to never talk about him. But, before Johnny died, and without telling me, he found our son. He took a picture, on the day he died, of Main Street in Poole. There was a café in the picture and I went in it the other day. I saw our son in there, working. Johnny's photograph was a message to me, to tell me where our son was. Is.'

Max put the kettle down and didn't say a word, just waited for her to carry on talking.

'I told my mother about it and she got so cross,' Heidi continued. 'She thinks that finding him again would be the worst thing I could do. I'm so exhausted by it all, and the one person I want to talk to about it isn't here. I don't know what to do. I don't feel I can trust my own ability to make decisions at the moment. I don't know how to feel. One minute I'm delighted that Johnny did this, the other I'm really cross with him.'

She shrugged, wiping a tear from her eye.

'Johnny was a good man,' Max said. 'He would never have done anything to hurt you. He loved you, Heidi; I've always known that. Everyone has always known that. Perhaps, by doing this, by taking that photo, he wanted to leave you a gift? I can imagine him thinking like that.'

Heidi started pacing the workshop, relieved that finally someone understood.

'Yes,' she said. 'That's how I want to see it, but my mother doesn't see it that way.'

'Perhaps it's a generational thing or because it reminds her of a difficult time in both your lives,' Max said. 'Of course you need to tread carefully, but in my opinion, life is too short to be ruled by your head. Meeting your son might be the most wonderful thing you ever do.'

Heidi hugged Max, grateful for him being hopeful and positive about the possibility of meeting William.

'I won't know until I try, will I?' she said.

He shook his head. 'No,' he said. 'You never know until you try.'

He turned away from her and continued with the tea-making, before stopping and putting the kettle down.

'Have you got any wine in your fridge?' he asked. 'And any bread?'

'Yes,' she said. 'Both.'

'Do you have any plans for dinner?' he asked, picking up the parcel of mackerel.

Heidi shook her head. 'No,' she said. 'Zoe isn't back until tomorrow.'

He smiled.

'Give me half an hour and I'll do us a little barbecue in the garden and cook the mackerel,' he said. 'Then you can tell me more about William. If he's anything like Johnny, I want to meet him.'

Heidi thanked him, and while he sorted out the barbecue, she thought about how she should contact William. Phone? Email? Letter? She could drive to the café right now.

Quickly, she pulled out a piece of notepaper and dashed down a note.

Dear William,

I believe my husband Johnny Eagle has been in contact with you. I would love to also be in touch with you and have some news. Please email me at heidi@eaglesworkshop.co.uk if you're happy to meet me.

Short and sweet. Nothing too emotional. Quickly, she folded it in half, tucked it into an envelope, stuck on a stamp and put it in her pocket. A great weight lifted from her shoulders. Later, she would check the full address of the Blackbird Café and post it. If Johnny's death had taught her anything, it was that life was too short not to. And Max was right. You never knew until you tried.

The smell of the barbecue being lit filled her nostrils, and for the first time in ages, Heidi felt a little jolt of happiness.

Chapter Twelve

The sea was the grey of school trousers and the sky a few shades lighter. The colour perfectly reflected Heidi's mood. She'd been in for a swim, but today the water felt like treacle. Her arms ached and her leg kick felt uneven, so after a few minutes, she'd given up.

After drying off in the beach hut and having a hot drink, she stomped along the beach, head down, hands balled into fists. The note she'd written to William was bothering her. After her initial enthusiasm, it had taken two days before she found the courage to post it. Then she had waited next to the postbox, questioning out loud whether she should fish it out again with a coat hanger or ambush the postman. A passer-by had given her a wide berth and a nervous smile.

Doubt about whether she was doing the right thing assailed her. Envisaging a conversation with William was impossible. She would have to break the news of Johnny's death – perhaps, as a grieving widow, he would consider her a burden.

Stopping for a moment to look out again at the sea, she kicked at stones and shells on the beach. If only her own mindset was more stable. One moment she felt high as a kite, thinking that she might meet her son. The next she plummeted into darkness. She envied people who went through life on an even keel.

The worst thing was that Rosalind disapproved, and she hadn't even spoken to Scarlet and Zoe. They were her priority, yet she'd sidelined them. Any sensible person would have spoken to them first, then they could have decided what to do as a family. She'd made excuses to herself. Scarlet was in the throes of a new relationship with Frankie and dealing with Charlie; Zoe had returned from her weekend with Leo in a positive mood – the break had done her good. The last thing she wanted was to give them both another shock. But was it fair to hide the truth from them?

'Oh God,' she whispered to herself. 'I should have told them first.'

She continued to walk along the beach, feeling cold and pathetic, when her phone rang. It was Walter, from the flat underneath Rosalind's.

'It's nothing too serious,' said Walter, 'but your mum tripped up in the garden and hurt her knee. I've bandaged it up for her – I used to be a nurse, by the way. She's lying on her bed with her knee up. I've made her a tomato sandwich, but I'm sure she'd like to see you.'

Heidi wondered if that was true – they hadn't spoken since their awful argument.

'I'm down at the beach; I'll be two minutes,' she said, heading up off the beach and towards the flats. It was Walter who greeted her at Rosalind's door, ushering her inside, while he stood awkwardly in a blue-and-white-striped apron over his shorts and T-shirt.

'Walter!' called Rosalind from her bedroom. 'Who's that?'

Heidi raised her eyebrows at Walter, who lifted his conspiratorially in reply.

'It's me, Mother,' called Heidi, then turned to Walter. 'Thank you, Walter, for helping her and for calling me.'

'That's no problem, my dear,' he said. 'Your mother's a great friend, so full of life. I've helped bandage her knee and given her some painkillers. Some of my strong ones – codeine.'

He stopped to stretch out his back. 'She's been telling me about Eagles,' he said. 'And I wondered if you could take on one of my armchairs? It's a bit soggy in the middle. Soggy bottom.'

'Yes,' she said. 'There might be a bit of a delay though. I've got a lot on.'

'Oh,' he said. 'I'm not sure how long I can wait.'

He trailed off and Heidi was about to ask why, when his eyes misted over. He cleared his throat.

'My wife,' he said quickly. 'It's my wife's chair.'

Heidi frowned. She didn't know anything about Walter's wife – Rosalind had never told her – but his eyes were so full of pain that she quickly tried to make him feel better.

'I'll prioritise it,' she said. 'I can collect it, any time.'

'Thank you, dear,' he said brightly, untying the apron and laying it gently across the chair. 'I'll leave you and your mother to it. Just bang on the ceiling if you need anything. That's what Rosalind does. I don't mind at all – night or day. I can't sleep anyway.'

Heidi closed the door behind Walter and went through to her mother's bedroom. It was spartan – a photograph of Alan on the bedside table, a lamp, a glass of water, her glasses and a book about garden flowers.

'I know I don't look my best,' said Rosalind, propping herself up in bed. 'I've only got half my face on. But neither would you if you'd spent half the morning with your head in a hedge.'

'Mum,' said Heidi, unable to stop a tear leaking from her eye.

'Oh, Heidi,' Rosalind said, her voice softening. 'Save your tears. I'm fine.'

Heidi flushed with relief.

'What happened?' she asked.

Rosalind shrugged and sighed.

'I fell over,' she said. 'I was feeling light-headed, toppled over and got this sharp pain in my knee. Of course, bones my age can break easily, but it's not serious. I got a bit of broken glass in my knee and twisted it, but Walter helped me. He's awfully gentle. Used to be a nurse.'

'Light-headed?' Heidi said. 'Was that before or after Walter's codeine?'

'Before,' said Rosalind, giving her a pointed look. 'I often feel faint. I fainted in the bathroom last week, knocked the side of my head. I have low blood sugar apparently. Probably my age.'

Rosalind lifted up her hair and showed Heidi a scab above her ear.

'Why didn't you tell me?' said Heidi. 'Why is everyone with-holding information from me?'

Rosalind took Heidi's hand in hers and squeezed. 'It's hardly earth-shattering news,' she said. 'No need to be dramatic! Who else is withholding information from you?'

'Johnny, for a start,' Heidi said. 'And I had to hear from Zoe that Scarlet was having relationship troubles, and now you! I want to help my family. I don't want you all withholding information.'

Imagining the letter she'd written to William winging its way across town, Heidi dropped her gaze, suddenly aware of the hypocrisy of her words.

'I know you do,' Rosalind said gently. 'But please don't waste time worrying about me. Look, Heidi, I'm sorry about the other day when we fell out a little bit. I shouldn't have got so angry when you told me about William, but this is one of those situations I just know will not end w—'

Rosalind's voice trembled before her words faded to nothing. A beat passed between them.

'Why were you so cross?' Heidi said quietly. 'Does the thought of me meeting him frighten you? We've got nothing to lose by talking openly, have we? After all these years of keeping him a secret, locked away. I often wonder what it would have been like if I'd been able to keep him. Would it have been so terrible? I know you and Dad were horrified that I was so young, but couldn't we have overcome that? It was the 1980s and it was perfectly acceptable for unmarried girls to keep their babies.'

'Trollops,' said Rosalind, with a twinkle in her eye.

'No, not trollops,' said Heidi, shaking her head. 'Just young girls, in love with a boy and having a sexual relationship. I knew how to be safe, but we made a mistake.'

Rosalind sighed.

'It was complicated,' she said, shaking her head. 'I didn't want you to suffer – your life, your ambitions, your dreams, your reputation – I was so proud of you. I wanted you to have a full, free life. I was so angry, with you, myself… Oh it's so damn difficult to explain. You don't understand.'

Rosalind suddenly seemed defeated, her limbs slack.

'What don't I understand?' said Heidi. 'Try me.'

Rosalind's eyes were glassy and her cheeks cherry pink. She turned away from Heidi and stared out of the window for such a long time, Heidi wondered if she'd forgotten she was there.

'What don't I understand?' she repeated.

Rosalind turned back to face Heidi, her eyes filling with tears.

'You're so damned intent on making me confess all,' she said, her voice breaking. 'I was going to take this to the grave with me, but the reason I insisted you gave up William was because—'

She fell silent.

'Because what?' Heidi prompted. 'You can tell me.'

Rosalind's eyes slipped to her hands, and when she spoke, her words were barely audible.

'The same thing happened to me at the same age,' she whispered.

Heidi frowned. 'What do you mean the same thing?' she asked. 'Did you get pregnant?'

Rosalind leaned her head back against the pillow. 'I did,' she said faintly.

Heidi's heart thumped in her chest. 'And what?' she asked. 'You had an abortion?'

Rosalind was silent for ten seconds, but it felt like an hour.

'No,' she said. 'Abortion was virtually unheard of in my day. Illegal. My mother thought I was shameful and organised for me to go to one of my father's distant cousins in Brighton. I had a girl. I had to vow I would never try to contact her. And when the same thing then happened to you, I felt so guilty for not giving you the information you needed to protect yourself and I panicked. I reacted the wrong way. I just wanted to make the problem go away. I didn't want your life to be defined by a mistake. So, me and your father made the decision we did. It seemed right at the time. I never dreamed you'd go on to marry Johnny and have more children with him. I know I wronged you, and I'm so desperately sorry for that.'

Rosalind seemed to shrink under the bedspread. Heidi dug her nails into her palms.

'Are you going to say something?' Rosalind asked quietly. 'You normally have plenty to say.'

Heidi swallowed. 'I... I'm... just trying to take this in,' she muttered. 'So, somewhere out there I have a sister?'

'Half-sister,' Rosalind corrected. 'The father was my first love. We were terribly young and met at a dance. Clueless and head over heels.'

Heidi blinked. It seemed impossible that the mother she'd always known as a straight-down-the-line, chin-up and 'proper' person was ever head over heels.

'Do you know anything about her?' Heidi asked.

'Not much,' said Rosalind. 'I know that her new parents called her Tuesday, which was the day she was born.'

Rosalind paused, as if uncertain whether to say more.

'Go on,' said Heidi. 'You might as well.'

'About ten years ago she contacted me out of the blue,' said Rosalind, a deep frown line on her forehead. 'I nearly dropped dead with shock when her letter arrived. She told me she lived in Brighton and loved to travel. She sent me a photograph – it's in my glasses case in the drawer. Don't look now. Your father didn't even know about her, so I had to write back saying I wasn't interested in meeting her. It wasn't an easy letter to write, but I was putting your father and you first. She told me she had no children of her own.'

Heidi slumped back into her chair. Her head felt ready to explode.

'She wrote to you, and you told her you didn't want to know her?' Heidi cried, incredulous. 'How could you do that?'

'Because your father and you didn't know about her existence!' Rosalind snapped. 'I didn't see what good could come from any reunion. She had her own life and we had ours.'

'That must have broken her heart,' said Heidi.

Rosalind's shoulders sagged. 'Possibly,' she said sadly. 'But I hope that she'll understand that I didn't have a choice. What would your father have said? It probably would have killed him.'

'You always have a choice,' said Heidi.

'That's a pleasant thought, but it's not true,' her mother replied.

'But, even though you went through this,' Heidi asked, 'you still thought it was better for me to give up William?'

'Yes,' said Rosalind. 'I thought it was for the best. It was for the best.'

'And now? Now that Dad is dead and I know about Tuesday, would you like to meet her?'

Rosalind shook her head and dismissed the thought with a wave of her hand.

'I can't open up old wounds,' she said. 'I don't think there's any point. I had my chance and I turned it down. My loss.'

Rosalind's expression was stricken.

'I can't take all this in,' said Heidi.

'I know. I knew you'd be upset. That's why I've never told you. I'd planned to take this to my grave. I've carried it with me all these years. I wish I'd done things differently. I hope you don't hate me for keeping this from you?'

'No,' Heidi said. 'I'm not upset. I'm sorry for you, that's all. I'm sorry you had to suffer.'

Rosalind sighed. 'Well it's not as if any alternative was an option back then,' she said.

Heidi squeezed Rosalind's hand with as much kindness as she could communicate. Rosalind's eyes brimmed with tears.

'You could try crying,' Heidi choked. 'Just let it all out.'

'I can't,' said Rosalind, swiping her nose with a tissue. 'If I start, I won't stop, and what good would that do to anyone? There's no use in crying. Oh, Heidi love, I'm tired now. Those tablets Walter gave me…'

Rosalind turned on her side and, like a light being flicked off, closed her eyes and fell into a deep sleep.

After a few minutes sitting completely still by the bed, Heidi looked in the bedside drawer and found the glasses case containing the photograph of Tuesday. She shared many of Rosalind's features.

Trying not to disturb Rosalind, Heidi took a photograph of it with her mobile, softly kissed her mother's cheek and crept out the room.

Leaving the flats, Heidi was struck by a thought about wounds: bandages covered cuts and bruises, signalling to others to offer sympathy. But what about the invisible wounds people carried in their hearts? There were no bandages for those, yet the scars ran deep and lasted a lifetime. If there were physical bandages for emotional hurts, perhaps people would be kinder to one another.

Chapter Thirteen

The email arrived into Heidi's pocket during dinner at Pizza Express. She was out with Scarlet and Zoe and usually hated the intrusion of mobile phones on family life. It made her stomach sink to see a table of people sitting together but all silently staring at their phones. Johnny's rule had been that unless you worked for Médecins Sans Frontières, there was no need to have your mobile lined up next to your knife and fork. But she couldn't resist.

'Why are you checking your phone, Mum?' said Scarlet, raising her eyebrows. 'You know what Dad used to say. No phones unless—'

'I know,' she said. 'Unless you work for Médecins San Frontières.'

They all laughed, but Heidi felt as though she'd had an electric shock. With a shaking hand she pushed her phone back into her pocket. The sight of William's name in her inbox made her incapable of swallowing another mouthful of pizza. She lifted her water glass to her lips and gulped the cold liquid, trying not to give away her internal panic. Zoe cleared her throat.

'You know when Leo and I were in Scotland?' said Zoe. 'We, well, we were talking about maybe taking a year out together. I might defer my application to Plymouth.'

Heidi was taken aback by Zoe's change of heart. Taken aback and worried – she didn't want Johnny's death to throw her daughter off course.

Scarlet and Zoe were looking at her, expecting an answer, but she was battling with the urge to read William's email.

'I don't think that's a good idea,' said Heidi hurriedly. 'You've always been dead set on nursing. I think you should carry on with your original plan. What would you do with a year out?'

Zoe shrugged and sighed.

'I just think we might need a bit of time out,' she said quietly. 'Leo wants to work and save up some money.'

'I think it would be a mistake,' said Heidi. 'I don't think you've thought it through properly. Just because you had a nice weekend in Scotland doesn't mean you should take a year out.'

'I knew you'd say that,' Zoe said, rolling her eyes. 'You're so uptight about everything. Dad was the laid-back one.'

Heidi sucked in her breath. Zoe's words stung and she was aware of her hypocrisy. She leaned back in her chair, glancing at the people sitting at the other tables. There were young couples not much older than Zoe or Scarlet, locked in conversation, hanging off each other's words. It was times like these when she missed Johnny dreadfully. Usually, in this setting he'd be deeply engaged in the conversation, injecting humour and stories. He'd enjoy the pizza, gobble up the leftovers, pour Heidi a glass of water while he had a beer. Ask her if she liked her pizza. Whether she wanted to try a slice of his. Small things. Gone.

Right now, he'd probably say: step back a little, let Zoe be. She's a sensible young woman. She needs to make her own decisions. He had always been reassuring and helped make important decisions, but now, without him here, everything was up to her. It wasn't that she couldn't cope or didn't know her own mind – she did. But she had become so used to running decisions about their daughters past Johnny. Discussing them. Sharing the responsibility.

Her phone buzzed once more, and her stomach turned over again. She slipped her hand into her pocket and felt the outline of her phone. She held her breath.

'So, how *was* your weekend in Scotland?' said Scarlet, attempting to break the tension. 'Did Leo take his bloody ukulele?'

'He's really good at the ukulele!' said Zoe. 'It was lovely. I... we—'

'I bet you went hiking with your map and compass,' said Scarlet, 'like scouts. And then had a cup of tea and a teacake as a treat.'

'Hey,' said Zoe. 'Stop making fun of us.'

Heidi couldn't wait a moment longer. She stood up abruptly.

'Sorry, girls,' she said. 'I have to use the bathroom.'

Walking through the restaurant and up the spiral staircase towards the ladies, Heidi hummed the theme tune to *Dallas*. 'Calm down,' she told herself, her head buzzing.

The noise of clattering plates, cutlery, laughter, conversation and a baby crying seemed to amplify, and Heidi felt the urge to go outside and fill her lungs with fresh air.

Pushing open the door of the ladies, she went into a cubicle, took her phone out of her pocket and opened her email.

And there it was. An email – no, two emails – from William. Her hand shot to her face as she covered her eyes, reading William's words between splayed fingers. He was brief.

Heidi,

I received your letter. I was shocked to hear from you but pleased. Johnny had mentioned you when we met. How about Wednesday? 11 a.m.? At the café?

William

Then, in a second message:

PS: Will Johnny be coming with you? I haven't heard from him since we met. Is it because of the money? Tell him I will pay him back.

Heidi rested the side of her head on the cubicle wall. Her vision blurred as she reread the line that had snagged her heart: *I was shocked to hear from you but pleased.* She read it over and over.

The pizza and wine rose in her throat and her stomach clenched into a tight knot. She wondered for a moment if she might vomit. The emails had been sent minutes earlier and the image of William sitting at a computer, perhaps trying to work out what to type, burst into her thoughts. He had obviously been worrying about where Johnny had got to – and she would have to break the news of his death. Perhaps she should have done so in her letter, but wouldn't that have been worse?

She read his emails again, this time focusing on the mention of borrowed money. Johnny had given money to William. She thought of the £300 rolled up in a sock in Johnny's shoe. Why did William need money? How much had he borrowed? Perhaps he was in difficulty. Heidi swallowed. She didn't want to think of him in difficulty. It didn't go with the story she had created for him.

I was shocked to hear from you but pleased.

'Mum?' called Zoe's voice from outside the cubicle.

Tucking her phone back into her pocket, she wiped tears from her face with tissue. 'Yes?' she replied.

'Mum,' Zoe said. 'You've been in here for ages. Your pizza is cold. Are you sick?'

'No, no. I'm fine,' she said quickly, blowing her nose. 'I was just thinking about your dad.'

Heidi flushed the toilet and came out of the airless cubicle to wash her hands. Zoe's cheeks were bright pink as she draped her arms around her mother's waist and hugged her tight.

'We have each other,' said Zoe. 'Don't forget that. And Scarlet. And Grandma.'

'I know,' said Heidi. 'I was just missing your dad.'

She splashed her face with cold water, hating herself for lying to her precious daughter. Zoe slipped her arm through Heidi's and they left the ladies, weaving their way through the tables and back into the restaurant.

'So, Mum,' Zoe said, before they got back to the table. 'I know you don't like the idea, but I'm really serious about deferring and having a gap year. I *have* thought about this, you know. I haven't just randomly said it without having good reason.'

She stared at Heidi, as if trying to communicate another layer of information, but Heidi's mind was on William's email. On the money he owed Johnny. On Tuesday, out there somewhere. On her mother, no doubt regretting her confession. Everything around her looked the same, but in her heart she knew that her life had changed beyond recognition.

'I think we should talk through your options,' said Heidi. 'If you're serious about this.'

'Thank you,' said Zoe. 'Let's go for a walk by the sea. You look like you could do with some air.'

'Yes,' said Heidi, her voice trembling. 'Yes, I would like that. Let's get out of here.'

Chapter Fourteen

There are moments in life when you feel as if you're standing on the edge of a cliff, arms outstretched, wind in your hair, preparing to leap. Today was one of those moments. Hovering outside the Blackbird Café, her entire body shaking, Heidi was reminded of the time she climbed to the top of the Eiffel Tower and, to the fury of hundreds of people behind her, froze. She couldn't put one foot in front of the other.

'Come on,' she whispered to herself now, sliding her feet forward. 'Do it. Move.'

To passers-by she was just an unremarkable woman walking into an unremarkable café for a cup of coffee. But the reality couldn't be more different. Here, now, the past would join hands with the present. The secret she had been carrying for so many years would finally be exposed. At last, she would lay eyes on her son. Perhaps she would even hold him in her arms or plant a gentle kiss on his cheek. Would she be as he had imagined? Would he be shocked by her frizzy hair, or think her choice of clothes – grey jeans and a black jumper – too casual? Perhaps she should have made herself shinier: worn something smarter, a little more make-up. What if he was disappointed? She would know, instantly, if he was.

'For goodness' sake it's not an interview,' she muttered to herself. But in a way, it was. The biggest, most significant interview of her life.

'Are you coming in?' said a friendly female waitress, holding open the café door. 'We've plenty of free tables.'

Heidi stumbled backwards but managed half a smile. Trying not to hyperventilate, she entered the café and scanned the room but couldn't see anyone fitting William's description.

'Sorry, thank you,' she stuttered. 'I was miles away. Is, um, is William here? I was um, supposed to be…'

'No,' said the girl. 'He's not working today.'

Heidi's heart plummeted.

'Oh,' she said, feeling as though a rug had been pulled from beneath her feet. 'Oh, I see. I didn't realise. It is Wednesday, isn't it?'

'Yes,' the girl said, laughing. 'It was last time I looked.'

Heidi rubbed her forehead and wondered what to do. The girl was still staring at her and gestured towards a table. Not knowing what else to do, Heidi sat down and ordered a coffee.

The waitress gone, Heidi tried to regulate her breathing. William had obviously changed his mind. Perhaps he couldn't face her. Perhaps she had been stupid to expect him to come at all. They should have done this more formally, employed a mediator or met in a neutral place. A park. He wasn't going to want his colleagues watching him meet his biological mother for the first time, was he? Why had he ever suggested it?

Hands shaking, she checked her phone, to see if he had emailed her again, but there were no new mails. She reread his original email and checked that she had the time and day right, aware of the sweat running down her body underneath her jumper. The waitress put the coffee down in front of her and Heidi half smiled, nodding briefly in thanks.

Massaging her temples with her fingertips, she tried to regain control of the conflicting emotions pumping through her veins. Something made her look up and glance at the door. She blinked. Her heart thumped. Then she jolted back her chair. William. It was William, and he was looking at her, smiling shyly. On his left cheek was a single dimple. She swallowed.

'Heidi?' William said, approaching her with his eyes slightly lowered.

He's shy, she thought. Shy and worried. Shy and terrified. Pale. Was he tired? He looked tired.

He was the image of his father, even down to his choice of overcoat; black, collar up. Johnny had worn one similar, years ago. In his hand he carried a thin bunch of purple and pink freesias that were tied with a length of brown string.

Standing too quickly from her chair, she rocked the table and sent her cup of coffee skittering onto the floor, where it cracked. Everyone in the café turned to stare. Colour rose in her face.

'Oh,' she said, lifting her hands to her lips and shaking her head, scooping down to pick up the cup. 'I'm so sorry.'

William crouched down to help pick up the broken pieces. Briefly their eyes met – he had beautiful pale-brown eyes – and they stared at each other for a long moment, a small smile spreading over their lips.

'Hello, William,' Heidi said. 'I'm sorry about the cup.'

'Don't worry,' he said. 'It's not an antique. Shall we get up or are you happy on the floor?'

He smiled and words failed her. She felt ridiculous, hopeless, inadequate.

'This is…' she started. 'I'm… yes, let's sit at the table.'

'These are for you,' he said, handing her the freesias.

'Thank you,' she said. 'They're beautiful. I love freesias.'

Her head flooded with questions. Had Johnny told William everything about her? Had he talked about what happened when they had William? Instinctively she wanted to explain everything immediately and urgently, so that he might understand.

'I'll order another coffee,' said William, handing the pieces to a waitress – presumably a friend of his – with a dustpan and brush. Heidi observed his trembling hands and longed to put him at ease. But she couldn't stop staring at him.

Leaning forward on his chair, on the very edge of it, elbow on the table, chin resting in his hand, his little finger beat out a rhythm on his cheekbone. The muscles in his cheeks twitched a little as if he was clenching his jaw. On closer inspection, his features were just like Johnny's though his skin was paler and the area under his eyes had a faint violet colour. She felt a wave of concern, but a crazy little laugh erupted from her. She put her hand to her mouth.

'I can't stop looking at you,' she said. 'Sorry. You're just so similar to Johnny. You're almost exactly like him.'

'I'm pretty nervous,' William said, changing position, so that both elbows were on the table, making the coffee cups wobble. 'It's so strange to meet you. I've always wondered… ever since I found out that I was adopted. Meeting Johnny blew me away. As you say, we're pretty similar. It was a little like looking in the mirror.'

Heidi chastised herself for not getting in there with the news about Johnny first. Tears stung her eyes.

'William,' she said, clearing her throat. 'I know we've only just this second met. But I'm afraid I have some awful news. It's about Johnny. I'm sorry to say that he died, suddenly. He had a heart condition and suffered a fatal heart attack. He was here, actually, in the street when he collapsed.'

'Here?' said William.

'Yes,' she said. 'On Wednesday the twelfth of April. Had you seen him?'

'No,' he said. 'I don't work on Wednesdays. He had started popping in sometimes though. Or walking past, anyway. Jesus, wow, I can't believe this.'

'I know,' said Heidi. 'I'm sorry; it's all such a shock. He didn't tell me that he'd contacted you. He sent me a photo of this street, of this café just before he died, and I discovered he'd tracked you down. It's a huge shock. All of this. I'm sorry, so sorry to tell you about Johnny. It must come as the most dreadful shock. Perhaps I should have told you in an email, but it seemed too cold.'

The colour drained from William's face. He went completely white.

Heidi reached tentatively across the table and rested her hand briefly on his arm.

'I'm sorry,' she said again, her lips quivering as she battled not to cry. 'I know it's a lot to take in.'

William withdrew his arm gently and fished a small bottle out of his pocket. It was a mini bottle of rum. He poured it into his coffee, then took a glug straight from the bottle. An alarm bell sounded in her head.

'Takes the edge off,' he said, with a small sad smile.

'How many times did you meet up with Johnny?' asked Heidi gently.

'Three times,' he said. 'I liked him. We talked about photography. I've always enjoyed taking photos. He didn't tell me he had a heart condition. Why didn't he say anything?'

'I don't know,' said Heidi, biting her bottom lip. 'He was doing well, making great progress. It came as a shock to us all.'

'That's a lot to process,' said William, shaking his head. 'So, you had a funeral and everything?'

'Yes,' she said. 'I didn't know about you then. I'm sorry.'

He nodded.

'I thought life was on the up when he got in touch,' he said. 'I was stupidly making all these plans for what we could do together. And now he's dead. I'm sorry for you, losing your husband like that.'

'Thank you,' said Heidi, swallowing down the burning lump in her throat. 'Did Johnny tell you much about us, me and about your adoption?'

William bit his bottom lip. 'A little,' he said. 'He told me you were both young when you got pregnant with me. He told me that I have two sisters, but I don't think they know about my existence, do they? I'm the skeleton in the cupboard.'

He let out a small laugh. Heidi twisted uncomfortably in her chair.

'I've always thought about you,' she said, trying not to break down. 'I'm overwhelmed to meet you, William – really I am. I know this will take time to sink in, but I'd love to get to know you.'

'You might not like me,' he said, trying to joke but exposing his vulnerability.

'I already do,' she said gently. 'You seem like a lovely person.'

He raised his eyebrows. His leg was jigging under the table. He shook his head and repeatedly rubbed his jawline, as if trying to remove a stain.

'Can't get my head around this,' he said. Again, he dipped into his pocket for the bottle of rum and took a swig.

'That won't help in the long run,' Heidi couldn't help but say.

He totally ignored her, and she wished she hadn't spoken. She opened her bag and fished inside for the Polaroid photograph of William wrapped up in a blanket on the rose chair. Tentatively, she showed it to him.

'This is you,' she said, 'on the day you were born. Did Johnny show you this?'

He nodded, picking up the photo and looking at it carefully.

'Yes,' he said. 'I can hardly believe that's me.'

Heidi smiled and looked at the photo herself.

'Yes,' she said. 'That's you. We sat together on that beautiful chair for many precious hours. That chair has always stuck in my mind – the thought of you and I sitting there, in the window, with the sun coming through. I think about that a lot. Every day.'

William chewed his lip, looking uncomfortable.

'Where do you live?' she asked, trying to change tack.

'In a bit of a dump,' he said. 'I had a house, but it's a long story. I live in my mate's studio flat for now.'

'Do you have any other family close by?' she asked, resisting the urge to ask about his adoptive parents. Had they been good to him?

'I have a six-year-old son,' he said. 'But my partner has him. I get to see him occasionally. Again, it's a long story.'

A grandson! Her heart leaped.

'Oh my goodness, I had no idea!' she ventured. 'I'd love to meet him. What's his name? Do you have a photograph? You must miss him.'

'I do miss him,' he said. 'My own fault though. He's Fred – Freddy. I don't have a picture on me. Plenty at home though.'

William's mobile bleeped and he quickly looked at it, apologising under his breath, but saying he 'just needed to check it'. Whatever the message was, it changed his mood. He went as stiff as a board.

'Are you alright?' said Heidi. 'I'd like to talk to you about everything properly, but perhaps it's all too much now, today, like this? Would you be happy to meet again? Maybe we could walk along the beach or something? I can bring photographs next time, of my daughters, your sisters, Scarlet and Zoe.'

He seemed utterly distracted, as if he was already halfway out of the door.

'It's so good to—' Heidi started, but he interrupted.

'About the money that Johnny gave me,' he said quietly. She could see he was embarrassed. 'Did he mention that I needed more? There was another £300 he said he could bring and—'

William's cheeks were blazing red. Heidi swallowed and her stomach twisted into a ball. She thought of the roll of notes in Johnny's shoe.

'He didn't mention any of this to me,' she said. 'I didn't even know he'd found you! What do you need money for? How much more do you need?'

His scraped at an invisible mark on the table with his fingernail.

'I need… need… it for Freddy,' he stammered. 'It's his birthday coming up and I promised his mum I'd get him a games console, and I promised I'd find the money for her to get her drains, I mean guttering sorted out… plus I owe her. I'll pay you back, of course.

Another five hundred should probably do it. Sort the drains – I mean guttering – and Fred's present.'

Heidi closed her eyes for a long second. She should have been prepared for this. It was a risk, but if she didn't speak her mind now, she knew she'd regret it.

'Well there's one thing we have in common, William,' she said. 'We're both terrible liars. Now why don't you tell me what you really need it for?'

And then William's expression completely changed, and a darkness fell, as if clouds had covered the sun and all the lights in the café had been switched off.

Chapter Fifteen

She failed the interview. Spectacularly. She couldn't have done a worse job if she'd tried. Furious with herself, Heidi followed William out into the street.

'William, I'm sorry!' she called after him. 'Wait! Please. Have I upset you?'

He stopped dead and spun around to face her, his eyes wild.

'Have you upset me?' he spat. 'First you reject me, then you don't even tell me Johnny is dead and now you call me a liar. Well fuck that. I don't need anyone else in my life calling me a liar.'

Heidi stood still, speechless, as he walked further down the street.

'I'm sorry!' she shouted after him, her voice breaking. 'Send me your bank details and I'll transfer that money, no problem. I want to help!'

His pace slowed slightly, and she wondered if he might stop, but then he picked up speed, turned the corner and disappeared out of sight. She wondered if she should run after him but stopped herself. She needed to take a moment to digest what was happening – not chase after William and completely wreck their new, fragile, barely existent relationship.

'What a disaster,' she whispered.

Tears in her eyes, she returned to the café to pick up her bag, where the entire café had obviously heard her yelling and were now staring at her.

'What are you looking at?' she yelled before leaving, feeling bemused, blindsided and sorry. If only Johnny had given her the heads-up about William and the money, and what he was like. If only he was here.

'Thanks, Johnny,' she hissed as she headed quickly back to the van. 'Why the hell didn't you tell me?'

She was half shouting as she walked. Other people in the street looked at her with a mixture of fear and sympathy. Closing her eyes, she suppressed the urge to scream. It wasn't fair to feel angry with Johnny when he wasn't here to defend himself, but that's exactly what she did feel. Anger. Fury. Rage.

Groaning, she looked up at the sky, where a gaggle of noisy Canadian geese flew overhead in the shape of an arrow. You could hear the sound of their powerful wings flapping. She envied their freedom.

Arriving at the Morris, she pushed the key in the lock.

'I wish you'd told me, Johnny!' she said again, the anger suddenly draining out of her. 'Then we could have done this together. Why would you think it was a good idea to leave me out of all this?'

'He wanted to suss him out first,' said a male voice from behind her.

She turned on her heels and saw Max standing in the car park, his hands pushed into his pockets, concern in his eyes.

'He wanted to suss him out and get to know him, so that on your birthday, he could introduce you to William and give you the best surprise.'

Heidi stared at Max, her vision blurring. She shook her head, trying to straighten her thoughts.

'You knew?' she asked, incredulous. 'He told you?'

Max approached Heidi slowly and carefully, with his palms raised, as if she was a wild animal, likely to bite off his hand.

'He did,' he said, offering her an apologetic smile. 'He swore me to secrecy. He had it all planned – the birthday surprise. I was just a sounding board. I felt shitty about it straight away, and I argued with him about it. Then he had to go and die on us, and I didn't think it was my place to say anything to you! But, thank God, you got there yourself. What do you do when your best friend asks you to keep a secret – a proper secret? I'm a loyal person. He would have done the same thing for me. He had your interests at heart. I tried to tell him otherwise, but he wasn't having it.'

'Bloody hell,' she said. 'Isn't that taking loyalty a bit far?'

'No,' said Max. 'Johnny was my friend. I wanted to do the right thing by him.'

Heidi's head pounded.

'But what are you doing here?' she asked, confused. 'Don't tell me you followed me here.'

'Of course not!' he said, with a small laugh. 'I parked here and saw the van – you can hardly miss it – and I wondered if you were going to see William. I thought I'd wait for you in case you needed someone to talk to. When Johnny had his first heart attack, he said if anything ever happened to him, to look out for you. That's all I'm doing. Shall we sit inside the van for a moment?'

Heidi sighed, nodded and opened up the van. She sat in the driver's seat and Max in the passenger seat. Max rested his hand on Heidi's forearm and, after a few moments, she briefly rested her head on his shoulder, his warmth making her want to cry.

'Did you meet William then?' he said.

She nodded and leaned her head back against the seat.

'This has been so crazy,' she said, wiping tears from her eyes. 'I've waited years to meet William. I've thought about him every day. I've dreamed of meeting him, seen people in the street and thought *could that be you?* And now I've messed it all up.'

'Why do you say that?' said Max.

Heidi sat upright and explained what had happened in the café.

'You're human, Heidi,' Max said. 'It's an emotional experience and highly charged. It's going to take time for you both to adjust. Have you arranged to meet again?'

Heidi shook her head. 'We didn't leave on the best terms,' she said. 'I wish I could talk to Johnny. He'd know what to do.'

'Tell him anyway,' Max said. 'I've heard you chatting to him in the workshop.'

'Am I losing my mind?' Heidi said.

'No,' he said. 'I do the same. When Jane died, I planted a pear tree and sprinkled her ashes around it. She loved pears, so it seemed fitting. And now I talk to the tree a lot. She probably wishes I'd just stop burdening her with all my problems!'

Heidi was relieved to laugh. She rubbed at a crick in her neck. 'Ouch,' she said, massaging her right shoulder. 'I'm so stressed out. My shoulders are up to my ears and my neck is as stiff as a post. I need to get my head straight. I'm ricocheting from one problem to another.'

'I've got an idea,' Max said. 'What are you doing after this?'

Heidi checked her watch. It was almost lunchtime and she hadn't even made a start on any work yet. Thinking of the backlog made her body flame with heat. If she didn't get a grip on it all, she would go under.

'Work,' she said. 'I've so many orders to fulfil.'

'I can help. No problem,' he said. 'But before we do that, come for a swim first. Go home and grab your kit then meet me at Southbourne beach. We haven't been for a swim together in ages.'

'I can't today,' said Heidi. 'I've too much to do.'

'I won't take no for an answer,' Max said. 'It'll take an hour out of your day and make you feel so much better. You know that better than I do. The health benefits are proven. People right back to the eighteenth century thought that swimming in the sea had a curative and therapeutic effect. That's why people started flocking here, to Bournemouth, to swim – to recover.'

'I know, I know, but I'm just so busy,' Heidi started but Max lifted a finger to his lips.

'Come on,' he said. 'Let's go.'

Max got out the van and Heidi sat in silence for a moment, thinking of her disastrous meeting with William. Blinking away tears, she started up the engine when her mobile rang. Glancing at it, she saw Scarlet's number and immediately picked up. Through tears, Scarlet said she needed to get away from Charlie – he was behaving like a stalker. Heidi felt hugely protective of Scarlet and, also, guilty for being so consumed with William. Her family was falling apart. She wiped her nose with a tissue and pulled herself together.

'Come home,' Heidi told Scarlet. 'Come home today and bring Frankie.'

An hour later, Heidi stood knee-deep in the cold seawater, in her Speedo swimsuit, goggles and a bright-yellow swimming hat. The sea was invitingly flat and almost silver, with wispy pale-pink clouds hovering above. The beach was empty apart from a couple of dog walkers and a Lycra-clad cyclist, speeding along the promenade. A feeling of calm washed over her.

'You're hardcore not wearing a wetsuit,' said Max, who was wearing his, plus wetsuit socks.

She shook her head. 'I just prefer it without,' she said. 'I feel more free, but I can't stay in long – partly because it's cold but also because Scarlet's coming home. Relationship troubles.'

Max was jumping up and down on the spot, warming up.

'I remember those,' Max said, giving Heidi a look. She gave him a shove and rolled her eyes.

'Right,' she said. 'Are you ready?'

Max grinned and nodded, then they headed into the water. Heidi pulled down her goggles and went deeper, bending her knees so more of her body was submerged, until eventually, her whole body was under. The icy water numbed her skin, and when she put her face in, her lips tingled with cold.

'Okay?' Max asked, giving her the thumbs up. 'Shall we swim?'

Heidi returned his thumbs up. Her skin buzzed as she moved through the water and focused on each stroke. For that moment, the sea was all that mattered. She felt aware only of the sound of the water, the cold against her skin and, when she lifted her head out of the water to take a breath, the vast blue sky above. For several hundred metres, she swam side by side with Max, until they came to a natural pause for breath, treading water in the gentle waves.

'Thanks, Max,' she said. 'You were right. After this morning, I needed this.'

Floating on her back in a star shape and staring up at the pale-blue sky, she heard William's harsh words. *First you reject me.* She heard a familiar tune in her mind and flipped back over onto her stomach before they started to swim slowly back towards the shore.

'I think my mother was right,' she said to Max. 'I should have listened to her.'

'The first meeting was bound to be difficult,' said Max. 'Don't give up. Your mum is just worrying about you. Fearful of the unknown.'

Heidi thought of Tuesday – the letter that Rosalind had written to her saying she didn't want to be in touch must have been so hard for Tuesday to swallow.

'My mother told me a secret the other day,' said Heidi. 'She told me that, apparently, I have a half-sister, who was also adopted. She's never met her, never spoken of her. It all came spilling out when I spoke to her about William. I think that's why she's always reacted so strongly about this whole situation.'

'No!' Max said, treading water. 'Really? So that's why she was so furious with you. Will you try to find her? What's her name?'

'Tuesday Snow,' she said. 'There can't be many out there…'

Max laughed. 'No,' he said. 'I'll look her up, unless you don't want me to.'

'I'm not sure I have the strength,' said Heidi. 'But I suppose it wouldn't hurt to have a look.'

'Your family is full of surprises,' said Max. 'Race you!'

They swam back to the beach, and Heidi clambered out of the water, her skin bright pink with cold. Drying herself quickly, she pulled on her clothes, her freezing fingers fumbling with the zips. Max, still in his wetsuit, was scrolling on his mobile.

'How old would Tuesday be?' he asked.

'About sixty-two or three, I guess,' she said. 'She also said that she lived in Brighton. But, Max, maybe we shouldn't look her up. I should speak to my mother first. She wants to keep everything buried in the past – you know what she's like. Perhaps it's easier for her to cope with. She's suffered a lot too.'

Max pushed his phone into his bag.

'But what about you?' he asked. 'What do you want?'

Heidi blinked and smiled at him.

'Thought so,' he said. 'I'm going in for a bit longer. I've got my wetsuit on, so I can stay in a while yet.'

'You've already started looking, haven't you?' said Heidi, warmth gradually flooding through her. 'Haven't you?'

But Max was already running towards the sea and splashing into the waves.

Chapter Sixteen

In the kitchen, Heidi scanned the collection of vintage teapots on the windowsill. She chose the green one, in the shape of an apple, probably from the 1950s. Filling it with water and a teabag, she placed it on the table with two gold teacups, in front of Scarlet and her girlfriend, Frankie. The backdrop of the bright-blue kitchen wall framed them beautifully.

'I love all the colour in your house,' Frankie said. 'There's so much grey everywhere usually.'

'Thank you, Frankie,' Heidi said. 'I do love colour, despite not wearing any myself.'

Heidi had instantly liked Frankie. Ever since she'd walked into the house, she was full of compliments and warmth. Now, she was scanning the framed photographs on the walls, the postcards and photos stuck with magnets to the fridge – and the shelves lined with recipe books Heidi rarely looked at these days. There were several plants on those shelves too – which she hoped Frankie didn't look at – all in desperate need of watering.

'Excuse my swimming hair,' said Heidi, catching sight of her reflection and pointing at her curls, which stood from her head like a wire brush. On the radiator in the corner, Heidi's swimming costume and cap were drying, and the faint smell of sea salt, not yet showered off, emanated from her skin.

'You went swimming with Max then,' Scarlet said. 'That's a bit cosy isn't it?'

'Don't be daft!' Heidi replied. 'Max is a great friend. He's been our friend for years – you know that.'

'But why ask you to go swimming?' said Scarlet sulkily. 'What does he want from you?'

'He doesn't want anything!' Heidi replied. 'We used to go swimming a lot when we were younger. Calm down, Scarlet – you're always so suspicious of people! Milk, Frankie?'

'Please,' Frankie said, adding a teaspoon of sugar to her cup.

'Scarlet?' Heidi asked, hovering over her cup with the milk. 'Milk?'

'No,' said Scarlet. 'I'm meat, dairy and sugar free, as from yesterday. We all should be. If you watch that documentary, *Cowspiracy*, you'd give up meat and dairy instantly. You know what I was saying about being more honest with myself – I realised I actually don't want to eat animals. And perhaps if Dad hadn't been such a carnivore, his heart wouldn't have suffered.'

Heidi glanced at Frankie, who opened her mouth to speak, but Heidi got there first.

'I think that's brilliant,' said Heidi. 'I admire you.'

'Oh, you're so lovely,' said Frankie. 'My parents would refuse to feed me if I went vegan. They're full-on meat and two veg.'

'Everyone's different, I suppose,' Heidi replied.

'That's exactly the thing though,' said Frankie. 'My parents can't accept that people are different. They don't like it. Anything that departs from the norm is seen as weird or unnatural. Even if it's food-based. I've tried so many times to get them interested in the unconventional side of life, but they won't have it. Not interested. It's normal or nothing.'

'I'm not really sure if there is a "normal",' said Heidi, not knowing how to respond to Frankie's disloyalty towards her parents. She wondered if Scarlet gave her the same treatment in other people's homes.

'Exactly!' said Frankie. 'One of the reasons I love Scarlet so much is that she's not afraid to be who she is, even though Charlie doesn't like it.'

Scarlet glanced at Heidi. Frankie was an attractive young woman. Her face was pink with a combination of vulnerability and fire, her blue eyes flickering about the kitchen as if searching for an escape route. Dressed in a black sweatshirt, tucked into black jeans, she was tall and athletic and wore her mobile on a thin multicoloured rope around her neck, like a long necklace. Heidi thought this a bit unnecessary, but perhaps it was preferable to clutching it, as all the young people did these days.

'Are you going to tell me why you were so upset on the phone, Scarlet?' Heidi asked. 'What's going on with Charlie?'

'Charlie's an absolute prick,' said Scarlet. 'I detest him. I wish I'd never set eyes on him or had ever been out with him. He's arrogant, pig-headed, selfish – I can't think of enough bad things to say about him.'

'Don't hold back,' said Frankie, giving Scarlet a secret smile.

Charlie, it materialised, had been making Scarlet and Frankie's life hell – shouting abuse at them in the street, banging on the door of Scarlet's flat late at night, begging to be let in and once – the final straw – letting himself into the flat through the bathroom window when both women were out and falling asleep on the couch, terrifying them on their return. After that Scarlet had refused any contact whatsoever and blocked his calls. He responded by turning up at college that morning and threatening her. It was then she'd warned she'd call the police and had complained to the university about him. The worse thing, she said, was that he'd been the one acting like a victim, so that other people felt sorry for him and blamed her.

'He's stalking me,' said Scarlet. 'He emails me, calls me, follows me.'

'He's not accepting that your relationship is over, is he?' asked Heidi, leaning back in her chair, trying to understand. 'His heart is broken and now, I suppose, he's trying to get his own back. His pride is dented.'

'So what if his pride is dented?' said Scarlet. 'Christ, who cares?'

'I doubt he's thinking clearly,' continued Heidi. 'It doesn't sound like the Charlie you used to describe.'

Scarlet leaped up from her seat.

'Mum! You can't just say "his pride is dented" in that forgiving voice of yours,' she spat. 'He's a nightmare. I can look after myself, but he needs warning off. That's why I told the university about him. It's like he's a man possessed! You read it in the news that a jilted lover gets obsessed and ends up murdering someone. Well that might just be me. Chopped into pieces and stuffed in a suitcase and thrown onto a skip for the foxes to sniff out! I knew you'd be all soft-hearted about it. Why are you defending him? If only Dad were still here, he'd offer to punch his lights out or…'

Heidi swallowed. 'You're right,' she said instantly, her voice wavering. 'Your dad would have done something. Remember the time he went to that customer's house who had been rude to me and threatened him? I'm sorry, Scarlet. Don't take what I said the wrong way. Please, I didn't mean anything other than working out what was going on in his head.'

Scarlet broke down into sudden tears and Heidi gulped down the ache in her throat. Scarlet's cry had always torn through Heidi's skin and squeezed her heart – probably because she didn't cry much at all. She tried to take hold of Scarlet's hand, but she drew it away, out of reach, and folded her arms across her chest.

'But why are you defending Charlie?' she said.

'Scarlet, I'm seriously not defending him,' Heidi started, glancing at Frankie, whose cheeks were burning a brighter shade of pink. 'I was only trying to understand the situation better—'

But before she could say any more, Scarlet tutted and moved to leave the kitchen. Both Frankie and Heidi got up from their seats to follow her, and Heidi stopped.

'Sorry,' said Heidi. 'You go. She'll want you. I'll talk to her when she's calmed down a bit.'

As she spoke, she realised she knew virtually nothing about Frankie, yet she had deferred to her to comfort her daughter. Did that make her a bad mother? It struck her suddenly that when her girls had been younger, she'd thoroughly vetted their friends, as much as was possible, but as they became young adults, she knew less and less about who they spent their time with. Perhaps Charlie was a danger to Scarlet. Perhaps he was some kind of stalker. She would have to do something about this herself. Drive to the university and tell him to back off.

'Heidi – I mean, Mrs Eagle,' said Frankie, reappearing at the kitchen door, her phone swinging around her neck like a clock pendulum.

'Heidi's fine,' said Heidi with a smile.

'I just want to say sorry about your husband, about Scarlet's dad. Scarlet's told me all about him and how he... he was a lot of fun. It must be so difficult for you all, with it being so sudden. Sounds like he was a lovely man.'

When she finished speaking, she exhaled as if it had been an effort to get the words out. Heidi managed a small nod.

'Thank you,' she said to Frankie, feeling her lips contort as she fought the urge to cry. 'Thank you for saying that. He was a lovely man.'

Frankie smiled, and then she asked a question which showed her kindness. 'What was he like?'

Heidi gulped. Most people avoided this topic of conversation like the plague, yet Frankie had dived into the heart of it. She'd asked a question about Johnny. She picked up a photograph of him grinning as he held up a stained-glass window he'd found in a skip.

'Oh God, it's hard to know where to start,' said Heidi. 'He was kind and thoughtful. The sort of person who would offer to help with anything. Silly things, like if we were stuck trying to get something down from a shelf or couldn't get the computer to work, he'd be there, by your side to help. He'd give my feet a rub after a hard day. Make me a drink and ask me how I felt. He rang the girls most days, just to check in. He knew Scarlet so well. She's got a tendency to explode, but he could make her laugh again in the snap of a finger. He'd pull silly faces, pretend to hide his head under a pillow when she shouted, that kind of thing. Sounds daft, but we needed him to even us out. I know Scarlet really misses him. I'm not doing very well, really. I've always needed Johnny to make me a better mum. He made me more patient, kinder, calmer. Oh dear, sorry, Frankie.'

Heidi wiped her eyes and sank down on a chair, utterly deflated. Suddenly the kitchen door swung open again and Scarlet burst into the room. She threw her arms around Heidi.

'You are doing well,' she said, through tears. 'You're doing a brilliant job. I'm sorry to have shouted at you. I'm sorry; I'm all over the place.'

They embraced and hung on to each other for a few long moments before parting.

'Welcome to our house, Frankie,' said Heidi, rolling her eyes. 'Why don't you both stay for a few days? Perhaps Charlie will back off a bit if you're not around. Out of sight, out of mind. And if he doesn't, I'll break his fingers or chop off his testicles with a blunt knife. Seriously though, we can report him to the police if it gets worse.'

Frankie laughed. Scarlet rolled her eyes.

'It's not like we can't look after ourselves, Mum,' said Scarlet, on the defensive. 'I just panicked today.'

'I know,' said Heidi, 'but it would be nice, for me and for your sister, to get to know Frankie.'

Frankie grinned. 'Thanks. My parents aren't quite as understanding as you about me having a girlfriend. They wanted to marry me off to a rich boy. When I told them I was gay, they told me I wasn't welcome in their home. Bit draconian, isn't it? They've allowed me back since, but we have to be in each other's company in short bursts. We're polar opposites, despite being blood relations.'

Heidi's thoughts returned to William.

'They're probably just products of their own upbringing or experience,' Heidi said. 'Perhaps they'll come around in time. In my experience, people make mistakes, say the wrong thing and then find it hard to admit they're wrong.'

Scarlet rolled her eyes. 'Here we go again!' she said. 'Forgive and forget. Actually, I think you're wrong. I think we should be accountable for our actions and, if we make a mistake, take the rap.'

Heidi knew she should stay quiet, but she was thinking about the fact that possibly one day soon, she would need Scarlet's understanding – and forgiveness.

'But what if you need someone's forgiveness at some point?' Heidi asked. 'Life doesn't always turn out the way you want it to.'

'I won't,' insisted Scarlet. 'I'm never going to do anything I regret, because I'll always think about what I'm going to do before I do it. It's simple really.'

Heidi turned away from Scarlet and Frankie and put her teacup in the sink. She turned on the tap and closed her eyes for a moment as an image from the café flashed into her head. *Nothing's ever simple*, she thought but didn't say.

Chapter Seventeen

Heidi pulled out a pearl drop earring that was trapped in the back of the cocktail chair she was stripping down. Holding the earring by the hook, she turned it over in her hand and wondered if it belonged to Annie. Perhaps it was a recent misplacement, or perhaps it had been there for decades. Imagining Annie, or someone else, searching everywhere for it made her heart contract a little. Each piece of furniture she worked on held so many stories. If only furniture could talk!

Absorbed by her work, she jumped when Max rapped on the workshop door and let himself in. From the expression on his face, something was wrong.

'Max?' she said. 'Everything okay?'

'You're going to need to sit down,' he said. 'Are you alone?'

She sat down.

'Scarlet and Frankie are inside,' she said. 'My heart's hammering here. What's going on?'

Max's cheeks were flushed, as if he'd been running. Under his arm he carried a laptop. He placed it down on the worktable, where the cocktail chair was balanced upside down, and pulled up another chair, throwing his jacket over the back of it, before quickly sitting down. Remembering their conversation on the beach, Heidi's stomach flipped. Was this about Tuesday?

'I have something to show you,' he said, the screen in front of him lighting up.

Heidi pulled her chair closer to Max and, with a pounding heart, watched as he tapped.

'Are you ready for this?' he said. 'I can't believe how easy this was.'

'Is this—?' Heidi began.

'Yes, it's about Tuesday,' he said. 'I went home after our swim and just typed her name into Facebook. Only a few people popped up. This Tuesday is sixty-three, lives in Brighton and runs a catering business from a vintage, converted horsebox. She looks quite like your mother, but it's difficult for me to know for sure. Do you want me to show you? You've seen her photograph, so you'll know straight away if it's her.'

Heidi blinked and nodded.

'Okay,' he said. 'So, I just type it in and… here she is, or at least, I think this is her?'

A circle popped up on the left side of the screen, the lens of a camera, and inside the circle was a photograph of a woman, dressed in a striped apron over a bright dress and sandals. She stood smiling, with her head to one side, in front of a pale-blue vintage horsebox. She had curly pink hair, pinned up, and piercing blue eyes. Her nose was narrow and straight, her lips full and red. She looked younger than sixty-three. The way she stood, with one shoulder slightly lower than the other, as if about to turn away, was familiar. There was no doubt about it – she was the woman in the photograph in Rosalind's glasses case.

Heidi leaned back in her chair and rocked her head backwards, before returning her gaze to the screen.

'Oh my God, yes, it's her,' she said, exhaling heavily.

She stared at the screen for longer, until her eyes watered. A few months ago, her life was straightforward. Now, it felt almost unrecognisable. As if she'd gone to sleep in a life she knew and woken up in someone else's, like falling asleep on a long-haul flight and waking up in a dramatically different landscape.

Max rested his warm hand on her shoulder and squeezed gently.

'What do you think?' said Max. 'I think she looks great!'

Heidi couldn't find any words, so she simply nodded, trying to stop the tears leaking from her eyes.

'Damn, this is too much, isn't it?' said Max. 'After William, it's too much. Do you know what? You don't need to do anything just because I've found this Facebook page. The fact is that you know now that she's out there and maybe that's enough?'

'I don't know,' she started. 'I don't know how I feel.' Heidi managed a smile. 'I always wanted a sibling,' she said quietly. 'I hated being an only child. But her nose is just like mine. It's weird. What should I do? Should I send her a message?'

'Don't do anything yet,' said Max. 'You've enough on your plate.'

'But what if my mother dies,' said Heidi, 'without ever having met her?'

'Your mother doesn't look like she's about to die, Heidi,' said Max. 'She's only hurt her knee.'

'She's an expert in hiding how she really feels,' Heidi said, thinking back to the fainting spells Rosalind had mentioned, then looking again at Tuesday and trying to ascertain what sort of person she was. She decided she looked lovely. Warm. Kind. Fun. 'Thanks for helping me, Max.'

He put his arms around Heidi and pulled her towards him for a big friendly hug.

'I just need to handle this all so carefully,' said Heidi. 'I've got William there on the one hand, and now Tuesday. The girls know nothing at all and they have their own problems to deal with. It could get messy. It's already messy. Without Johnny… it's all too messy.'

'Life's messy,' said Max. 'People are messy, this workshop is messy, your hair is—'

Heidi gave him a mock punch.

'I don't even have a Facebook account,' she said. 'If I wanted to send her a message, I couldn't. Oh, actually I have the workshop account. I could use that, couldn't I?'

'It's so simple,' Max said. 'You could easily message her. You don't even need to send her a request because she has a business account. You simply need to type in a message and send. It's almost too simple.'

Simple. Scarlet had used the same word. Heidi almost laughed out loud at the idea that anything in her life was remotely simple.

Jerking forward suddenly to avoid a fat black fly that had come from nowhere and was buzzing in her face, she tried to bat it away and accidentally knocked the laptop, which toppled off the worktable and fell. Lightning fast, Max moved and caught it but had stretched across Heidi and, as she also tried to catch the laptop, she fell into him and they lay in a twisted embrace.

'My God, Max, I'm so sorry,' she said, blushing a shade of boiling red as she tried to sit back upright. 'That fly! It was like a bomber jet.'

They laughed as they unwound themselves from one another and rescued the laptop. At that moment Heidi noticed two figures in the doorway. Scarlet and Frankie.

'Mum,' Scarlet said, her voice deadly serious. 'I cannot believe that you would do this. Dad has only just died and you're snuggling up with Max! Have you been waiting for this moment?'

While Scarlet ranted, Frankie was moving nervously from foot to foot, pulling the cuffs of her sweatshirt over her hands. Max cleared his throat.

'Scarlet!' said Heidi, fuming. 'Will you just stop this? I knocked the laptop off the table; we both moved to catch it at the same time and got rather twisted up. It's absolutely nothing more than that. How can you even think that? Your dad was my world! For goodness' sake.'

Max stood, pulled his jacket from the back of the chair and put it on.

'It really was just as your mum says,' Max said. 'There's nothing untoward going on, Scarlet, I assure you.'

Scarlet's face was ashen with fury.

'I promise you, Scarlet,' said Heidi. 'You mustn't jump to conclusions. Max is your dad's friend and my friend, and absolutely nothing more.'

She glanced at Max, who looked momentarily glum. Scarlet sighed. Frankie took hold of her hand.

'I just popped in to say we're going out for a pint,' she said moodily. 'I don't know how long we'll be.'

Her gaze rested on the screen of the laptop, before she frowned and moved slightly closer.

'Who's Tuesday?' said Scarlet. 'She looks just like Grandma!'

'Nobody,' said Heidi firmly, before snapping shut the laptop. 'Now go for a pint and I'll see you later for dinner.'

With the girls gone, Heidi felt utterly flustered. The atmosphere between herself and Max had fallen flat.

'Sorry about that,' she said. 'Scarlet's nerves are quite frayed at the moment. Her ex-boyfriend is being a pain.'

'Don't worry about it,' Max said, followed by what sounded like forced laughter. 'Maybe now I'm here I'd better get on with something useful? I'll put the radio on to distract us from the bombshell I've just dropped.'

They worked quietly alongside one another, occasionally asking the other a question but mostly listening to the radio.

When Max eventually left at just before 7 p.m., there were no lights on in the house; the girls were still out. Loneliness put its hands around Heidi's throat and squeezed.

Hands trembling, she opened up her own laptop and brought up the Eagles Facebook account. Pausing for a breath, she ignored the fear in her heart and typed out a message to Tuesday, explaining who she was and how she'd discovered her, telling her she'd love to hear from her. Pressed send. Closed down the computer. Amazing, she thought, how just a few words typed in a few seconds had the potential to change lives. She could easily have not typed that message. She could easily have not written to William. Yet she'd done both. Had loneliness motivated her to reach out? Curiosity? Or something else, deeper. Love?

'Mum?' said Scarlet from the door. 'Why are you still working? Are you coming inside? We're really hungry. Shall we cook dinner?

Sorry about earlier. Frankie said I was unfair. I miss Dad, that's all. I know you do too. I love you.'

Heidi felt choked with tears and gratitude. She was wanted. Needed. Required to help with dinner. Loved.

Turning away from her daughter to switch off the lights, she cleared her throat. 'Yes, love, I'm coming now,' she said. 'I love you too.'

Chapter Eighteen

After their disastrous meeting, Heidi sent William an apologetic email, asking for his bank details so she could transfer money, but hadn't received a reply. One morning, unable to bear it any longer, Heidi returned to the Blackbird Café. She sat at the same table as before and scanned every inch of the café, stealing glimpses of the entrance to the kitchen whenever she could. There was no sign of William, but perhaps this wasn't his shift. When a waitress came to the table, she ordered a coffee and asked after him.

'I'm sorry, William doesn't work here anymore,' she said.

'He doesn't work here anymore?' Heidi asked, feeling desolate. Had he left in order to escape any contact with her? How would she ever contact him again?

'No,' the waitress confirmed. 'Not since last Monday.'

'Why did he leave?' Heidi said, trying not to show how desperately unhappy she felt. 'Did he get a new job?'

The girl's eyes fell to the floor and she repositioned herself so that the boss couldn't see her. Her cheeks flamed.

'No,' she whispered. 'He got… you know… there was an argument and he was asked to leave.'

Heidi blinked and whispered, 'Why?'

'I shouldn't say,' the waitress said, 'but he was spending too much time on "breaks" in the bookies, when he should have been in here. I think he has a bit of a problem.'

Heidi's face burned. 'Oh right,' she said, wiping the prickly sweat from her forehead. 'Poor him.'

The waitress shrugged, obviously unsure if she felt any sympathy towards him, which made Heidi feel highly defensive.

'Perhaps you shouldn't go around telling everyone about what happened,' Heidi snapped. 'It's hardly fair.'

'You asked!' said the waitress, suddenly sullen.

Heidi sighed and shook her head.

'Sorry,' she said hurriedly, chastising herself because this girl might be the only link she had to finding out where he lived. 'I'm sorry. I was worried for him. *Am* worried for him. I'm a... new friend of his. Do you know where he lives?'

'No clue!' the waitress said. 'In the bookies!'

Heidi frowned, but before she could ask another question, the waitress was called over to serve another customer. Heidi didn't drink the coffee. She left too much money on the table and slipped out of the café. She didn't want the waitress's words to be true – perhaps they weren't true. Was William a gambler? Johnny had given him money and she'd agreed to lend him money too. Was he using it to gamble, or did he owe money to someone? What was going on in his life? Hideous scenarios unfolded in her head. William involved with loan sharks, bailiffs – and worse. Beaten up and alone in the gutter. Held up at knifepoint outside his front door. Perhaps William had lost his way. Her body burned with the desire to track him down and help him.

She walked past the betting shop next door – and her heart sank into her boots.

'Oh, William,' she whispered as she looked in through the window, at the 'beast of a bet' and 'place your bets' signage. She peered through the door. There were two men inside, neither of them William.

Heidi walked along the street, with no direction or clue what to do next. She knew how gambling could destroy people. Temptation was everywhere: on TV, on mobile phones, on the Internet, on the high street, in the corner shops.

Entering a One Stop shop, Heidi chose a sandwich and waited in a queue to pay, staring at the displays of scratch cards, her mind whirring. A trickle of sweat ran down her spine.

Checking a phone message from Zoe, she was only half aware of a commotion at the checkout, when a man behind her raised his voice and shouted: 'Get a ruddy move on, will you?'

Almost cricking her neck as she turned to check he wasn't talking to her, she side-stepped out of the queue and saw a man at the till, wearing a black sweatshirt, with his hood up, digging his hands into his pocket, clearly trying to find his wallet. Heidi glanced at his basket: a pack of cornflakes. A pint of milk. A tin of beans. One banana. You'd think they'd let him off.

'Have you forgotten your wallet, love?' she heard the cashier say. 'Or don't you have enough on you? Maybe you could come back? Only there's a bit of a queue, love.'

Heidi's cheeks blazed. She hated situations like this, when a simple act of kindness would defuse the situation completely. She moved towards the cashier, pulling her purse from her bag.

'Excuse me,' she said quietly. 'I'll get this shopping if you've forgotten your wallet.'

The man was looking in the opposite direction but turned to face her. Heidi stumbled backwards, her hand over her mouth.

'William?' she gasped. 'I had no idea it was you. Sorry. Look, can I pay for this?'

'Hurry up, will you?' someone in the queue shouted, while Heidi fumbled in her purse and pulled out a £10 note. The cashier quickly gave her change.

'For God's sake!' said someone else from behind her, while another said, 'Bless you, dear.' But Heidi was oblivious. She didn't look at anyone as she followed William out of the shop and onto the pavement, her heart banging. He walked quickly, his hood up, and for one dreadful moment she thought he was going to carry on walking and not turn around at all, so she called out his name. He stopped and waited for her, as she half jogged to join him.

'Why did you follow me to the supermarket?' he said. She tried to conceal her pain.

'William,' she said. 'I wasn't following you. I honestly didn't know that was you. I went into the café and they said you'd left, so I was walking around here, trying to work out what to do and then, there you were in the shop. Serendipity.'

She smiled and handed him the bag of shopping.

'I… just forgot my wallet in there,' he said. 'I don't need you to rescue me. I would have gone back later.'

She tried not to stare at the wallet poking out of his pocket.

'Oh, I know that,' she said. 'But I would have done the same for anyone in the hope that someone would help me out when I'm in a tight spot because we all get in them at one time or another.'

'I'm not in a tight…' he said, his sentence drifting into a sigh. He clenched his jaw.

'Are you alright?' Heidi cut in, gently touching his arm, before letting her hand fall away again. 'I emailed you. You seem, I mean… why did you leave your job?'

'I don't want to serve coffee for the rest of my life,' he said angrily. 'I actually wanted to be a photographer. I was working as a freelancer, but it's difficult to get really established without all the latest digital equipment and my ex – she's not helping. I had a small room in our house as a place to work, but now, well, that's a distant memory.'

Photography. He had that in common with Johnny. She remembered now that he'd mentioned it during their first meeting, and despite the bleak situation, this common interest delighted her.

They stood in silence for a moment and rain began to fall. Gently at first and then ferociously, drenching Heidi and William in a matter of seconds. But neither of them moved.

People in the street dashed into doorways or pulled umbrellas from their bags, but William stayed completely still, as if he didn't even notice the rain. Though he was there in body, all six-foot-something of him, Heidi thought he seemed far away. She desperately wanted to know what was going through his mind. Heart thumping in concern, she felt at a loss to know what to say. Did she have any right to ask questions and delve into his life?

Finally plucking up her courage, she pulled the car keys from her pocket.

'Can I give you a lift home?' she asked. 'I think it's raining.'

Her attempt at humour fell flat.

'No, no,' he said. 'I can walk. I'm not far from here. I'm already wet. The rain doesn't bother me.'

He gave her a small, unconvincing smile, and the dimple appeared. Thunder rattled across the sky and the rain became hailstones.

'Please?' Heidi said, covering her eyes. 'Please let me just give you a lift so we can talk for a few more moments.'

With a reluctant shrug, William followed Heidi to the Morris. Hardly daring to breathe in case he changed his mind, she opened the passenger door and ushered him inside.

'Climb in,' she said. 'You'll have to give me directions.'

In the car, William pointed ahead, then stared out of the window without making conversation other than to say left, right or straight on. Heidi glanced at him repeatedly, marvelling at how similar to Johnny he was physically, but also taking in how battered his clothes were and that his shoes – a pair of black-and-white-checked Vans, like the ones in the suitcase, had a big hole in them at the toe. Had Johnny bought them for William and intended to give them to him?

They drove past vast houses in well-maintained roads, and then moved into roads of terraced housing and blocks of flats, some of which were quite run-down.

'I can get out here and walk the rest,' he said when they turned into a long residential road mostly comprising blocks of flats. 'Listen, I'm sorry about the other day. I was rude to you. You didn't deserve it at all. You've only just lost your husband. I'm not normally like that. That's not me. This isn't me.'

'That's okay,' said Heidi gently. 'But it's still raining. Are you sure? Just let me find a place to pull over.'

She indicated to pull into a space and turned off the engine.

'Cool car,' he said suddenly, a light flickering in his eyes.

'Thanks,' she said. 'It was Johnny's. He loved vintage cars. Probably would have had a whole collection if he'd had the money. Do you live here then?'

She looked around, wondering which was his home. Nowhere looked very homely or inviting.

'I'm staying with a friend,' he said. 'Just for a few weeks.'

'You don't have your own place?' Heidi asked.

'I did,' he said. 'But as I explained last time, my partner and I broke up. She wanted me to move out so we could have some breathing space. I've not been able to afford my own place as well as still paying for her stuff. It's literally impossible.'

Heidi was bursting with questions, but she could see from William's expression that he wanted her to stop asking them.

'Can I come in for a cup of tea?' she asked. She knew she was pushing it, but she couldn't leave it like this.

William pressed the back of his head against the headrest and rubbed at an invisible mark on his forehead. She knew he was uncomfortable but crossed her fingers, hoping he'd say yes.

'It's a bit of a bachelor pad,' he said. 'You won't like it. Maybe another time. I wasn't expecting—'

'I don't care if it's a dump,' she said quickly. 'I've stayed in my fair share. Please?'

He shrugged. 'If you insist. But don't say I didn't warn you.'

The rain relented, and shafts of golden sunlight poured through cracks in the grey clouds. She wanted to comment on it to William but, registering his negative demeanour, she didn't think he would be interested and think her superficial.

'Look at that,' he said, gesturing towards the break in the clouds. Heidi grinned.

'Reminds me of that children's story where the wind and the sun compete in trying to get a child to take off his coat. The wind blows and blows and exhausts itself trying, but the child just holds his coat tighter to him. The sun comes out and he instantly takes his coat off.'

He smiled, in a lopsided way that took her straight back to Johnny.

They walked a few hundred yards before reaching a block of flats. There was a patch of grass in front it, a communal area for bins and a shared entrance, with a panel of labelled buzzers. Some had names written on in pen; others were blank. A bicycle with no wheels was locked to a post. He unlocked the front door and held it open for Heidi.

'Eighth floor,' he said. 'Shall we get the lift?'

Heidi entered the lift, her eyes scanning a poster which said: 'Are you being held against your will?' above a picture of a young woman in the corner of a room, with her hands over her head. Someone had obviously emptied their bladder in there too. She tried not to appear disgusted.

When they jolted to a halt, William showed her into his friend's flat and gave her a quick tour, which lasted seconds.

'Living room and kitchenette,' he said. 'Toilet, Ian's bedroom. As you can see, it's on the cramped side.'

He waved her into the living room and it was immediately clear to Heidi that William was sleeping on the sofa. There was a sleeping bag there, and a rucksack on the floor, with a picture of a little boy balanced up against it, a teddy bear in the crook of his arm. Freddy?

'Tea?' he asked.

'Yes please,' she said, following William into the kitchen. She did her best not to react with despair as her eyes passed the beans on toast mouldering on a plate, a teacup full to the brim with cigarette ends and a black bin bag of rubbish that had at least been extracted from the dustbin but had not been taken out of the flat and smelled awful. There were empty beer cans all over the place too.

'Christ, sorry,' William said, quickly tying up the bin bag and putting it outside the front door, before hurling an armful of cans into another bag. Heidi focused all her efforts on finding something to celebrate.

'I like the windows,' she said stiffly. 'There's a lot of light.'

William went over to the window and flung one of them open. He grabbed a can of spray deodorant from a shelf and sprayed for ten seconds, before flapping his hand around in the air and apologising.

'I've made it worse,' he said. 'Sorry about this. Ian likes to party. He invites his mates back and, well, the place gets into a state. I've tried to tidy it up, but I can't be cleaning up after him. I try to stay out as much as possible, working, and just crash here at night. Well I did.'

'It's okay…' she started. 'I've brought up teenagers. I was young once.'

She immediately regretted her words. Clearing her throat and blushing madly, she finished her sentence. 'It wouldn't take long to sort this out. A pair of marigolds and a couple of hours.'

'It's since I lost my job,' he said. 'I can't find the motivation. Let me clear this for you.'

Frantically, he moved the sleeping bag and some clothes off the sofa, pushing them into a corner. He returned to the kitchen, opened the fridge, sniffed the milk, poured a splash into her cup and handed her the tea, didn't have one himself and sat down. He gestured for her to take a seat next to him on the sofa. Smiling, she sat, trying not to notice the dust balls on the carpet. He jogged his knee up and down, tapping his foot.

'So,' Heidi said. 'What happened about your job? The waitress said there was an argument.'

'She shouldn't be going around telling everyone everything!' he said, too loud. 'But yes, I got the sack. I had nipped out for my lunch break and was too long.'

He glanced at his phone.

'I need to go,' he said, suddenly leaping up. 'I'm picking up my son from school today.'

'Are you bringing him here?' she said, trying to hide the concern in her tone.

'No,' he replied. 'I take him to his mum's and I sit there for an hour before she gets back from work. I'd love to be able to take him out, but she prefers I stay at home… so, I better go. Sorry.'

He stuffed a few things into a bag – some bars of chocolate and a stuffed rabbit.

'Right,' she said, placing down her cup of tea and standing, her mind fizzing with questions. 'Can I… can I come again? There's so much to talk about. I could help you out a bit too maybe. If you'd let me. I've got marigolds.'

He stared at her for a long moment, seemed confused, half shrugged and then was distracted by another message appearing on his mobile. She noticed a change in his body language – that he'd retreated again into a private world of whatever preoccupied him. She watched him move around the kitchen and discreetly take a small bottle from the cupboard which he put into his pocket. She opened her mouth to speak but thought better of it. She picked up a digital camera from the side. Johnny had had one similar. She turned it over in her hands.

'Johnny had one like this,' she said gently.

'It's his,' William said. 'He lent it to me, but the battery's gone. He didn't lend me the charger. He said he'd bring it next time we met, but that never happened. There never was a next time.'

Heidi smiled at the thought of Johnny lending William his favourite camera.

'I can take it home and charge it,' she said.

'I better go or I'm going to be late,' William said, agitated. 'Yes, thanks.'

Heidi slipped the camera into her bag and followed him towards the front door. When he nipped into the bathroom, she quickly slipped a £20 note under his sleeping bag. Outside, she was relieved to be released from the claustrophobic atmosphere of the flat and the lift.

'Can I drive you?' she asked, but he shook his head and said it was quicker on foot.

William said goodbye and walked quickly in the opposite direction to where she was parked. She raised a hand in farewell, wondering if he might turn around again, but he didn't. She waited until he was almost out of view when suddenly, he half turned to face in her direction. He lifted his hand. Her heart leaped. She waved madly in return, her body moving with the effort, earning a curious glare from a woman walking past, dragging two tiny children with her.

'Sorry,' Heidi said to the woman, 'just waving to my son.'

Son. My son. She repeated the words over and over in her head as she walked down the road. My son. My son. My son.

Chapter Nineteen

'Mum!' shouted Zoe as soon as Heidi walked into the house. 'Where on earth have you been? I've been trying to get hold of you!'

Heidi dropped her bag to the floor and took off her coat, grabbing her phone from the pocket. There were eight missed calls. Zoe's face was pink with anxiety and Leo lurked behind her, his hands shoved into his pockets, long fringe obscuring his eyes.

'What's wrong?' Heidi said, resting a hand on her daughter's shoulder. 'Is it Scarlet? Your grandma? I'm so sorry, my ringtone was on silent. I went for a walk and lost track of time. I'm hopeless with this phone!'

Zoe grabbed Heidi by the hand and pulled her into the kitchen, where she quickly pushed the door shut behind them. The kitchen was littered with snack debris: a bag of sliced bread was open near the toaster, alongside a tub of butter and a jar of Marmite, lid off. Immediately, she started putting things away.

'Something really weird has just happened,' said Zoe, gesticulating wildly. 'This woman came to the door and said she wanted to see you. She was peering over my shoulder into the house as if she wanted to get inside and search it!'

Heidi frowned, thinking that maybe one of her customers was disgruntled because she was late with a job.

'Was it one of the customers?' said Heidi. 'They're not supposed to come to the house; that's why I have the workshop, but it could be someone who's waited too long and…'

Heidi's words drifted off. Zoe shook her head.

'No,' she said. 'I asked her if she was a customer and she said no and that it was a personal matter. She asked who I was and what my name was. I didn't know whether to tell her! She wanted to come in and wait for you in the house. Really pushy.'

Zoe looked incredulous and Heidi widened her eyes.

'I said that I didn't know what time you'd be back,' she continued, 'and I asked whether she had a number I could get you to call her on instead. She scribbled on this piece of paper and said she'd wait in the Anchor until 7 p.m. So that's another two hours.'

Zoe handed her the piece of paper. There was a phone number written in black pen. Heidi's head was spinning. Was this someone to do with William? Or…

'Did she give you her name?' asked Heidi. 'What did she look like?'

'She said her name was Tuesday,' said Zoe. 'Never heard anyone called Tuesday before. She made a joke of it, she said: "I know it's Friday but I'm Tuesday" before laughing madly. She's quite loud and in your face. She had loads of curly hair under a bright red beret. Her hair was dyed pink, despite her being in her what, late fifties, early sixties? Something about her totally freaked me out. And you, Leo – didn't she freak you out too?'

Leo nodded and said, 'Yeah, totally freaked me out,' then quickly checked his phone, his transitional object.

The blood drained from Heidi's face and she felt as if she was floating above herself and watching events unfold. Tuesday had come to her house. Yes, Heidi had given her address, thinking that Tuesday might like to write to her if not respond directly on Facebook, but had never dreamed for a single moment that she would arrive at the door. Wasn't that a little forward?

'Oh God,' said Heidi, sinking into a kitchen chair, her bag flopping onto the floor, Johnny's camera catching her eye.

'What is it, Mum?' said Zoe.

'It's nothing to worry about,' said Heidi. 'Just someone I got in touch with and didn't expect to hear from. It's a bit complicated. Look, I'll explain it all later if that's okay. I should go and see her while she's waiting in the pub. Are you okay to get yourselves some dinner? There's a pizza and salad in the fridge.'

Zoe sighed and looked suddenly wan. Heidi stood up, her mind already walking towards the pub.

'Yes, sure,' she said. 'But, Mum, there's something I need to talk to you about too. You're always so busy, I feel like I need to make an appointment with you. If you're not working, you're out somewhere – I don't know where.'

Heidi already had one arm pushed into her coat and was picking up her bag.

'Is this about deferring your course?' said Heidi. 'Because we can talk when I get back? I promise. I won't be long.'

Zoe turned away from her and faced a cupboard where the cereal was kept, which she opened and closed without purpose.

'Fine,' said Zoe, her voice almost a whisper.

Heidi hesitated, feeling torn, but she knew the discussion could wait – and Tuesday wouldn't. She left the kitchen as it was, opened the front door and rushed out into the cold darkness.

The Anchor was an oven. Hot air and noise blasted Heidi's senses. They lived close by, yet she'd been inside the pub only a handful of times. Johnny had enjoyed a pint there with Max, but the pub wasn't really Heidi's scene. Now, gingerly, she walked in and moved through the groups of people either holding drinks and chatting or waiting to be served. Her entire body pounded with the drum of her heart; her legs felt made of air and her mouth dry. Her gaze fell on a woman sitting at a table in the corner, sipping a glass of red wine. Nobody could miss that pink hair. There was no doubt in her mind that it was Tuesday. And sensing that someone was staring at her – in that peculiar way humans do – Tuesday looked up. Their eyes met in a moment of startled recognition, before Tuesday leaped up from her seat and waved enthusiastically, all teeth and big eyes.

'Heidi?' Tuesday yelled. 'Is that you? Yes, it's you!'

Several people in the pub turned to see who was bellowing but quickly returned to their drinks and conversation. Heidi moved to the table Tuesday was sitting at, not knowing what she was going to say, but it didn't matter because Tuesday had that covered.

'It's SO wonderful to meet you!' she said, throwing her arms around Heidi and pulling her close into her body. Heidi was overwhelmed by fragrance, a scent she recognised as patchouli oil.

'This is my half-sister!' she said to the table of people who had turned to see what the commotion was about. They smiled and returned to their drinks.

'My half-sister,' Tuesday continued. 'I can't bloody well believe it. I was overwhelmed to get your message, Heidi. It just popped up! I was going to email you back, but I thought "no", I'll do this properly and I'll turn up in person! Why wait any longer? I'm not a woman to do things by half. Do you know, I once bought everyone at a packed bar a shot of sambuca? I don't know why. I just thought "Why not?" and everyone was so pleased and happy until some bright spark told me I was just lonely and wanted people to notice me. He had a point, I suppose – why do you think I have pink hair? But anyway. Will you have a red wine? I bought a bottle and got a glass for you. Presumptuous of me, I know, but if you're anything like me… I said to myself, if you don't come I'll drink the lot! Drown my sorrows. If you'd rather have something else, I'll go straight to the bar and get you whatever you like. I'm so delighted to meet you, I can hardly believe I'm here and I can't stop talking, can I? Right that's it, I'll stop.'

Tuesday pinched her lips closed with her fingers but still continued to make murmuring noises as if the words were struggling to get out. Heidi erupted with laughter and Tuesday released her lips, joining her. Heidi was struck by Tuesday's radiance. Pink hair, red lips, blue eyes and a golden complexion. A coral-coloured blouse and a string of pinkish beads. A giant, smiling peach. Tuesday held up the bottle of wine, ready to pour.

'Thank you,' Heidi said, her voice tremulous. 'Thank you. I'm… I'm… quite stunned actually.'

She took off her coat, feeling incredibly hot under Tuesday's grinning gaze.

'I'm so very happy to meet you!' Tuesday said again, pouring Heidi a glass of wine full to the brim. 'This feels bizarre, doesn't it? To think, we share genes! I've always wanted a sister! One exactly like you.'

'Me too,' mumbled Heidi, embarrassed but also delighted.

Heidi swallowed a big gulp of the wine, followed by another and another, until her glass was empty, before placing it back down on the table. Tuesday immediately refilled it – and she drank again.

'I have so many questions,' said Tuesday. 'I've wondered what my mother is like my entire life – and of course I didn't know I had a sibling. Yet here you are. And you have children and a family, and I just met Zoe – what a lovely girl. Those eyes! What's our mother like? I know we have different fathers, but that's all I know. Tell me everything. I want to know everything. I've always wanted to know the details, since I was nine years old, when I was told about the adoption. I wondered what perfume she wore, whether she worked, what colours she liked, poems, quiet or loud, her strengths and weaknesses.'

Heidi gulped. 'Gosh, well, perfume, she wore Guerlain's Mitsouko when I was a child. Now she wears a rose fragrance from somewhere; I'm not sure where. She wears flowy clothes and lots of prints, a bit like you. I'm not aware of her reading much poetry, but she enjoyed fiction. She still does – often has her nose in a book. Though gardening is what she enjoys at the moment. She thinks Monty Don is marvellous. She's not an actually loud person, but she's quietly loud. She can make her presence known with her posture. She is a "chin up" type of person. I haven't seen her cry very often. Her weaknesses, hmm, that's a difficult one. I think she hasn't known how to cope in certain situations and rather than be honest, she's buried the way she really feels. If that makes any sense! And she can't say no to a fresh cream chocolate eclair.'

Tuesday's eyes were wide open, and she sat perfectly still, listening to the details, absorbed.

'I've said too much,' said Heidi, aware that Rosalind didn't even know about this meeting and would not approve. 'Do you feel any resentment towards her?'

Heidi took another gulp of her wine. It seemed that the future was hanging on Tuesday's response, because what she said might be how William felt. Did he, beside the many problems he seemed to have, resent Heidi? Perhaps he blamed her for everything that had gone wrong in his life.

'Not at all,' said Tuesday emphatically. 'I was brought up to believe that my biological mother had done a kind thing by putting me up for adoption. That she was a young girl, unmarried at a time when that was frowned upon, and didn't really have a choice then, in the 1950s. Besides, my mum and dad are wonderful. They've recently moved to France, which was their dream. I'll miss them. I told my mum that I was coming today and she was fully supportive. Does Rosalind live locally? She wrote to me some years ago in reply to a letter from me, saying it wasn't the right time for us to be in contact, but I guess now, she's decided it is time and asked you to be in touch with me?'

Heidi froze. Of course she hadn't told Rosalind that she'd contacted Tuesday – and she knew that she wouldn't take the news that they'd met well. She blushed.

'I… I… yes she does live close by, but…' started Heidi, before taking another gulp of wine. 'I haven't… I don't…'

'Oh,' said Tuesday, her expression suddenly stricken. 'You haven't told her you emailed me?'

Heidi was crushed by Tuesday's disappointment. 'Not yet,' she said. 'But I'm planning to. I will do. Tomorrow. I thought I'd wait to see if you got back in touch first. And now you have, so I will.'

There was a moment of silent tension between them and Heidi felt terribly guilty.

'Don't worry,' said Tuesday, working hard to conceal any hurt she felt. 'Let's get to know each other first. Meeting you is more than enough!'

Tuesday ordered a second bottle of wine and they sat huddled in the corner for the next hour and a half. Heidi drank more wine than she had in months. Tuesday told Heidi about her life; growing up in London with her adopted brother, a teacher for a mother and a scientist for a father. There had been a love affair with an German chef that lasted almost a decade and when it broke down, nobody else compared. She lost energy when she spoke about him; as if the memory literally drained her. But, she said, buoying herself up, she loved horses and the outdoors and cooking. She ran a mobile catering business, from an adapted pale-blue converted vintage horsebox, attending festivals and weddings and any outdoor event. She spoke with passion and energy – the words spilling out of her – and every now and then she nervously clutched her bead necklace, moving it back and forth around her neck.

'Every year I go on holiday to Germany to—' Tuesday started, before stopping. 'Actually, I won't go into that now. I'm not proud of myself.'

Heidi frowned, guessing that perhaps she visited the German chef – and that perhaps he wasn't single.

'We all do things we're not proud of,' said Heidi hurriedly, the wine temporarily expelling her anxiety. Her head spun with the alcohol, and her lips felt rubbery as she talked, but once she started talking, she also couldn't stop. Though she'd talked a little to Simone about her feelings since Johnny's death, now she unbuttoned completely and told Tuesday almost everything – Johnny's sudden death, finding William. Tuesday was suitably stunned and full of sympathy.

'Have you told your daughters about me?' said Tuesday.

Heidi shook her head. 'Not yet,' she said. 'They've had a lot to take in recently.'

'Yes,' she said. 'It sounds like it. I'd love to meet them properly. When can I meet them? I'm desperate to meet them – my nieces! How about now?'

Swept up in Tuesday's enthusiasm, Heidi tried to think clearly, but her brain was muddled by wine and weary with emotion.

'Um, I should probably—' she began, but Tuesday interrupted.

'I'm sorry, I'm being too forward,' she said. 'It's one of my faults. I put people off with my eagerness. Why don't I come over at the weekend instead? I'll bring a pudding and I can get to know your girls. Perhaps you can persuade Rosalind to come along too? Life is short. Let's seize the moment, Heidi. It's the only way to live life.'

Heidi nodded, overwhelmed and drunk. 'Perhaps it is,' she managed to say, a faint, distant alarm ringing in her ears.

By the time she arrived home, Zoe had already gone to bed. Heidi hovered outside her daughter's closed bedroom door, wanting to rush in and shake her awake, to tell her about Tuesday. And William. But though her mind was swimming, rational thought pushed to the surface. When she spoke to Zoe and Scarlet, she needed to be clear-headed and calm, not slurring her words. Tonight, she was drunk. More drunk than she'd been in a long time. It was nice actually, she thought, to be drunk. The world felt softer.

She splashed her face with cold water and patted it dry with a towel, then stared at her reflection, thinking about Tuesday. She'd liked her – a lot. Tomorrow she would speak to Rosalind and tell her that she was a lovely person. Perhaps by meeting her like this, she was only doing what Johnny was doing when he met William.

'Oh, Johnny,' she sighed as she stumbled into her bedroom and closed the door.

She lay on Johnny's side of the bed, still fully dressed. In the darkness, the ceiling appeared to move in waves. Her ears were ringing with snippets of Tuesday's conversation, and images of William's flat ran, like broken scenes from a film, in her mind. How she longed to speak to Johnny and hear his voice. Where was he now?

Pulling a pillow from his side into her stomach, she hugged it tight, her mind wandering to the bag of William's shopping that he'd left in the car and of Johnny's camera, which needed to be charged. She sat up and checked the clock, the numbers swimming before her eyes. Midnight. Perhaps she could charge the camera now, so she could return it – and the shopping – to William in the morning. That would give her another excuse to see him. She felt compelled to see him, to help him. She knew he was in difficulty.

She resisted the strong, alcohol-driven urge to go now, on foot. To run there. To hammer on the door. Her heart pounded with anticipation, but she knew she must sleep. She must still her thoughts.

Half pulling the duvet over herself, she squeezed her eyes shut and waited for sleep.

Chapter Twenty

Sleep didn't come, not really. At 4 a.m., Heidi decided to get up, because there was no point tossing and turning for another two hours.

Creeping downstairs, she retrieved the camera from her bag and went outside to charge the battery. This would give her the perfect excuse to visit William again – and to give him the bag of food shopping. Remembering the cornflakes and milk in the bag, she felt a new sense of urgency. That was his breakfast. If she didn't get there quickly, he wouldn't have anything for breakfast!

Buoyed by her decision to go straight away, she waited a few minutes until there was enough power in the battery for her to view the photos on the camera. Then, she pressed the play button and the first image floored her.

'Johnny,' she said to the empty room, unable to tear her eyes away from the beautiful photograph of her husband, taken at a table in the Blackbird Café, a window behind him framing him in gentle golden sunlight. William had captured him perfectly. Johnny's mouth was slightly open, mid-laugh, and he was leaning forward in his chair, hands on his knees. The warmth in his eyes and the joy in his expression proved to Heidi everything she needed to know about his feelings towards William. He seemed lit from within, absolutely present in a precious moment.

'Wow,' Heidi said, gently scrolling through several more images of Johnny. William had taken at least a dozen shots and each one felt, to Heidi, like a gift.

'Mum?' said Zoe, from the doorway. 'Are you alright? Couldn't you sleep?'

Heidi looked up, the wine from the previous night suddenly making itself known as a monumental headache. She lifted a hand to her forehead and rubbed.

'No, I couldn't sleep,' she said. 'Bit of a headache. Are you okay? Why are you up? Shouldn't you go back to bed?'

'I could ask you the same question. What are you doing out here?' Zoe said, rubbing her eyes. 'I waited up for you last night, but you stayed out so late. It's like we've reversed roles! I want to know about that woman. Tuesday. Who is she?'

Heidi swallowed, aware that she didn't have much time if she was to reach William's house in time for breakfast. If she told Zoe about Tuesday now, she'd ask questions, and Heidi needed to give her time. Also, how could she tell her about Tuesday without telling her about William?

'I know I seem secretive,' said Heidi, stuffing the camera into a bag with the battery charger. 'But I need to talk to both of you – Scarlet and you – together. A few things have happened. Big things, since Dad died.'

'What big things? He wasn't having an affair, was he?' asked Zoe. 'With Tuesday? Not Dad. He'd never do that!'

'No,' said Heidi. 'It's nothing like that. Not at all. Dad would never do that.'

'Then why not tell me now?' said Zoe, frowning. 'I'm fed up with this!'

Heidi felt guilty. Zoe was being punished and it wasn't fair, but she needed Scarlet and Zoe to be together when she explained. Now wasn't the right moment.

'I've got to go out,' Heidi said. 'I've got to return this camera to someone before 9 a.m. They need it… for an event. I'll speak to you later.'

Heidi hated herself for lying and was amazed at how easily the lies tripped from her lips.

'It's as if you're avoiding me,' Zoe said sadly. 'Why are you avoiding me?'

Heidi hugged Zoe and kissed the top of her head.

'Darling, I'm not,' she said. 'Let's say this evening we'll talk about everything. Are you seeing Leo today?'

Zoe stared down at her hands and shook her head. Heidi gently lifted Zoe's chin.

'Has something happened?' said Heidi.

Zoe shrugged and sighed. 'I'll explain later,' she said moodily, mocking Heidi's words.

Heidi frowned. She knew Zoe needed her, but she also felt a burning compulsion to take the shopping and camera to William – it was as if their future relationship depended on her doing this. She was desperate to prove to him she was a woman of her word. That he could rely on her.

'Okay,' she said, squeezing Zoe's shoulder. 'Sorry to be in a rush; I'll see you at dinnertime. Scarlet's coming home for the weekend so we'll all be together.'

Zoe didn't reply; she just went back to the house. Heidi followed and grabbed William's bag of shopping and stuffed it with the pair of Vans and extra things from the kitchen cupboards. Pasta. Baked beans. Tin of custard. Bag of apples. A round of Dairylea triangles. Two packets of biscuits. A pack of bacon. Six carrots. Two pints of milk. A packet of peanuts and a box of chocolates Frankie had given her for letting her stay over. There was hardly anything left in the house.

'I'll pick more up later,' she said, aware that she had a lot to do 'later'.

Stealing out of the front door, she placed the bag of food on the passenger seat of the Morris van and sped towards William's flat.

But when she parked up outside, she felt suddenly apprehensive. What if he wasn't there, or had a guest?

It doesn't matter, she thought, making her way towards the flat entrance, where the bicycle without tyres was still locked up. She took the lift to the eighth floor and knocked on the front door of the flat, but nobody answered. She rapped again, harder this time.

'William!' she called, feeling desperate. 'William!'

There was movement from inside the flat and the noise of something crashing to the floor. She pressed her ear up against the door.

'William!' she called urgently. She thought of Zoe at home, resigned to being shoved to the bottom of Heidi's to-do list – and felt suddenly desolate and tearful, confused by her own behaviour. Why was she putting William first, when she barely knew him?

What am I doing? she thought, giving the door one final furious thwack with the side of her fist and a kick with her boot. A small part of her wanted to kick the door down. There was the sound of footsteps and of a man clearing his throat.

'Heidi?' came a quiet voice from behind the door. 'Is that you?'

It was William. By the sound of his sleepy voice, she'd obviously woken him up.

'Yes,' said Heidi. 'I have some breakfast for you. And the camera battery charger, in case you needed it. I was passing by. Can you let me in?'

Heidi's words were met with silence. Her heartbeat whooshed in her ears. After what felt like an eternity, he unlocked the door. Rather than open the door wide and let her in, he simply poked his nose through the gap.

'Passing by at this hour?' he said. 'I don't need the camera today. It's yours anyway. It's Johnny's. It's not mine.'

The smell of alcohol on his breath hit her like a thump on the nose.

'I'm sure he'd want you to have it. Are you going to let me in?' she said. 'I've got some other things to give you. Some shoes. And you left your shopping in the car.'

'No,' he said. 'I—'

Heidi pushed her boot into the gap in the door. Surprised, he raised his eyes to meet hers.

'What the hell?' he said.

'Let me in,' she insisted. 'Please.'

Her desperation was palpable. He lifted his index finger to his lips. 'Ian's here,' he said. 'It's not the best time to visit.'

William sent her a wary smile. But Heidi would not be deterred. She bit her lip and followed William through the flat past closed bedroom doors – where she could hear the sound of someone snoring – and through to the living room. On the floor next to the sofa where William had been sleeping was an empty bottle of vodka. Heidi's heart sank into her boots, and he registered her disappointment.

'I told you not to come in,' he said. 'It's a bad time. My life hasn't always been like this. I haven't anywhere else to go at the moment but it's temporary.'

Heidi desperately wanted to ask about his adopted family. Wasn't there anyone else he could rely on?

'What about your parents?' she asked bravely. 'Could you stay with them?'

He shook his head. 'Both my parents are dead,' he said.

Heidi swallowed. 'I'm sorry,' she said.

'My dad, Fred, died in an accident when I was a toddler, then my mum got together with someone else. Then my mum died. I do have some distant relations, but we're not close.'

'I'm so desperately sorry,' Heidi said, her heart pounding. 'When did your mum die?'

Heidi dug her fingers into the sofa fabric, hoping that it wasn't when he was still a child.

'My mum—' started William. 'My mum passed away when I was eighteen. It was just me and her for a while, but she didn't have an easy time with her new partner. I tried to look after her, but… she was a good person. She loved me and I loved her. We were a team.'

There was so much he wasn't saying. William choked a little on his words and Heidi physically ached with his pain. She sat down next to him.

'Look,' he said. 'I'm not sure what you're doing here. My life's a bit complicated at the moment. Sleeping here like this, I—'

He stopped speaking and Heidi gently rested her hand on his knee.

'Drink some water,' she said. 'I'll find somewhere for you to stay. I'll just need a bit of time to explain to my girls.'

He stared at her, incredulous. 'You don't even know me,' he started. 'If I were you, I'd turn around and never come back.'

'No, you wouldn't,' she said. 'If your son was in trouble, you'd help him. I want to help you. Why wouldn't I want to help?'

'But it's different,' he said. 'Completely different. I'm not your son. What I mean is, I might be biologically, but…'

His words stung, but Heidi understood.

'I know what you mean,' she replied. 'It would be different if your parents were still around to help you, but they're not. Johnny started this whole thing, by finding you, and there's no way I can walk away from you. My girls will be fine. They'll love you.'

William's face turned pink and he briefly reached out to Heidi, to touch her arm. She picked up the bag of shopping.

'Here's your shopping,' she said. 'I thought you might need a few extras. These shoes were in Johnny's cupboard. I think he bought them for you.'

They both looked at the bag.

'Thank you,' he said. 'But look, if you're on some kind of guilt trip…'

'No, it's not that,' she said. 'I'm just being myself. I know what it's like to be at rock bottom. I almost forgot to say that those photos you took of Johnny are beautiful. You're good. I don't think you should give up on your dream. When you're back on your feet, perhaps you can take it up again.'

A stripe of sunshine fell into the room at the edges of the grey curtains, and for a brief moment, Heidi felt hopeful. She stood up and opened them, letting the light flood the room.

'It'll work out,' she said, looking down at the street outside. 'That's what Johnny used to say to me. Nothing can be that bad.'

She turned back to face William, who was sitting, arms folded, staring into space.

'There's something you should know,' he said in a half whisper. 'And you're not going to like it.'

Chapter Twenty-One

The time had come. Heidi couldn't let another day pass without speaking frankly to Scarlet and Zoe. No excuse.

'There's something you should know,' she said, echoing William. Scarlet and Zoe were watching the TV together – a cookery show – and she couldn't compete with the narrator's incessant chatter. Heidi picked up the remote control and switched it off. Earlier, she had practised her speech in front of the mirror but now, her mind was blank. Could she really tell Scarlet and Zoe not only about Tuesday but about William? She had to. Could she really expect them to accept that she had a son? Let alone a son with various problems. Sweat burst onto her forehead. The music to *Dallas* played out in her head. She cleared her throat. Her nerves were frayed. This was terrifying.

'What are you doing, Mum?' shouted Scarlet. 'We were watching that! Now I don't know if Michael's soufflé collapsed!'

'Sshhh,' said Zoe, sitting up straight, knowing that this was the moment Heidi would tell them about Tuesday. 'Mum's going to tell us something.'

'I need to tell you something,' Heidi said, her voice shaking.

'You were right,' said Scarlet sarcastically. 'She's going to tell us something. Get on with it then – I don't want to miss the end of the show!'

Zoe threw a cushion at Scarlet, who jokingly screamed before Zoe hushed her once again. Heidi stood in front of the TV, then moved towards the couch, where she perched on the edge. Her hands shook. Her eyes travelled around the room, which suddenly seemed neglected. The mossy green walls needed redecorating, the family photographs positioned in clusters on the shelves and windowsill needed dusting and the wilting plants were thirsty. The piano, once played every day by Johnny and Zoe, hadn't been touched for weeks.

'Is this about that lady last night?' said Zoe, pulling her hair into a ponytail on the top of her head. 'Tuesday?'

Zoe's cheeks were fever pink and her blue eyes shone like polished stones. She had on Johnny's enormous cream fisherman's sweater, which she'd barely removed since claiming it. By her side was a big bag of Monster Munch crisps. Scarlet, who had pulled off one glittery sock to inspect a toenail, painted blue, looked up.

'What lady?' said Scarlet. 'Tuesday. I recognise that name. Was that the woman's name on Facebook?'

Heidi held her hands up in the air to silence the girls.

'Yes, it's about Tuesday,' she said. 'This is very delicate, girls. I need you to be patient while I tell you the whole story.'

The girls glanced at one another, Scarlet widening her eyes in suspense.

'Your grandma, well, you know how proper she is and how reputation was very important to her family,' said Heidi. 'Well in 1957, she fell pregnant. Not by Grandad – she didn't know him until a few years later – but by another chap. She had the baby, but because she was unmarried, she had to put her up for adoption. It happened a lot in those times. Your grandma never told me about it, nor did she tell Grandad. She only told me recently because… well, because, well… because…'

This was her moment to make her announcement about William. But the words stuck in her throat like chunks of bread. She coughed, holding her throat.

'Because Dad died?' finished Scarlet. 'Poor Grandma! And so you contacted this woman, Tuesday, and she was here, last night? Why the bloody hell didn't you say anything? For God's sake, Mum, this is major news! You should have shared this with us!'

Heidi blanched at Scarlet's language. She was always full of opinions, reflective later.

'I've had a lot on my mind,' said Heidi. 'An awful lot has happened recently, I… your dad – he – before he died he took it upon himself to…'

Heidi fell silent. Words completely failed her. She had her daughters' undivided attention, but she simply couldn't bring herself to tell them about William. Especially after his confession that morning, which lurked in her thoughts like a storm cloud, threatening to break. He had explained that he was in serious debt to the tune of several thousand pounds. He had inherited some money when his mother died and, when he got together with Martha, he used some of it to set up a photography business and put a deposit down on a house. Then his photography business started to struggle and he couldn't pay some of the bills. He became desperate and, on a whim, went to a casino one night with a friend. He got lucky a couple of times and started to visit the bookies and tried online gambling. Soon the luck and money ran out, but by then, he was hooked. It was the reason he and Martha had split up.

Now, with maintenance to pay to Martha, and a very low income, bailiffs were chasing him for unpaid debts. He had shown her a clutch of letters from debt agencies, the content in bright red typeface, threatening him with legal action. He owed money to friends too. The shame and fear in his voice and written on his face was enough to break Heidi's heart. He had described how he'd tried to give up gambling, but because he could play on his mobile, it was too difficult to resist.

'I just want to be a good dad to Freddy,' he'd said. 'Each time I place a bet I think of how the winnings will help me provide for Freddy, but of course it doesn't work like that. I'm making an absolute mess of the whole thing. I'm a failure.'

Heidi had known that instant that she was going to help him. Others might walk away. But she would do anything to help.

Contact the debt-collection agencies, pay off the debt with savings she had, get him professional help if necessary. Give him a room to call home, so that he could make a fresh start. She was going to be the person to offer William hope. It's what Johnny would have done, *was* doing. Their son was broken and she was going to fix him.

'Did you like Tuesday?' said Zoe now. 'So, she's your half-sister and our half-aunt?'

Heidi thought about her meeting with Tuesday and felt a rush of excitement. She had enjoyed being with her, though her memories of what they'd discussed were a little hazy.

'Yes, I did like her,' she said. 'I would have told you straight away, but I didn't know how you would take that news.'

'Don't look so terrified; it's not like you have a secret love child, Mum!' Scarlet said, laughing.

Stars fizzed above Heidi as if she'd been knocked out.

'Can't believe Grandma had that secret for so long. I feel sorry for her. Has she met Tuesday?'

Heidi shook her head. 'Not yet.'

Zoe fell silent and looked close to tears. Heidi shook her head, moved to sit next to Zoe and held her hand.

'Don't be upset, Zoe,' Heidi said. 'Grandma will be fine with this news. Tuesday wants to come here at the weekend and meet you, but there's no pressure if it's too soon.'

'I don't mind,' said Zoe, with a small supportive smile. 'Do you think Grandma would mind if I spoke to her about it? I'd just like to know how she feels about it all. We don't really know much about her life at all, do we? This must have been painful for her.'

'Not yet,' said Heidi quickly. 'Just give me some time to talk to her.'

'What's she like?' said Scarlet. 'Tuesday. Is she like you?'

'She seems fun,' said Heidi, 'bright, passionate, full of life, generous, likes a drink and loves to cook. We drank too much the other night, probably nerves. She's a colourful person. I think you'll like her. She's got bright pink hair and runs a catering business from a converted horsebox. I wonder if maybe she's a little bit lonely.'

'Call her,' said Scarlet, the cookery show completely forgotten, 'and invite her round next weekend. I like the sound of anyone who's in her sixties with pink hair and a vintage horsebox.'

Chapter Twenty-Two

The dining-room table was set as if it was Christmas. Red napkins, round rattan placemats. The mostly matching vintage Wedgwood crockery reserved for special occasions and long cream candles in vintage pale-green glass holders – all arranged on an antique gold lace tablecloth. The sight of it made Heidi feel sad. They hadn't used the dining table in months. The last time would have been actual Christmas, when Johnny was alive, and as a treat, he'd allowed himself a slightly bigger dinner than usual. She had cleared the table of the last few months of post, paperwork and detritus, including a bicycle helmet and a vase of dried chrysanthemums that had gathered a layer of dust on each dead petal.

Chair cushions had been plumped up, disturbing a cloud of dust. A duster swept over the piano keys and the floorboards hoovered. The air was heavy with the scent of roast chicken, a nut roast for Scarlet and roast potatoes.

'You could go on one of those interior design shows,' said Zoe. 'This all looks so lovely.'

Heidi laughed. 'Hardly. But thank you. I don't want her to think we live in a slum.'

When she said the words, her thoughts went to William and his sofa-surfing lifestyle. Glancing at Zoe, she wondered what her daughter would say if she told her, now, about his existence.

'Today must really mean something,' Zoe said. 'I'm glad for you to have someone new in your family. It's nice.'

Heidi reached for Zoe's hand and squeezed, always grateful for her younger daughter's kindness. Today did matter to Heidi, an awful lot, but it was so much more than simply making a good impression on Tuesday. It was bigger than that. She wanted to prove to the girls that having a new person in the family could be a good thing. A good thing that wasn't to be feared, that would enrich all of their lives.

'Am I underdressed?' said Heidi, gesturing to her jeans and striped top, continuing to talk before she got an answer. 'Anything that's not my dungarees feels like a suit! Can you pick up those socks over there? How did they get there?'

'What's going on?' said Scarlet, yawning as she entered the room, still wearing her dressing gown, with her hair tied up in a floppy bun and yesterday's eyeliner smudged around her eyes. 'You look posh, Mum, in your smart jeans.'

'Scarlet!' said Heidi. 'Tuesday is coming in half an hour. Please can you get ready? This is important.'

Scarlet flopped onto a chair, pulled her phone from her dressing-gown pocket and started scrolling, but Heidi snatched it from her hands and pointed towards the stairs.

'Go!' she said. 'You need to get dressed.'

'Chill!' said Scarlet, stretching out. 'You're going to scare her off if you're like this. Just be your normal self.'

'I don't know what my normal self is anymore,' Heidi muttered to herself as she rushed through to the kitchen to check on the food.

Turning her attention to the sage and onion stuffing, she pushed her fingers into the bowl and started mixing. Again, she thought about William. While she was setting the table and making a roast dinner, he was sofa surfing, worrying about debt. Tempted by the games on his phone. A wife and child he loved but couldn't live with. His problems hung around his neck like a ball and chain. Not for long. She would make sure of that.

'Mum!' came a shout from the living room. It was Zoe. 'She's here! She's early! I've just seen her park up outside in a yellow Mini!'

Heidi's scalp tightened with nerves and anticipation. She yanked her hands out of the stuffing mix and held them under the cold-water tap, quickly drying them on a tea towel as she waited for the doorbell to ring. But there was no ring. Instead, came the sound of the front door opening.

'Hellooo!' came Tuesday's voice from the hallway. 'Can I let myself in? I'm here!'

Heidi's heart raced. She dashed out to the hallway, where Tuesday was standing, dressed in a red coat, a red beret and wearing bright red lipstick to match. A cloud of patchouli wafted inside with her. In her arms she held an enormous bunch of gladioli which she held out to Heidi.

'Thank you,' said Heidi, thinking back to William's freesias. 'They're magnificent.'

Tuesday took off her beret, and with her pink curls and bright eyes, she was quite dazzling. Placing down her bags – two large tote bags overflowing with wine and goodies – she held out her arms and greeted Heidi as if they were familiar siblings, or old friends, not new acquaintances.

'I've been desperate to see you again,' said Tuesday, giving a little bob with her knees when she said 'desperate'. 'I've been driving around for the last half hour, counting down the minutes. I just couldn't wait any longer. Look at your fabulous house! And your fabulous daughter, my niece. You must be—'

'The house is really not very fabulous,' said Heidi apologetically, hanging up a coat that had slipped from the coat pegs to the floor. 'But this is Zoe, my youngest daughter, and Scarlet is just...'

Tuesday released Heidi from her fragrant grip and hugged Zoe, who was standing shyly and stiff as a lamp post. At that moment, Scarlet bounded down the stairs wearing a short blue dress. She had reapplied her eye make-up and smelled like coconuts. She held out her hand confidently.

'I'm Scarlet,' she said. 'And this is my sister Zoe. We're very pleased to meet you.'

Tuesday went straight in for a hug. 'Scarlet,' she said. 'I wish I had been called Scarlet. You smell gorgeous!'

Heidi couldn't help cringe. Hugging strangers, no matter if blood related, was not something she, or Rosalind for that matter, would normally do. But Scarlet seemed to like it – and hugged her new aunt in return.

'I love your coat,' Scarlet said happily. 'You're like a rainbow. A burst of colour compared to my monotone mother! My girlfriend would like you.'

'Thanks, Scarlet!' said Heidi, glancing at her outfit and wishing she'd worn something brighter. Thinking back over the weeks since Johnny died, she wasn't sure she'd worn anything other than grey or black. Years ago, women wore black for an entire year to grieve – sometimes for the rest of their lives.

'Can I just say that this is a dream come true for me,' Tuesday said, smiling. 'And the most bizarre thing is that you all look a little bit like me! It's as if I'm in one of those hall of mirrors at the fairground.'

She laughed uproariously and paused to pull a bottle of Prosecco from her bag. She waved it in the air and grinned.

'This is cause for celebration,' she said. 'A remarkable day. I've been waiting for this forever.'

Heidi nodded and gestured towards the living room, slightly overwhelmed.

'What a great family room,' Tuesday said, crossing the room to the wall that was covered in pictures. 'It's lovely. And these photographs are exceptional. Is this… is this… Johnny? I'm so very sorry about your dad. I would have loved to have met him.'

The four women stood in front of the wall of photographs, looking up at the faces staring out. Heidi thought she must add the one of Johnny that William took. It was probably the most recent.

'Thank you,' said Zoe. 'We all miss him a lot, don't we?'

'Yes,' Heidi said. 'Of course we do. Very much. Most days I wake up and for a second I think he's still here and then the reality hits. I can't believe he's gone.'

'He looks very handsome,' said Tuesday gently. 'And kind. A lovely warm heart. I'm sure you still feel his presence here.'

Heidi smiled. Connecting with Johnny in some way felt like a wonderful prospect, even though she'd previously dismissed that kind of thing. But enough things had happened since he'd died – like their favourite song coming on the radio when she was thinking about him, or a seagull swooping down right next to her head, as if with a message – for her to feel there was some truth in it. It was a comforting thought anyway.

'Scarlet, can you get some glasses?' said Heidi. 'I'll just have a taste. Tuesday, would you like to take a seat in here? I'm preparing the lunch; it won't be long.'

Scarlet darted into the kitchen and returned with a tray. The excitement in the air was tangible. It made Heidi realise how long it had been since she'd invited anyone to their home for dinner. When each of them held a filled glass, Tuesday raised a toast.

'To new family,' she said. They all raised their glasses and took a sip.

'It's lovely to meet you,' said Scarlet. 'Exciting!'

From the kitchen came the sound of the timer going off, so Heidi quickly returned to the oven, followed by Tuesday and the girls.

'Can I help you at all?' Tuesday asked, looking around the kitchen. 'I love your home. It's so homely.'

Heidi removed the lid from a saucepan and turned off the heat. Her cheeks were bright pink with the warmth of cooking. She shook her head and smiled.

'You're the guest!' said Scarlet. 'We'll help. You sit here at the table.'

Scarlet pulled out a seat for Tuesday, who sat down and placed her glass on the table. Zoe sat down at the table too, while Scarlet stood near Heidi, who opened the oven and pulled out the tray of roasting chicken and potatoes.

'Mum said you run a catering business from a vintage horsebox,' said Scarlet. 'That's so cool. You'll have to tell us all about it.'

'Gosh, you're so very welcoming,' Tuesday said. 'It's a lot for you to process, I suppose, after your dad passing away, to suddenly have an aunt and a brother you didn't know about! How are you feeling about it all? I wondered if William might be here today. Your mum said something about him coming to stay, but we had a bit too much wine, so I'm hazy on the detail.'

With the roasting pan still in her oven-gloved hands, Heidi stood frozen to the spot, and opened and closed her mouth. The blood drained from her face and her stomach dipped. She recalled a flash of their drunken conversation in the pub, where she'd not been able to stop talking.

A heavy silence gripped the kitchen, like a huge pair of hands squeezing the air out of the room. Scarlet and Zoe stared at Heidi, brows furrowed, mouths agape.

'Sorry?' said Scarlet. 'I think you've got something a bit confused here... Mum? Did Grandma have another child?'

When Heidi couldn't find the words to answer or react in any way at all – other than to stand completely still with the roast chicken steaming before her – Scarlet's cheeks bloomed pink.

'Tuesday just said that we have a brother?' she said, more loudly. 'Not you, Mum.'

Heidi remained silent. Tuesday swallowed loudly.

'Mum, can you explain what's going on?' Zoe said.

Heidi felt as if she was sitting on a fairground waltzer and was being flung around the room from corner to corner, at high speed.

'Yes, I can explain,' Heidi said, her mouth so dry she felt as though she'd been eating sand. 'You do... you do...'

'Tell us then!' Scarlet said, shoving into Heidi's arm. She staggered and dropped the roasting tin. The chicken and potatoes bounced out of it and skated across the kitchen floor, in a pool of cooking oil. Everyone gaped.

'Oh, I—' Tuesday started, her hand over her mouth. 'Oh God, me and my big mouth. I'm so sorry; I had no idea you hadn't told—'

'We have a brother?' said Zoe. Her eyes were perfect circles. 'You have to be joking?'

Heidi searched her brain for a reply, to give them an answer they would approve of. But nothing came. Her head was air, and dots fizzed in front of her eyes before her knees gave way. Collapsing onto the floor, she flopped down on the kitchen tiles alongside the upturned chicken. And then Scarlet threw her glass at the wall.

Chapter Twenty-Three

Everything was ruined. Heidi stepped around the scattered roast potatoes, her feet crunching on broken glass. Scarlet had walked out. Music thundered through the ceiling from Zoe's bedroom – she'd locked herself in after tearfully but politely excusing herself upstairs. A stress headache split Heidi's brain in half. Her body filled with hapless rage and hot tears blurred her vision.

'How can you possibly have kept that secret from us?' Scarlet had yelled. 'I don't even feel like I know you anymore.'

Scarlet's sharp words pierced Heidi's heart. She felt angry, but her own rage wasn't directed at Scarlet or Zoe. Of course they would react to this news with disbelief and anger. They were in shock. Needed time. Questions answered. An explanation. Her girls had reacted normally. No, the rage she felt now was directed at Johnny. He had done this. He could have spoken to her months ago. He should have spoken to her. Sinking into a kitchen chair and resting her palms on the tabletop, she sighed.

'It's a horrible feeling,' she said to a bewildered and grim-faced Tuesday, who had her arms protectively wrapped around her waist, 'to be cross with the person you love the most in the world. But he's the one who got me in this situation. He found William. He didn't once talk to me about it. He lied to me about where he was going, who he was seeing. I tried to tell myself they were white lies, but are lies ever good? Surely the very existence of a secret means that someone is being deceived. And when is deceit good? If you're doing anything behind anyone's back, it's never good.'

She remembered Tuesday's confession about her holidays in Germany and what they likely meant and immediately apologised. Tuesday shook her head as if to say it didn't matter.

She squeezed her eyes closed and tipped back her head, balling her hands into fists and quelling the urge to scream at the top of her lungs. Tuesday gently rested her hand on Heidi's shoulder.

'Take a deep breath,' she said. 'Inhale for three and exhale for six counts. It really works.'

Heidi opened her eyes, did as Tuesday said, and offered her a small apologetic smile.

'You're in a lot of pain, Heidi,' Tuesday said. 'And I've just made it a hundred times worse. A million times worse. I'm so sorry. I got the wrong end of the stick at the pub. I'd had too much to drink. As usual, it's a bit of a theme.'

Heidi blinked away tears.

'No, I'm sorry. This is my reality,' said Heidi, bending down to pick up the chicken. 'It's not napkins and lace tablecloths. It's a bloody mess. One minute, my life was going along steadily, the next it's upside down. I keep blaming Johnny, but it's all my fault really. I have to be strong. I can't lose my way. I should have spoken to the girls long ago. But my son, William, he's got some problems, and I've been wary about telling the girls about those troubles. I wanted to help him first.'

'Oh, Heidi, you're not superhuman,' Tuesday said. 'I can't tell you how sorry I am.'

'It's not your fault,' said Heidi. 'I've been weak all along.'

Heidi registered that Zoe's music had been switched off and knew that she was listening through the ceiling.

'I should go and check on Zoe,' said Heidi, standing. 'I'm sorry that you've been subjected to this family drama. Not what you wanted, I expect, from your new half-sister that you were so excited about meeting!'

Heidi put her hands on her hips and exhaled. Her heart was pounding in her chest and sweat trickled down her neck. Suddenly the kitchen shapeshifted in front of her.

'Drink this,' said Tuesday, handing her a glass of Prosecco. 'You've had a shock.'

Heidi gulped it down. She winced but poured more into the glass and drank another, hoping that it would numb the pain a little.

'Would you like me to go out and look for Scarlet?' said Tuesday, glancing at the window, which was being hammered by rain and wind. 'Do you know where she might be? I know we've only just met, but I could at least find her and apologise to her for blurting that out, while you talk to Zoe. Again, I'm so sorry.'

'This was going to happen at some point,' said Heidi. 'Scarlet's girlfriend is in Southampton, so she might have called her, but actually she's left her mobile on the table. She might be on the beach. I think it's probably better to leave her to cool down on her own. I hope she hasn't gone to see my mother! Our mother!'

The women shared a look.

'Let me clean this up while you speak to Zoe,' said Tuesday. 'It's the least I can do. Cleaning is calming. If your house is in order, your mind is in order, or something like that. Tidy house, tidy mind, that's it!'

'That's the sort of thing my – our – mother would say,' said Heidi.

Tuesday pulled on the yellow rubber gloves and crouched down on the floor to pick up the potatoes. The hem of her skirt dipped in the pool of cooking oil, which instantly stained it.

'Your skirt!' said Heidi, still frozen to the spot. 'Oh God, your skirt will be ruined!'

'Oh, I don't care about my skirt; it's not important. I'll use my hair if I need to – it looks like a mop!' said Tuesday. 'Now go and see Zoe.'

Tuesday pointed towards the stairs and Heidi dragged her legs up them. Her limbs felt so heavy, as if she was pulling several other people with her as she moved. Knocking on Zoe's closed door, she tried to plan an explanation, but the words scrambled in her head. She knocked again and Zoe opened the door, her face ashen.

'Is it true then?' Zoe said, her face crumpling into tears. Heidi nodded.

'Can I come in?' she said, stepping over the threshold into Zoe's room. Heidi perched on the edge of the mattress and realised she hadn't been inside Zoe's room for more than a few minutes for ages. She scanned the things strewn about – a holiday brochure, half a packet of digestives, Johnny's grey fluffy dressing gown, a stack of washing, a pair of running shoes covered in mud and three empty bottles of strawberry milk and several lovely pencil drawings of a landscape on the wall. She felt guilty – she hadn't been there for Zoe. She hadn't given her enough time.

'I'm sorry you had to find out like that,' said Heidi as Zoe quickly pushed something under the bed with her foot. 'But when your dad and I were really young, I got pregnant and your grandma didn't want me to keep the baby. It was different then. I was doing my A levels and the pregnancy was an accident. Your grandma didn't want me to ruin my chances of getting a good education and a good job. She thought the baby would be better off going to a stable couple who had the means to bring up a child. I expect it was for the best. Your father and I never talked about it. We should have done. And we should have told you and Scarlet. But unbeknownst to me, before your dad died, he found our son. His name is William. I can only think that when your dad had his first heart attack it frightened him into thinking that he might not have long left, so he decided to find him. William had put his details onto a contact register so it wasn't difficult. I've been to meet him a couple of times. I wanted to suss him out first before I told you. I meant to talk to you that night that I told you about Tuesday, but I couldn't find the words. It's been a massive shock, all of it. Too much to process for you, I know.'

The rain stopped and sun flooded through the bedroom window, turning everything gold.

'What's he like?' Zoe asked through tears.

Heidi sighed, conjuring up a painful image of William in his friend's awful flat – and at One Stop, unable to pay for his shopping.

'He looks like the double of your dad and has a dimple on one cheek,' said Heidi, which made both of them smile. 'He has a child but has split from his partner, so it's a difficult time for him. He's great at photography, just like your dad. He's staying at a friend's house, but it's temporary. I was hoping to offer him our spare room to help him get back on his feet, but I know it's a lot to ask of you and your sister. Everything has happened at once. I think your dad planned it this way. He gave us something to deal with, something major, to keep us distracted from our grief. It wasn't enough to leave me with the business to run! How does it make you feel?'

Zoe shrugged, wrapping her arms tightly around the middle.

'How did you feel when you got pregnant all those years ago?' Zoe asked quietly.

Zoe was chewing the ends of a chunk of hair – something she used to do as a little girl when she was nervous.

'I felt frightened and ashamed because Grandma was ashamed of me, but I didn't know the truth and that she'd been through the same!' Heidi said. 'But I also felt curious about what was happening to my body. I didn't know what to do or what was best. Afterwards, after the baby was born and adopted, I fell apart a little bit. I couldn't cope with the fact that nobody talked about it to me. Even your dad. It was very odd.'

Zoe pushed her toe around an invisible spot on the carpet. Heidi knew that she was struggling not to cry. She reached over to Zoe and pulled her in for a hug.

'Try not to be too upset,' Heidi said. 'This changes nothing about my love for you and your sister. You come first. I love you both so much. I want to support you and help you through the loss of your dad, not make it all worse by dragging up the past, but obviously it's a difficult situation for me. You're only eighteen, Zoe, and you've been through so much recently. I just want you to be okay. I'll do anything to make sure you're okay.'

'I'd like to meet him,' said Zoe. 'If he looks like Dad, I'd like to meet him. I've always wanted an older brother.'

A tear escaped Heidi's eye. Zoe had a big, generous, unquestioningly good heart.

'Thank you, for being so kind,' said Heidi. 'We'll talk about it all again. Will you be okay if I go out? I need to find Scarlet, and I don't think she's going to have the same take as you on all this. Tuesday is downstairs. She's just cleaning up, then I expect she'll go. Poor Tuesday probably wishes she'd never met me! What an introduction!'

Zoe managed a small laugh, wiping away her tears with her sleeve. Heidi moved towards the door, picking up Johnny's dressing gown on the way and holding it to her nose. It still held the scent of him. She hung it on a peg on the back of Zoe's door.

'We should sort your room out,' Heidi said. 'But those drawings are lovely. When did you do them?'

'When I was up in Scotland,' said Zoe. 'Mum?'

'Yes?' said Heidi, about to leave the room. 'What is it?'

Zoe was trembling. Kneeling down to retrieve whatever it was from under the bed, she pulled a pregnancy testing stick out and handed it to Heidi, who stared at it for a long moment. The result was positive.

'Is this…' asked Heidi in a faint voice. 'Is it yours?'

Zoe nodded. Heidi sat down on the bed.

'If we're getting everything out in the open, I might as well show it to you,' Zoe whispered, trying not to cry. 'It happened before Dad died. I didn't realise for ages. You know how my periods are never regular, and I thought they'd stopped because I was upset about Dad. Then, when I found out, Leo talked me into making *us* official so that we could try to make a go of being together properly. He said it didn't matter that we were young, that it shouldn't change our lives and that he loved me and wanted to spend his life with me. When we went away for those few days, we went to Gretna Green… Leo used his savings and we paid for this one-night package in this hotel to… to… get married. I wasn't going to tell you, but, if we're telling each other our secrets, this is mine. I'm pregnant and I'm married.'

Slowly, Zoe pulled a necklace out from inside her jumper. On it hung a very slim gold wedding band. Heidi's jaw dropped.

Chapter Twenty-Four

'M-Married?' Heidi stuttered. 'Actually, legally married? And actually, definitely pregnant?'

Zoe nodded and lifted up the fisherman's jumper, where there was a clearly defined bump.

'Six months,' she said. 'Nearly seven.'

'Nearly seven months!' said Heidi, utterly stunned. How could she not have known?

'My bump is pretty small,' Zoe said. 'I've hidden it well under Dad's jumpers.'

Heidi felt overwhelming guilt and a sense of loss. If she had been more focused on her daughters, rather than distracted by William, she would have realised something major was going on. The arguments she'd had with Leo, Zoe's increased appetite, her refusal to take off that huge jumper and always wearing baggy clothing, but this was enormous. Life-changing. All those hopes she'd had for Zoe's future. Her nursing degree, the travel she'd talked of, the imagined opportunities. They were now on hold. How could she have missed this? She was also acutely aware that how she reacted would be imprinted on Zoe's heart for the rest of her life.

'This is my fault,' Heidi said, the colour draining from her face and pooling into her boots. Zoe burst out laughing.

'It is absolutely not your fault,' she said. 'I know all about the birds and the bees. I'm doing an A level in Human Biology! This was an accident. I know that this changes everything – but I can deal with it; I know I can. And I love Leo – he's a good person. We want to make a life together. Commit.'

Heidi's thoughts went to Leo. Heidi didn't know him well enough to know whether he was a good person. How long had they been together – eighteen months?

'Have you thought about what you'll do?' Heidi asked tentatively.

'I've given it a lot of thought,' Zoe said, swallowing. 'I mean, we'll have to live separately for a while but… eventually we can get somewhere together. A flat, you know, where I can grow plants and have a piano. Maybe closer to the sea. I know Leo loves me and supports me. He's nineteen soon, and he's looking for a job. I still want to be a nurse. We're going to work it out so we can both still do what we want. I don't see why we can't make it happen.'

Heidi could almost see the images inside Zoe's head: the movie-inspired apartment lit with strings of fairy lights and with huge floor cushions thrown casually on the floorboards. A life that wasn't reality, but on the other hand, she admired Zoe's resolve.

Zoe gazed hopefully at Heidi. In her childhood bedroom, painted dark blue when she was fourteen, decorated with vinyl stickers of seagulls, old photographs and certificates from school and with a collection of three old teddy bears perched on a shelf, she seemed out of place. As if she was wearing shoes that were much too small. Heidi was hurled through history back to the point in time she had discovered her own pregnancy. She had been desperate for Rosalind to comfort her and support her, only to be met with the opposite response. She hugged Zoe tight, kissing the top of her head.

'We can get through all of this together, and I will support you,' Heidi said firmly. 'Does Leo's family know?'

Zoe shook her head, crossing the room to open the window. Leo's family were unknown to Heidi, but Zoe rarely spent time at his. Almost their whole relationship had been conducted in this house, on camping trips, at the cinema, eating pizza.

'He thinks they'll be okay about it,' she said. 'He was hoping to go to York university, but he's looked locally and seen a course he likes and he's keen to take a year out to earn more money so that we can eventually be independent. For the time being, I think I need your help for a while longer, if you'll have me at home. I'd like to be at home. I've been feeling quite alone.'

Heidi swallowed, desperate not to say the wrong thing. She couldn't stand the thought of Zoe feeling alone.

'Oh, Zoe,' said Heidi. 'Of course I'll help you and Leo. Your sister will help. We'll find a way for you both to be able to study. Having a child doesn't mean your dreams end – maybe they change or maybe they just happen a little slower. You're at the heart of my life, you and Scarlet, just as your child will be at the heart of yours. Anything you need from me comes first, always. Look, we're getting ahead of ourselves. Have you seen a doctor?'

'No,' Zoe said. 'But I will. I can't believe that this happened to Grandma, then you and now me. It's completely mad.'

From downstairs came the sound of the front door opening and closing. For a second she imagined it was Johnny, and that any moment he would call out 'hello'. But Scarlet was home. There was a muffled 'goodbye' and then the front door opened and closed again. Poor Tuesday would never come back. Heidi felt unfathomably disappointed.

'It's not the same,' said Heidi, determined to shine a positive light on Zoe's situation. 'Life has changed. It's about how you handle these things. Just don't worry. It'll all be okay. Besides, Leo will share the responsibility with you. As you said, he's a good person.'

Heidi concealed any doubts she had, and Zoe fell silent as they listened to Scarlet climbing the stairs. She put her head around the door and cleared her throat.

'Are you talking about William?' Scarlet said, emphasising his name with distaste. 'Do you think you might like to tell me too, since I am your daughter? One of your many children! Look, Tuesday gave me this note downstairs. She's cleared up down there! Sorry about the glass.'

She handed Heidi the note: *I'm going to collect a few things. I'll be back later. Tuesday x*

Heidi stuffed the note in her pocket and briefly wondered what on earth Tuesday was going to collect and why she was coming back after the day they'd had. But she registered that she felt pleased too.

'So,' said Scarlet, taking a seat on the bed and tucking her feet under a corner of the duvet. 'Are you going to tell us the truth – finally?'

It was clear that Scarlet was going to punish Heidi as much as possible, but Heidi would have to grit her teeth and get through it with as much patience as possible.

'Of course, Scarlet, I'll tell you everything about William, but we were just talking about something else,' said Heidi, glancing at Zoe, who dropped her gaze.

'What?' said Scarlet. 'What now?'

'I'm… I'm… I'm… I'm… pregnant,' Zoe muttered. 'And… married.'

Scarlet's jaw dropped. 'Whoa,' she said. 'I was not expecting that! I thought I was supposed to be the crazy one.'

Registering the fear on her sister's face, Scarlet put her arms around Zoe and held her in a protective grip.

'So that's why your skin has been amazing,' she went on. 'It never used to glow like that. You've been looking like a peach for weeks. I thought you must have bought some of that miracle cream. Married though? What the…? When did you do that? Why did you do that? Now you're stuck with Leo playing his ukulele forever more!'

Zoe smiled and shrugged. 'I don't know,' she said. 'I got a bit swept up in trying to do the right thing. We thought, if we made some big decisions on our own, our families wouldn't try to meddle too much and get us to change our minds about going ahead with it all. To be perfectly honest, I'm scared. Terrified.'

'Don't worry, Zoe,' said Scarlet softly. 'We'll help – won't we, Mum?'

The plea in Scarlet's voice didn't escape Heidi. She nodded with as much confidence as she could muster. She must not let either daughter see the fear coursing through her.

'Of course we will,' said Heidi. 'Absolutely yes.'

Two hours later, Tuesday arrived with a shopping bag brimming with 'emergency provisions'. There were crisps, three bottles of wine, tins of coconut milk, vegetables, spices and maple syrup. She bustled back into the house, dropped the shopping bags on the kitchen floor and offered to make everyone a hot chocolate with a twist. Heidi noticed that she'd also brought with her a bag of clothes and that her toothbrush was poking out the top.

'Coconut cream, cacao, syrup and a dash of rum,' Tuesday continued. 'Honestly, it's just what you need in a time of crisis. It's got me through many lows!'

Unpacking the shopping bags, she paused and turned, blushing when she saw that Heidi had clocked the toothbrush. Quickly, she shoved it deeper into her bag and pushed it to the side of the room.

'Please tell me if you'd like me to go away,' she said, her voice dropping to a whisper. 'But I feel as though you could do with a helping hand. A bit of support. We've only just met, but I've nowhere to be and you seem as if you could use a friend. I can make myself useful. I have a hotel booked tonight, but it's not as nice as here.'

Tuesday gave a small, crushed laugh. Heidi's heart contracted. She seemed to hold her breath as she waited for Heidi's reply. Heidi worried about the fact she needed to talk more to Zoe and Scarlet, in private. But Tuesday's expression persuaded her otherwise.

'Yes,' she said. 'You're welcome to stay tonight.'

Tuesday's shoulders visibly dropped. 'Thank you,' she said. 'I didn't want to lose you all as soon as I found you.'

'Is there anyone you need to let know?' Heidi asked.

Tuesday's face fell. 'Nobody,' she said. 'Nobody at all. I'm all alone in the world.'

'Not anymore,' said Heidi.

Tuesday beamed. 'Thank you. I'm so glad I've met you. Do you think you can persuade Rosalind to meet me?'

Heidi frowned. Trying to get Rosalind to do anything she didn't really want to do was hard. She opened her mouth to say as much but was met with Tuesday's pleading eyes.

'Yes,' she found herself saying. 'I'm sure of it.'

All at once she was enveloped in patchouli, pink curls and warmth.

'Thank you,' said Tuesday. 'Thank you, thank you, thank you. Now let me make this hot chocolate. You are going to love it. It's vegan. By the way, I'm vegan – so I was quite relieved when the chicken didn't materialise.'

'You and Scarlet both,' said Heidi. 'She's vegan too. And don't worry, there was nut roast!'

'Oh that's great!' said Tuesday. 'We're all going to have fun together, aren't we?'

Heidi smiled, bemused, wondering if anything that had happened today could be described as 'fun'.

Chapter Twenty-Five

In her swimsuit and with her hair tied in a bun, Heidi walked determinedly into the sea and dropped her shoulders under the surface. The cold water was electrifying and made her gasp. But the cold cut through the confusion she felt about Zoe's revelation. However supportive Leo was, it was inevitable that Zoe's life would change more than his. He might choose to walk away from having a child – but would she ever be able to? Perhaps that was a non-feminist thought. Perhaps she was being unfair to Leo. She hoped so.

Swimming energetically, she turned her thoughts to her productive morning in the workshop. With every tack or piece of cloth that she had methodically removed from the armchair she was working on, she had felt more certain about what she had to do to help her family move forward. She had to take control. Make a plan.

Flipping onto her back and floating in a star shape, she stared at the vast pale-blue sky and seagulls, turning over thoughts in her head. When she grew cold, she swam back to shore, wrapped herself in a thick towel and dressed quickly, thinking about Tuesday and how much she longed to meet Rosalind. Heidi knew what she had to do.

Glancing up towards her mother's flat, she swallowed. Rosalind could be unpredictable and maybe, after all these years, it would be too much to ask. She may well refuse. But Heidi would try.

Half running up the beach, teeth chattering with cold, she crossed the road and buzzed the bell to Rosalind's flat. Her mother's voice burst through the intercom.

'Have you been swimming again?' she asked, when Heidi arrived at the door. 'Your hair is wet. You'll catch your death! I do worry about you. You've always had a reckless streak. I don't know where you got it from. Must have been your father. Can you remember when the silly man once ran ahead when we were on a family walk and climbed a tree to surprise us by jumping out at us, only to break his ankle!'

Heidi remembered. She had loved that about her dad – that and his devotion to making old furniture beautiful again. He had taught her everything she knew.

'I remember,' she said, following Rosalind into the flat. 'We thought he was joking, didn't we, when he couldn't walk? Poor Dad. I miss him.'

They smiled at one another.

'So many people to miss,' said Rosalind. 'I dream about them all, the dead people. Do you?'

Heidi nodded, taking in the folded checked blanket on the sofa, a copy of *Gardener's World* magazine and a small tube of rose hand cream – a brand she had used for decades. Rosalind was dressed in a long purple dress, with stockinged feet. She had on foundation, but no other make-up.

'Did you forget the rest of your make-up?' said Heidi.

'What do you mean?' said Rosalind, looking at herself in the mirror. 'Oh yes, I see what you're getting at. Must have got distracted. I look like I'm wearing a mask. That's what you used to say to me when you were a child and I was putting on my make-up: "Are you putting your mask on, Mummy?" I suppose I was really.'

'How's your knee?' Heidi asked. 'Is it feeling better?'

'Much better, thank you,' said Rosalind. 'Walter's been very attentive. He's a sweet man – poor dear has had a difficult time lately. We've become good pals.'

Heidi smiled. 'I'd like to talk to you for a minute. If you've got time?'

'I'm planning to sort out my baking cupboard this afternoon, but I can squeeze you in,' Rosalind joked.

'Why don't you sit down?' Heidi replied. 'I'll make us some tea.'

Out in the kitchen, as the kettle boiled, Heidi planned out what she would say. With two cups of tea placed on coasters on the table in front of them, she dropped onto the sofa next to Rosalind and gradually told her the whole story about Tuesday's appearance and her wish to meet Rosalind. Heidi's speech was met with stony silence. Rosalind stared directly ahead of her. The tea remained untouched, now cold and still as a quarry pond.

'Mum?' said Heidi.

Still Rosalind said nothing.

'Nod once if you'll at least consider meeting her,' Heidi said.

Rosalind did not move her head. She sat rigid as a post, her arms folded on her lap, her gaze fixed on a point in the far distance out of the window. Heidi chewed the inside of her cheek but wasn't prepared to be ignored.

'Would it be so bad to meet her for half an hour?' Heidi said. 'Just thirty minutes of your great big long life?'

'What can be achieved in half an hour?' Rosalind said quietly. 'You can't bake a cake in half an hour, let alone make up for a lifetime.'

'You haven't got to make up for a lifetime,' Heidi said gently. 'She simply wants to meet you, to see you in person, to say hello, for you to acknowledge her.'

Rosalind shook her head. 'Heidi,' she said. 'I'm not meeting her. I can't. I'm sorry, but it's not going to happen. I'm an old woman now. My life is quiet. I don't want all of this sudden noise.'

'What are you scared of?' Heidi asked gently.

'I'm not afraid. It's not fear,' Rosalind said. 'It's choice.' She stood and walked to the window, her hand resting gently on the windowsill. 'My choice.'

'But what about Tuesday's choices?' said Heidi. 'She hasn't had any power to make any choices about this. Can't you see it from her point of view?'

Rosalind turned towards Heidi. There were tears in her eyes, and Heidi knew she was wavering.

'Since Johnny died, I've looked at life differently,' continued Heidi. 'Everything can change in an instant. Literally an instant. With that in mind, shouldn't we be more open to things like this? I think you should meet Tuesday.'

Rosalind turned back to face the window, wiping her eyes with a tissue, which she quickly stuffed into her sleeve. The sea was now a shade of deep navy blue, streaked with white froth.

'What's she like?' she said quietly. 'What is Tuesday like?'

Heidi tried to suppress her smile.

'Absolutely lovely!' she said. 'Funny and generous and outspoken and a vegan. I didn't realise she was vegan at first, but she runs a vegan catering business from a vintage horsebox.'

'Vegan!' Rosalind said. 'Horsebox!'

'Yes, don't be so shocked,' said Heidi.

'Poor farmers,' said Rosalind. 'How will they ever survive?'

'They'll have to adapt, I suppose, like the rest of us when things change,' said Heidi.

'I'm too old to adapt,' Rosalind tried, but Heidi shook her head and checked her watch.

'She's waiting for you at my house,' she ventured. 'She's expecting you today. This afternoon. Now. She's baked some vegan brownies for you.'

Heidi was winging it. Rosalind froze.

'Heidi, this isn't a game show,' said Rosalind, her voice shaking. 'I can't possibly meet her today. I haven't even done my make-up properly, let alone sorted out the baking cupboard, and I'm busy. You're bullying me, for goodness' sake. Stop it.'

Rosalind's mouth was set in a firm line, but Heidi wasn't going to give up.

'You can't let her down,' she said. 'Just come with me for an hour.'

'I can't,' said Rosalind, her voice breaking now.

'You can,' said Heidi. 'Seriously, you'll like her. Just meet her, once, and then if you don't like how it goes, never mind.'

'But... I'm...' said Rosalind, her voice suddenly dropping to a whisper. 'What if she hates me? Look at me – I'm an old lady. I've got broken veins and a saggy neck. I've got so used to... to... being this tough old woman, pretending that I'm not affected by things, when inside... Inside I'm... scared that I've done everything wrong.'

Heidi crossed the room and put her arms around her mother. Rosalind's shoulders shuddered as she released a sob. Heidi held her for a moment and felt her mother's stiff body relax in her arms.

'She won't hate you,' said Heidi. 'Swallow your pride and confront your fears. Come on – let's go now. Once you've met her, you'll feel differently about the whole thing; I know it. It will no longer be this enormous unmentionable secret in your life. That will be a relief for you.'

Rosalind stood in the middle of the room like a child that didn't want to go to their first day at school. As vulnerable and fearful as Rosalind appeared, Heidi ploughed ahead with her plan.

'Right,' Heidi said. 'You finish your make-up and I'll get your coat.'

Heidi fetched Rosalind's coat and scarf from the hook in the hallway, realising her own hands were trembling.

'Come on,' she said in the most matter-of-fact tone she could muster. 'I've got a lot of things to sort out today. I can't hang around.'

Rosalind looked confused. But unused to Heidi's authoritative tone, she did as she was told. She quickly applied blusher and lipstick and followed Heidi out through the front door. It was only when they were at the top of the stairwell she realised she hadn't put on her shoes.

'I haven't got my shoes on!' said Rosalind, bustling back indoors and slipping them on.

They walked down to the car without another word. Heidi's heart cracked when she noticed Rosalind's hand was shaking too much to lock the seat belt. Heidi helped, without making a comment, and they drove in silence to Heidi's house, parking on the road a few doors down.

'Right,' Heidi said, turning off the engine.

Rosalind gripped hold of Heidi's hand and didn't let go.

'I can't do it,' she said urgently. 'I can't be any kind of mother to her. Not now.'

'She doesn't want a mother,' said Heidi kindly and calmly. 'She already has one that she loves very much. She just wants to meet you. Nothing more than that. It's a matter of finding out where she's from, who she's from. The girls are there with her. Try to relax. I think, if you don't do this now, you'll always wonder what would have happened.'

Rosalind was so pale, Heidi worried for an awful moment that she might be about to faint.

'Are you feeling alright?' she said. 'You're not going to die on me, are you?'

'Of course I'm not feeling alright!' said Rosalind. 'But you seem determined that I do this. And no I'm not going to die. Good God, I wouldn't want to inconvenience you!'

Rosalind opened the passenger door, got out and slammed it shut. Heidi leaped out of the car and walked by Rosalind's side to the front door and opened it.

'Hello!' she called out. 'We're here.'

There was a hush from the living room, followed by the appearance of Scarlet in the hallway.

'Grandma,' she said, reaching out her hand to Rosalind. 'We're sitting in the living room. Come through and meet Tuesday.'

Heidi smiled gratefully at Scarlet. 'I'm going out,' she said.

'You're going out?' spluttered Rosalind, staring at her in astonishment. 'You can't go out!'

'Come with me, Grandma,' Scarlet said. 'We're having vegan hot chocolate.'

Rosalind blinked. Heidi noticed that her whole body was trembling and, for a moment, she was tempted to stay. But before anyone could say another word, Heidi closed the front door behind her and returned to the car, consumed with anxiety. She instructed herself to calm down. Rosalind and Tuesday were adults. This was their story. She had simply put them together on the same page.

Swallowing down the ache in her throat, she focused on the next stage of her plan. William. It was a risk, but she'd made a plan and she was sticking to it.

Chapter Twenty-Six

'I know I'm doing the right thing, Johnny,' Heidi said as she drove to Poole, towards William's flat. 'I know he needs our help. You knew too. That's what you were trying to tell me.'

Pulling up outside William's flat, parking on a double yellow line, Heidi's chest was tight with anticipation. There was nothing she wanted more than to have everyone – Zoe, Scarlet, Rosalind, Tuesday and William – together in her home. Taking a deep breath, she walked up to William's flat and knocked.

Nobody answered the door, so after calling his name a couple of times, she tried the handle and, finding it unlocked, let herself in. Inching past a bag of rubbish on its way out to the communal bins, Heidi's heart thumped.

'Hello?' she called gently as she entered the living room and found William, stretched out on the sofa, fast asleep, hugging a half-empty bottle of Jack Daniel's like a hot-water bottle. She checked her watch. It was 1 p.m. His face was pale and his hair unwashed. Running her eyes over the kitchen counters, she swallowed. There were yet more empty cans of beer on the kitchen and a greasy empty pizza box. The curtains were closed, and the air was stale with the smell of unwashed plates and something male... feet and armpits.

'William,' she said, shaking his arm. 'Wake up. William, wake up!'

He opened his eyes a crack and, seeing her face above him, immediately closed them again, groaning. She shook him again, noticing his mobile abandoned on the carpet by the sofa.

'What are you doing here?' he mumbled, pulling a pillow over his head.

'Have a shower and grab some clothes,' she said. 'You're coming with me.'

William opened his eyes again, wider this time, frowned and moved into a sitting position, rubbing his eyes with his palms. Noticing the bottle of whiskey, he pushed it under the covers. He looked up at her, blinking, his dark hair flopping over his forehead. Irritation and anxiety ripped through her – she hardly knew William, yet she knew she had no choice but to take him under her wing, whatever the consequences.

'Get up,' she said more firmly. 'I'm taking you to my house where you can have a decent meal and a proper bed for a couple of nights.'

She paused, though she wanted to launch into a tirade of what he might contract if he stayed living in this flat.

'But…' he said, shaking his head. 'Freddy… I've got to collect…'

Heidi picked up William's mobile and passed it to him.

'Contact your partner and tell her you're unwell today,' she said. 'You need to get yourself together. You're not doing Freddy any favours by letting him see you like this. Children remember things. They notice things. You'd be better off taking some time out.'

He glared at her, but Heidi remained resolute.

'I mean it,' she said, opening the curtains. 'If you don't tell Martha you're unwell, I will. Go and have a shower and I'll see you in a few minutes. Don't be long.'

William stood, squinting in the sunlight that was now beaming into the flat, dust particles shining in the light like bubbles. He rubbed his face. 'Okay,' he croaked. 'Give me five minutes.'

Silently, Heidi sighed with relief, collected her bag and started to walk out.

'Heidi?' said William, from behind her.

'Yes?' she said.

'Thanks,' he said. 'I don't deserve your kindness. I'm not normally like this.'

Heidi smiled. 'Neither am I,' she said, before letting the door close behind her.

Waiting in the car, Heidi sat in silence, watching people pass by on the street. Ordinary-looking people – in couples, on their own, with children – but what secrets were they carrying? Heidi and Johnny had carried their secret for their entire marriage. It amazed her how they'd managed to not talk about William – not even a word. It had been too painful, and there had been that question, that awful doubt in her mind, that Johnny resented her for agreeing to the adoption.

She cast her mind back to their wedding day – there had been a tiny part of her that wanted to run away and disappear, because if she married Johnny, she knew they would have other children and would spend a lifetime saying they had two children, when in fact they had three. What if she hadn't married him? Would it all have been easier to compartmentalise?

Heidi put her head to one side, contemplating this, but was interrupted by the appearance of William at the passenger door, a rucksack on his back. He opened the door and ducked his head down. He looked brighter – scrubbed – now he'd showered.

'Are you sure about this?' he asked.

Heidi nodded. 'I'm sure. Do you have everything you need?'

'All my things are still with Martha and Freddy,' he said. 'I'm mostly living out of a bag.'

As they drove, Heidi tried not to think about what might be unfolding at home, but she wondered if Zoe had confided in Rosalind about her pregnancy. Rosalind would be feeling incredibly emotional, and bringing William into the mix now was a lot for everyone to take in, but the alternative was to wait longer. She'd waited too long as it was.

'Will your daughters be there?' said William nervously.

'Yes,' she said. 'Scarlet and Zoe. Also, my mother and my half-sister Tuesday. They're all there.'

William tapped his feet in the footwell. 'I'm not sure I'm up for that,' he said, shocked. 'I thought it was just the two of us. I don't think I'll know what to say to—'

'You'll be alright,' she said. 'They're good people. Kind. Welcoming. Don't worry. This is new for all of us. We can muddle through.'

'I don't think I…' William said, pulling at the neckline of his jumper, then clutching his rucksack and unzipping a pocket before zipping it up again. He started to sweat. When she slowed down at the traffic lights, it crossed her mind that he might open the door and make a run for it. The Morris didn't have a central locking system, otherwise she would have been tempted.

'Honestly,' she said kindly. 'Try not to worry. They're not scary. They're your family, William. They'll all welcome you.'

She tried to sound confident, despite the doubt niggling her.

After what felt like an eternity, she pulled into the street and parked up outside the house.

'We're here,' she said, with a feeling of relief. 'Let's go and say hello.'

William exhaled. He had paled to the shade of milk, and his forehead was coated in a film of sweat. He stared straight forward and held his breath.

'Relax,' she said, feeling utterly unrelaxed. 'It's just a few people, some food and a place to sleep.'

William opened the car door and followed Heidi to the house. Heidi showed him in through the front door, welcomed by the sound of Rosalind's laughter coming from the front room. Rosalind, who had been shaking with fear hours earlier! Relief washed over her – at least she was okay.

Aware that William was lurking on the doorstep behind her, she gestured to him to follow. His demeanour changed from trying to be brave to sheer terror. She smiled encouragingly at him, despite her own sense of trepidation.

'Hello!' she called out, pushing open the door to the living room, where Zoe, Scarlet, Rosalind and Tuesday were arranged on the sofas. The fragrance of hot chocolate filled the air and there was a ginger cake, half eaten, on the coffee table in front of them. Someone had got out the photos – a cardboard shoebox stuffed with a muddled collection of old family photographs – and they were spread out over the table. The women all looked in her direction. Heart hammering like the percussion section of an orchestra, she turned towards William and reached out her hand. He didn't take it but clung to his rucksack as if it was a life ring.

'Hello,' said Tuesday, smiling.

Heidi lurked in the doorway, then took a deep breath.

'I'd like you to meet William,' she said. 'I've invited him to stay for a couple of nights. Hopefully it will give us all a chance to get to know each other a little bit.'

Silence fell. Zoe's eyes widened and Scarlet's jaw dropped. Tuesday was still wearing that welcoming smile and Rosalind forced one. Heidi immediately panicked. Perhaps this was a terrible idea.

She twisted around to face William, but he was no longer there. He was leaving through the front door. Panic tightened across her chest and her throat burned.

'William!' she said, following him out onto the street. She called his name again. Behind her, bundled in the doorway were Scarlet, Zoe, Tuesday and Rosalind, all looking shocked.

'You could have been more welcoming!' Heidi chastised them. 'At least said hello!'

'We didn't get a chance!' said Zoe. 'Of course we'd say hello.'

Heidi felt guilty. Zoe was always so sweet. She was also pregnant. Her entire life was changing, and Heidi needed to be more sensitive.

Shielding her eyes from the light, she scanned the pavement, left and right and, beyond some parked cars, saw William disappear around the corner in the direction of the sea.

'Damn it.' Quickly, she broke into a run and followed him as he headed towards the beach. She picked up her pace to try to catch up with him, Zoe and Scarlet following closely behind.

'He's just going down to the beach,' said Zoe. 'Don't worry, Mum. He can't get far unless he's a really good swimmer.'

Waiting to cross the road, Heidi held on to Zoe and Scarlet's hands briefly and pulled them with her over to the other side. It brought back a memory of years ago, when they were little and walking to school. Who had walked William to school? Who had held his small hand in theirs?

'He's over there.' Scarlet pointed to a bench when they reached the beach. Someone had tied a bunch of carnations to it, which were now bedraggled and bent in the wind. Slowly, the three of them approached, wind whipping sand into their eyes. A golden Labrador sniffed William's feet and he gently patted the dog's head, not looking up.

'William?' said Heidi. Zoe was by her side, but Scarlet hung back. 'Why did you run off back there?'

'Why do you think he ran off?' said Zoe. 'I'd run off if you introduced me to a room full of strange women! Hello, William, I'm Zoe. It's good to meet you. You look so much like Dad. You even have his dimple.'

Zoe held out her hand and William gave her a small, wary smile. He stood from the bench and shook her hand briefly before letting go.

'Good to meet you too,' he said. 'I'm sorry. I wasn't expecting any of this to happen today, and when I got to the house and you were all there, I thought I should have bought flowers, or wine, or…'

Heidi pulled Scarlet into the group. She was uncharacteristically quiet.

'This is Scarlet,' said Heidi.

'Hi,' he said, lifting his hand in a small wave.

'Hi,' she said, giving him a brief wave in return, before folding her arms across her chest. 'You really do look like Dad. How old are you?'

'Thirty-six,' William said, rubbing his jaw nervously before he smiled – making him look even more like Johnny.

Though he was smiling, his eyes blazed with something – resentment? Fear? Heidi's heart and stomach turned somersaults as she grappled to work out how to handle him. A dark cloud positioned itself above them and rain began to fall.

'Shall we go back?' said Heidi. 'William, will you come back with us? Please? Looks like it's going to pour.'

'Come on,' said Zoe. 'We're not that bad. Are we, Scarlet?'

Heidi was grateful to Zoe. So grateful. But Scarlet was another story. She gave a slight shake of her head, which wasn't a confirmation of anything, kicked at a pile of sand with her toe and didn't say a word. A cold wind blew.

Chapter Twenty-Seven

Making coffee as fast as she possibly could with trembling hands, humming a tune as she worked, Heidi accidentally sloshed boiling water over her wrist.

'Ouch!' she said, briefly running her skin under the cold-water tap, before deciding a few blisters didn't matter in the scheme of things. Getting the coffee into the living room at lightning speed was more important. The conversation she could half hear was stilted, and she desperately wanted to get in there to ease the situation. Hurriedly putting two cups of coffee onto a tray, she headed back into the living room, placing the tray down on the table, before handing a cup to William and taking one for herself.

'Thank you,' he said, before taking a sip.

Zoe was holding up a photograph of Johnny taken years ago that she'd found in the photo box. She held it up near William's face. Nobody could deny that William was his son – they were physically incredibly similar.

'This is so weird,' Zoe said. 'Your eyes, they're exactly – I mean exactly – like Dad's. And your smile, with the dimple, it's amazing.'

William was quiet and pale, and perched on the edge of an armchair, his knee jogging up and down. He smiled at Zoe and murmured in agreement. 'I guess so,' he said.

Detecting his discomfort, Heidi almost snapped at Zoe to put the photo down, but she knew that Zoe was doing her best.

'So,' she said to distract them both. 'How is everyone getting along?'

Her question was met with a moment of silence.

'You're certainly dropping plenty of bombshells today, Heidi,' Rosalind said with a quick laugh. 'It's one hell of a family reunion.'

Heidi cleared her throat, anxiety making her scalp prickle with pins and needles. She smiled quickly at Rosalind, who looked at her apologetically.

'Sorry,' she said. 'Just trying to break the ice.'

'I suppose it's hard to know where to start,' said Zoe, still trying to help ease the situation. 'Where did you grow up, William?'

William sat stiffly in his chair and gave scant information about his childhood. He grew up in Exeter with his mum and dad, but then his dad died and his mum got together with another man, who had a son of his own. He studied photography, and after his mum died, he applied for his birth certificate and discovered that his birth parents were from Dorset – and that was when he moved here. He met Martha and they had a son, Freddy. He'd joined the adoption contact register and put a notice up on a reunion website, with his date of birth and his biological parents' names and found that Johnny was searching for him.

'And you worked as a photographer, didn't you?' said Heidi. 'Johnny loved photography, didn't he, girls? He was good at it too.'

Scarlet chewed a fingernail and nodded. Zoe took out a few photographs from the box and laid them on the table, illustrating the point.

'I'm new to the family too,' said Tuesday. 'It's obviously a strange time for everyone. And today is the first day I've met my birth mother.'

She turned to smile at Rosalind.

'It's been very good to meet you, Tuesday,' Rosalind replied. 'I've spent all these years worrying and trying to be tough about my past, when here you are, a lovely young woman who could almost be my sister.'

Tuesday smiled. 'Not so young,' she said, with a smile. 'I don't know how much you know, William, but I was adopted when I was a baby and met Heidi a week ago. She's been so welcoming. I'm staying at a hotel down the road for a while longer. What was it like for you, to meet Johnny?'

Heidi felt grateful to Tuesday for trying to keep the conversation going, when the atmosphere was tense and Scarlet in particular was making it felt that she didn't welcome him. Right now she was scrolling down her phone. Perhaps the fact that William was so physically similar to Johnny was unnerving her?

'Great,' he said. 'Meeting Johnny was amazing. Mind-blowing. I'm gutted that I didn't know him for longer.'

Heidi felt guilty. If they'd confronted this earlier in their marriage, they could have had longer – years potentially – with William in their lives. Zoe, Heidi and Tuesday smiled at him in encouragement.

'Do any of you play?' William asked, nodding at the piano. Heidi pointed at Zoe, who hid her face behind a cushion. Peeping over the top of it, she rolled her eyes.

'Dad was the virtuoso,' she said. 'I just play a little bit.'

'A little bit!' said Rosalind. 'You're just as good as your dad. I know you want to go into nursing, but you could just as easily be a pianist! You can do whatever you want. How I'd love to be young and free like you.'

Zoe glanced at Heidi, who gave a small shake of her head. Now wasn't the time for Zoe's recent revelation to come under the spotlight. Rosalind was bound to have an opinion about Zoe's news, so she would speak to her separately.

'Do you play?' Heidi asked William.

'A little,' he said. 'We had a piano when I was growing up, but I'm self-taught. I didn't have lessons. I can't read music. I just play by ear.'

'Let's hear you then,' said Scarlet, crossing her arms over her chest.

'Oh no,' said William, shying away from the offer.

'Go on,' said Scarlet, as if challenging him. 'Show us your skills.'

'Okay,' he said, moving to the piano. He played a piece that Johnny had in his repertoire – 'The Entertainer'. When William finished, he was blushing. He turned around and smiled warily.

'Was I that bad?' he said.

'No, you were brilliant,' said Heidi. 'Johnny used to play that piece, that's all. It's just strange that you should choose to play it too.'

'It's not strange!' said Scarlet. 'For God's sake, Mum, that's one of the most played pieces on the piano. Don't go adding meaning to everything.'

William stood from the piano and moved to the window, where he looked out at the garden, his hands stuffed in his pockets. Heidi sensed he was restless, very possibly overwhelmed, but was desperate for him to relax. Desperate for him to like them all, to accept them into his life.

'William,' she said. 'Why don't I show you outside? The workshop was one of Johnny's favourite places to be.'

Leaving the living room, she felt Scarlet's eyes burning into her back. She turned and smiled, hoping for positivity. Zoe nodded encouragingly and gave her the thumbs up, while Scarlet concentrated on a fingernail.

In the workshop, Heidi smiled. This was Johnny's favourite space and she knew he would have wanted William to see it. She glanced at the green pot on the shelf while William looked at the tools, the haberdashery cabinet stuffed with fabric, Annie's 'Barry' chair and the kissing chair. She thought he liked it.

'It's cold in here, so feel free to borrow a coat,' she said, pointing to Johnny's jacket on the back of the door. 'It's one of Johnny's.'

'No, no. You're alright thanks,' he snapped.

Heidi glanced up at him. 'What is it? Have I said something wrong? Is it all too much?'

He shook his head and sighed.

'It's all this comparison with Johnny,' he said. 'It makes me feel uncomfortable. I'm not him. I'm a totally separate person. None of you know me, and I don't know you either. We're strangers, virtually. This is all messing with my head.'

'Sorry,' she said. 'Nobody means to make you feel uncomfortable.'

'Scarlet doesn't like me,' he said. 'I can tell you that for nothing.'

Heidi felt a flash of anger. Scarlet could be so wonderfully open, charming and loving, but she seemed intent on making William's visit difficult.

'Give her time,' Heidi said. 'She's a prickly person sometimes. Wary. She can be a little defensive, but it's not personal. Come on – let me show you around here. Would you like to get involved? I could really do with some help. Nothing too much – sanding, varnishing, collection and delivery. If you helped out in here, you could stay for a week or so perhaps. I could pay you. You could have a break from your friend's flat and...'

Heidi let her sentence drift. She didn't say and 'stop drinking' or 'stop gambling' though that's what she thought.

He stared at her as if she was completely crazy.

'You don't need to do this,' he said. 'It doesn't feel right.'

'Just until you're back on your feet,' she said hurriedly. 'I'd do this for anyone.'

He bristled and she regretted her words. 'Not anyone. But what I mean is, I'd like you to stay. I'd love it. I think Johnny wanted this. He wanted us to get to know each other. And you're in a difficult situation at the moment.'

'Johnny may have wanted it, but what about you?' he said.

'Of course me,' she said softly.

'But...' he said. 'How will I get to Freddy? I don't have a car. I sound pathetic. A man my age. I did have a car, but I had to sell it to pay off a debt. God, I hate myself.'

He sat on a chair and put his hands in front of his face.

'You're not pathetic,' said Heidi. 'Don't say that. You've just lost your way. I lost my way once.'

'I so want to be a good dad to Freddy,' he said. 'If there's one thing I want to do, it's to be a good dad. But I'm failing.'

Heidi's heart broke. She wanted him to carry on talking, but he fell silent.

'You can borrow my car,' she said. 'The Morris van. I hardly use it when I'm working. Otherwise, you can catch the bus. Please say you'll stay a while. It would mean so much.'

Heidi stopped short of begging him to let her help him.

'I'm offering you an olive branch,' she said. 'That's all. What do you say?'

'Okay.' He nodded, running his hand over an old-fashioned blanket box she was re-covering in William Morris fabric. 'As long as I can do something to help.'

'Of course,' she said, trying to conceal her delight. 'Now, let me show you something I've kept since you were born.'

She opened the filing cabinet and rummaged to the bottom of the drawer, pulling out the cash tin. Unlocking it, she gently lifted out the dancing-clown trinket box and handed it to him.

'Johnny gave this to me on my seventeenth birthday,' she said. 'The day you were born. I've kept the photos in it ever since. Open the drawer and you'll see.'

'So we share a birthday?' he said, opening the drawer and looking at the photograph of her sitting on the rose chair with him in her arms. She nodded.

'You look so young,' he said.

'I guess I was,' she replied. 'I just love this photo. Despite the circumstances, it was a special moment. I sat on that beautiful chair – the seat was embroidered with roses – and I held you for hours. I've looked for a similar chair ever since but never found one. I often wonder what became of it and who has it now. This little trinket box, it's the one thing I had to keep you close to me. As well as my memories, of course.'

William smiled sadly and looked towards the door, where Zoe was standing.

'Mum, William,' she said. 'Tuesday's opened a bottle of wine if you'd like a drink? And we've ordered an Indian takeaway – just a mix of dishes. We thought everyone would be getting hungry. I hope that's okay with you?'

Heidi held her breath. 'Will you stay?' she asked.

'Yeah,' William said, brightening and handing her back the trinket box and photo. 'Thank you.'

In the house, wine flowed and tongues loosened. William talked about the café – the customers who told him their life stories, the cake with the chef's wedding ring inside. At one point, Heidi showed William up to the spare room, where he put down his bag, and she noticed he was swaying. She tried to give him water, but he laughed and said, 'Water's for animals,' which Tuesday found very funny. But the more he drank, the less happy Heidi felt. By 8.30 p.m., he was drunk. He reached out for the wine and knocked a bowl of leftover lentil dhal to the floor, where it soaked into the rug.

Leaping up from his seat, he staggered to the kitchen and grabbed a cloth. Heidi followed him and poured him a glass of water.

'Don't worry about the dhal,' she said. 'I think you've had enough to drink, don't you?'

He faced her, swaying a little and blinking slowly.

'What?' he said. 'I'm not a kid.'

'I know,' she said. 'But I'd say this to any guest I felt had drunk too much.'

'Would you?' he asked, frowning. 'That's a bit controlling, isn't it?'

'When Johnny had his first heart attack, it made me feel differently about alcohol,' she said. 'He had to cut down, so we all did. I'm not used to everyone drinking so much.'

William blinked and swayed, then opened his mouth to speak, but was interrupted by Tuesday's voice calling from the living room.

'I've found the horoscopes in my magazine,' she yelled. 'Who wants to know theirs?'

'Me!' called William, leaving Heidi alone in the kitchen. 'I'd like to know what else life is going to hurl at me.'

Slowly, she followed him back into the living room.

'What's your star sign?' Tuesday asked William.

'Cancer,' he said. 'Same as Heidi.'

Tuesday scanned the magazine page and started to read.

'Beware of new acquaintances,' she said. 'They may not turn out to be who you hoped they'd be and your heart might get—'

Her face fell and she stopped talking. William glanced at Heidi, his eyes dark and shiny. Heidi busied herself collecting plates.

'Oh,' Tuesday said. 'It's all a load of rubbish. It's all made up anyway.'

Tuesday turned to Rosalind, who was yawning. 'Rosalind, you're almost asleep. Shall I get you a taxi? I'll come with you to see your home. I'd love to see where you live.'

Rosalind looked worn out. Tuesday stood up and, as she did so, the magazine slipped to the floor.

Scarlet picked it up and finished off the horoscope: 'They may not turn out to be who you hoped they'd be and your heart might get broken,' she said.

'Scarlet,' said Heidi. 'Put it down.'

William's demeanour completely changed. He flopped back into the Chesterfield, checked his phone, then excused himself and headed for the stairs.

'Goodnight,' Zoe called after him.

'Goodnight,' he called back gruffly. 'Sorry, I… I'm tired. Thanks for the evening and everything.'

After Rosalind and Tuesday left, Heidi had expected to be able to talk to Scarlet and Zoe, but Scarlet pulled on her trainers and stuffed her jumper into her rucksack.

'Where are you going?' asked Heidi. 'It's 9 p.m.'

'Frankie's coming to get me,' she said. 'I'm going back to Southampton.'

'Oh,' said Heidi. 'Is that because of William staying the night? Don't you like him? You don't seem to like him.'

'I don't know him, Mum,' Scarlet said. 'I don't know why he's here. Why doesn't he have his own place? He's a grown man! And he got drunk, on our first-ever meeting. Would you do that?'

'Sometimes people get into difficulty,' Heidi explained. 'Sometimes people need a hand to get back on their feet. I'm offering him that.'

'He's a total stranger and I don't trust him,' Scarlet said. 'And I don't think you should either.'

Her phone beeped and she checked the screen.

'Frankie's outside,' she said. 'I'll call you tomorrow.'

Heidi hugged Scarlet goodbye and watched her get into Frankie's car. Closing the front door, she said goodnight to Zoe who was already half asleep, then headed upstairs. She could hear the sound of William's voice coming through his door and hovered outside it, trying to listen. He was arguing with someone, his voice harsh and raised. Then came the sound of something – his phone? – being thrown to the floor.

In the process of tiptoeing away, she stopped dead when she heard the muffled sound of him weeping. Her heart cracked open, but what was she to do?

Chapter Twenty-Eight

Heidi carried the stoneware pot of Johnny's ashes into the garden. Sitting on a green-and-white-striped deckchair in a spot of sunshine, she rested the pot on her lap. She frowned, thinking of William.

A week had passed since she'd invited him to stay, and mostly he kept to himself, spending a lot of time in his room or travelling to pick up Freddy from school. He had worked alongside herself and Max, where he was quiet and hesitant about the tasks he was given but hard-working. What bothered her the most was how he seemed continually distracted. She'd repeatedly said he could talk to her, if he needed to, tell her how he was feeling, but he remained buttoned up.

'I wish he'd confide in me more,' she told the ashes. 'And, Johnny, there's something bothering me. I don't know what I've done with it, you know how forgetful I can be, but some money has gone missing.'

She stopped speaking, fearing she might cry.

'What did you say?' said Max from behind her, making her jump. 'Are you talking to yourself again, Heidi?'

Heidi almost cricked her neck as she whipped round to face him. He was grinning, wiping his hands on a towel and dusting sawdust from his work apron.

'Coffee?' cried Tuesday from the back door, coming outside to join them. 'Max, I've got you a vegan brownie to try. I'll bring them out.'

Max took a seat next to Heidi while Tuesday crashed around in the kitchen, collecting cups and plates.

'She likes you,' said Heidi quietly. 'Tuesday likes you.'

Max's face darkened. 'Heidi, I…' he started, but let his words trail off.

'She seems to be here a lot. Is she staying in Bournemouth?'

Heidi nodded. 'For the time being,' she said. 'She likes it here. I don't think she misses anyone in Brighton.'

'So, what were you talking to Johnny about?' he asked.

'Oh, nothing important. I was just wondering about some cash I can't seem to find,' Heidi said. 'I had £100 in the workshop – one of the customers paid in cash – and I think I've mislaid it. Have you seen it?'

Their gazes locked. Max rubbed his chin.

'You've mislaid it?' he asked doubtfully.

'Definitely,' she said. 'You know what I'm like. Keep your eyes open in case I've dropped it in a drawer or into a toolbox.'

'Okay,' he said, 'I'll do that. Have you checked in with William? Maybe he's seen it?'

Heidi shook her head, but when William came out of the workshop for a coffee, Max asked him directly. Heidi's heart thumped in her chest.

'Haven't seen it,' William said quickly. 'Did you want me to deliver that kissing chair you've finished? I can drop it on the way over to collect Freddy if you like?'

Heidi felt relieved. He was proving himself to be an asset. It was all she could do not to throw her arms around him.

'Yes,' she said. 'Thanks, William.'

'Brownies!' said Tuesday, bringing out a tray of cakes and coffee. 'Brownies for the workers. Max, would you like to try one?'

Heidi gave Max a small, secretive smile. He cleared his throat.

'Thank you, Tuesday,' he said. 'Yes please.'

The arrangement was a simple one. William would take the Morris van and drop the tête-à-tête chair at Karen's address. It should have been easy. But two hours later, Karen called to ask where the chair was. She'd waited in all afternoon, but there was no sign.

'We sent it over hours ago,' Heidi said, confused and glancing over at Max, who looked up from his work. 'William brought it over in the Morris. He can't have got the wrong address. I don't understand.'

She listened as Karen explained that she'd been watching out the window and she hadn't seen the Morris at all. Panic laced her voice.

'Don't worry,' Heidi said, 'we can't have lost a chair. I'll get back to you as soon as I know where it is.'

Heidi put the phone down, unease slinking across her shoulders. Max was still looking at her.

'Karen says the chair didn't arrive,' she said lightly. 'I'll phone William. Must be some explanation.'

William's phone rang out. Checking her watch, she realised he should be with Freddy, the grandson she was desperate to meet. Perhaps Freddy was poorly or something. Perhaps he'd had to collect him earlier than usual? Yes, that would be it.

Despite wanting to believe that was true, a voice inside her head told her she was being a fool. She called William several more times, and on the fourth time, he picked it up. There was music in the background of wherever he was. Didn't sound like a school. And he didn't seem to be holding the phone to his mouth properly because his speech was muffled.

'Who is it?' he slurred. 'Martha? Is that you again? You can't stop me seeing my boy. I'll find the money!'

Heidi gasped.

'Martha?' he said again. 'Is that you?'

'It's Heidi,' she said loudly. 'Don't you dare drive my car in that state. Where are you? Tell me where you are. I'll collect you.'

William fell silent, then mumbled the name of a pub she recognised as being nearby.

'Wait there,' she instructed. 'Do not move. I'm coming to collect you. I need to get that bloody chair.'

He had ended the call. Shaking, she put the mobile down on the table and exhaled.

'Come on,' Max said, without needing to ask the details. 'Let's go and find him. I'll drive.'

Closing up the workshop and turning over the We Are Closed sign, they headed towards Max's van. Heidi sat in the passenger seat and gave him the name of the pub, twisting her hands in her lap.

'That money,' she said quietly. 'I thought it was me at first, but I'm pretty sure it's…'

She let her sentence drift, unable to say his name.

'You think William took it?' Max said.

Heidi's silence said it all.

The pub was awful. The sort of establishment Heidi would avoid at all costs. Max offered to go inside, and when he finally brought William out, he was swaying, his eyes were red and narrow, and he reeked of alcohol.

'Give me the keys to the car,' she said, holding out her hand. 'What the hell are you doing? Aren't you supposed to be with Freddy?'

William rubbed his eyes and tried to focus on Heidi.

'Martha won't let me pick him up anymore,' he mumbled, hanging his head. 'Told me I wasn't giving her enough money and that she was going to see a solicitor about getting a divorce and applying for full custody over him. Says I'm untrustworthy. Weak. A failure. But that's my boy. That's my BOY! I love him. I love my boy.'

William dropped to his knees, tears dripping from his red eyes. Heat rose in Heidi's face.

'I know,' she said calmly. 'It'll be okay. I know you love your son. I know you must be in pain right now.'

'What do you fucking know about loving your son?' he spluttered. 'You gave yours away!'

'That's enough,' said Max. 'Stand up, William. Stand up and tell us where the chair is. It's not in the van.'

William said nothing. Max repeated his question. 'Where is the chair?'

'Sold it,' William muttered. 'I got the cash and… I had a bet. Just one last bet. I wanted to buy Freddy something; I wanted to be a good dad.'

'You sold it!' shrieked Heidi. 'You need to tell me where you sold it. I have to get that back. Karen will be devastated. Our reputation will be ruined!'

'Who cares about the chair?' William said. 'All I care about is my boy.'

'*I* care about the chair!' Heidi said. 'This is my business. Your dad's business. This is my life.'

'He's not my dad,' he said, glaring at her. 'And you're not my mum. My mum is dead. Just sod off and leave me alone. I don't know why you came to find me – though you obviously like collecting bits of junk.'

Max pushed William in the chest. He stumbled backwards into the wall.

'Don't speak to her like that,' Max said. 'You've no bloody right! She's bending over backwards to accommodate you, you selfish git!'

'Thank you, Max, but I can fight my own battles,' Heidi said, as calmly as she could. 'Just tell me who's got the chair?'

'Pokesdown Antiques,' William said, pointing vaguely in the direction of a shop Heidi knew very well. She closed her eyes – relieved. She knew the owner and hoped that she could convince him to sell her back the chair, though she'd probably have to pay him twice as much.

'You wait in the Morris, in the passenger seat,' she instructed William. 'Max, please could you drive your van up to Pokesdown Antiques. I'll pop in and speak to the owner.'

Max nodded, glaring at William, before jumping into his van, with Heidi in the passenger seat.

'Hope he doesn't do anything else daft,' Max said.

Heidi held up the car keys. 'He can't go anywhere. I've locked the doors.'

In the antiques shop, Heidi negotiated for the return of the chair, paying Jimmy, the owner of the shop, his money back, tearfully explaining there had been a misunderstanding. With the chair in the back of the van, they returned to the Morris, where William had fallen asleep and was loudly snoring.

'What are you going to do, Heidi?' asked Max. 'You can't take this on. He needs professional help.'

Heidi got into the driver's seat of the Morris and wound down the window, smiling at Max.

'Then I'll help him,' she said.

'You don't have to,' he said. 'You have enough to cope with. Zoe's expecting. Scarlet's a handful. Tuesday's here. You've just lost Johnny.'

Heidi sighed. 'But he's lost and he's my son. What choice do I have?'

'I knew you'd say that. I just think you need to be careful. I'll drop the chair off to Karen, okay?'

'Thank you,' Heidi said, before driving home with a sleeping William by her side. She took a detour, to give him time to snooze, before drawing up outside the house, where she pulled on the handbrake, switched off the engine and rested her head against the headrest. Sliding her gaze left, she watched William wake, blink and frown, before he turned to her and then dropped his eyes to his hands. Rubbing his face, he mumbled something inaudible about Freddy.

'Let's go in,' said Heidi. 'Then you can sleep this off and I'll bring you some headache tablets and some water.'

'I feel like I'm fourteen years old,' he said. 'I'm so ashamed. Why are you doing this?'

Heidi got out the car and headed towards the house without saying anything. William stumbled behind her and lurched in through the front door, where Zoe was pulling on her coat, about to go out.

'What's with him?' she asked.

Heidi hung her keys up on the hook and started to take off his coat.

'He's unwell,' she said, then addressed William. 'Why don't you go up and have a lie-down?'

William nodded bleakly and climbed the stairs, gripping on to the bannister, while Heidi threw her arm around Zoe's shoulders and guided her towards the kitchen, so she couldn't study William.

'How are you feeling, Zoe?' she asked as cheerfully as she could. 'I was thinking we should celebrate your news. Invite some friends over, Leo's parents – everyone – and do something fun? It's been so long since we had any kind of party. What do you think?'

'A party?' said Zoe. 'Really? I'm not sure our news will be met with a celebratory response! Everyone will probably be shocked and think we're too young.'

'Well I'm celebrating your news,' Heidi said. 'I think if we take the lead then everyone else will follow. Sometimes you've just got to – I don't know how to put it – pretend you're not in any doubt. Perhaps people will appreciate a get-together for a happy occasion.'

Their conversation was interrupted by a sudden crash from upstairs – William knocking into furniture or falling over.

'What's going on with William?' Zoe frowned. 'He looked like he was swaying. Was he drunk?'

Zoe's face was creased with concern.

'No,' said Heidi, clearing her throat. 'He's got a bug, I think.'

'You know what you said about pretending?' Zoe said, raising her eyebrows. 'I think you might be good at it.'

Chapter Twenty-Nine

Heidi tried to ignore the *Dallas* theme tune playing at the edges of her thoughts while a customer told her about a chaise longue that she wanted reupholstering, with cushions to match. She nodded now and again but wasn't really listening. She was worrying about William. She wanted to help him, but if she meddled too much, would he leave? If she didn't try to help him, would he sink further into an abyss? She sighed a deep sigh, mulling his words over in her head. Shame. Failure. She didn't want to frighten him away when he was so vulnerable. He had only just come into her life – she couldn't risk losing him so quickly.

'… and I've chosen red velvet… because that's my favourite colour and that will look good, won't it?' the customer said, finally pausing for breath. 'What do you think? Can you do it?'

'Yes,' Heidi said, blinking. 'Yes.'

'You think "yes"?' the customer said, frowning. 'You think yes to red velvet?'

'R-Red velvet, yes,' stuttered Heidi.

The customer gave her a tight smile.

'So, when are you looking to bring the piece in for us?' Heidi continued.

'Well I've just spent twenty minutes explaining that you'll need to pick it up yourselves,' she said. 'I only have a push bike.'

'Right,' said Heidi, fishing a pen and some paper from the tabletop to hide her blush. 'Well you can't bring in a chaise longue on a push bike, can you? Of course we can collect it. Can you give me your address and we'll get that organised?'

Heidi took down the woman's details, and after she left, she slumped down on a chair and put her head in her hands.

She was disturbed by a knock on the workshop door. It was William, looking hungover and sorry for himself.

'Can I talk to you?' he asked.

'Yes,' Heidi said. 'Come in.'

William took a seat and Heidi noticed that his hands were shaking. Whether that was nerves or alcohol, she wasn't sure.

'I'm sorry about the chair,' he said. 'I really am. I don't recognise myself anymore. I had a call from Martha a few nights ago. She said she was going to stop my visits to Freddy because I'm late with the maintenance I pay. She was so cold. I wanted to prove to her I could get the money, that I wasn't as hopeless as she thinks.'

Heidi wanted to jump in and talk, make a speech about how you can turn your life around if you really put your mind to it, but she said nothing – to give him more time to talk.

'I…' he started. 'I thought maybe if I had a bet, I'd get lucky and then get some money together. I know I have a problem. I have a big problem. I told you about the debt I'm in, but I can't stop gambling. It's got me, around the throat, and even when I tell myself over and over to stop, I can't. And each time I give in to the compulsion, I imagine that this will be the time I make a big win so I can win back Martha and be with Freddy more. I'd just like to get back on my feet and not be living off you like this.'

'You're not living off me,' said Heidi. 'And I would imagine that Martha is lashing out because she's frightened. You need to be completely honest with her.'

He hung his head.

'I've promised her I'm going to change,' he said. 'I'm going to stop being this way before it gets completely out of hand. It already is.'

Heidi felt sweat prickle her forehead. She thought of the £100 that had gone missing.

'William, have you taken some cash from the workshop?' she asked.

William's eyes shone. He nodded once, his mouth twitching.

'I'm sorry,' he said. 'I'm so ashamed. How could I do this to you? It's as if I'm not in control.'

'You're being self-destructive,' she said, 'and I don't know why, but perhaps it helps you cope with something, breaking up with Martha?'

'I was doing it before then,' he said. 'The gambling and the drinking were the reason Martha asked me to leave. Perhaps it was something else, something in my past.'

Heidi froze. Was this all her fault?

'I'm going to stop,' he said. 'I've had enough.'

Heidi worried that if she spoke, she would cry. She took a deep breath.

'I think you can get through this,' she said. 'With my help and maybe some professional help, if you'll allow me to look into that for you.'

They were interrupted by Tuesday bursting in through the door, wearing a bright blue dress and rainbow-coloured beads. She had a scarf tied around her hair, which stuck up on her head like a child's scribble.

'Zoe says you're planning a party?' she said, beaming. 'Heidi, there's nothing I love more than a party. Please can I help you? I make the most delicious canapés you've ever tasted, and I've been known to make a cocktail or two in my time. Sorry, have I interrupted something?'

'Don't worry,' said Heidi. 'Yes, of course, your help would be brilliant. Thank you.'

William stood up and started moving some tools around.

'Will you be inviting Max?' Tuesday asked, raising her eyebrows.

'Of course, yes. Why?' Heidi asked.

'I think he's rather nice,' said Tuesday, letting out one of her explosive laughs.

'Oh, I thought so,' said Heidi, grinning. 'Yes, he would of course be coming. He's one of the family these days. But, Tuesday, you know Max lost his wife not too long ago. He might not be ready for—'

Tuesday waved her hand in front of her face. 'I'm not trying to marry the man,' she said. 'I just think we could have a little bit of fun together.'

Though she smiled at Tuesday's comment, she felt protective of Max and didn't want him to get hurt. Perhaps she was overthinking it. She pushed the feeling away and looked at William.

'I hope you'll come too,' she said to him. 'You're one of the family too.'

William half smiled, and something in his eyes made Heidi blush. She had an acute sense that William felt nothing of the sort.

Chapter Thirty

Heidi pushed her toes into the cold sand. Wrapped in her towel, she sat on a camping chair while Rosalind stayed inside the beach hut with a blanket draped over her back like a resting racehorse, making tea. The air smelled of the ocean, mingled with Calor gas and chips. Still in the sea after swimming all the way to the pier, Max was now heading in their direction, powering through the swell. He swam confidently and steadily, as if he could carry on going until he reached France without even looking up.

Rosalind cleared her throat then stirred the sugar in Heidi's tea so vigorously Heidi wondered if the cup would crack.

'What is it, Mum?' she asked, glancing up at the sky, squinting in the sun. It was the brightest blue, the sea one shade darker, the sky and sea melting together on the horizon. The beach was her happy space, no matter how hard Rosalind stirred her tea.

Rosalind passed her the cup and sighed an enormous sigh.

'What?' asked Heidi, smiling up at her. 'What are you sighing about?'

'Tuesday told me about William,' she replied. 'About what he did. I don't know how you can still have him in your home, Heidi. If he's stealing from you, what's next? Quite frankly I'm speechless. He's not exactly turned out to be the fairy-tale son you were hoping for, has he?'

'You seem to have a lot to say for someone who's speechless,' said Heidi, feeling hurt. She put down the tea and rubbed her hair dry with a smaller towel. 'And what right did Tuesday have to tell you that?' she said. 'Why's she gossiping about things that don't concern her?'

Rosalind pursed her lips and tutted, pulling a chocolate digestive from the packet and balancing it on her knee.

'She's not gossiping. She's worried for you,' she said. 'As am I. Maybe you've jumped in too deep, too soon.'

'You can talk!' said Heidi. 'When she's not with me, Tuesday is at your flat every single day.'

Heidi was surprised at the envy in her voice. Was she jealous?

'She's helping me with a few things, and we're getting to know each other better,' said Rosalind. 'That's all. She's a lovely person.'

Heidi bit her lip. Rosalind had changed her tune somewhat.

She pulled on her jogging bottoms and jumper, and sat down on a deckchair, with the towel wrapped around her wet hair. She had to stay focused on what Johnny wanted, whatever everyone around her said.

'Good,' said Heidi. 'I mean, I'm pleased – really I am.'

'Did Tuesday tell you about her plans?' said Rosalind.

'No. What plans?'

'She wants to move here,' Rosalind said. 'With her parents living in France now she says there's not much holding her in Brighton. She's looking at a flat just around the corner from me. She says she can do her job anywhere.'

'You certainly have a spring in your step,' Heidi replied, unable to help herself. 'Now that Tuesday is here.'

'Now, now. You're not jealous, darling, are you? Don't be. There's nothing to be jealous of.'

'I'm not jealous,' said Heidi. 'Well, I suppose I'm disappointed that things aren't so good with William as they are with you and Tuesday. But I'm glad for you.'

Rosalind put her hand on Heidi's shoulder and squeezed.

'I'm sorry it's turned out this way,' she said gently. 'Perhaps you should let it go for now and focus on your girls.'

'I'm doing what I think is right and what Johnny wanted,' she said, with the most positive smile she could muster. 'And I'm still focused on the girls. I'm going to have a celebration for Zoe, actually, Mum. There's something I should tell you.'

'About her pregnancy and elopement?' said Rosalind.

'How do you know?' Heidi asked.

'Tuesday,' said Rosalind. 'She's very well informed.'

Heidi tried not to react, but inside she felt irritated with Tuesday for sharing her daughter's private news.

'And?' said Heidi. 'What do you think?'

'She's very young...' started Rosalind.

Heidi and Rosalind exchanged a knowing glance.

'I think she's the sort of person who can make it work,' said Heidi. 'She has her head screwed on, and I've offered to help them. They can live with me.'

'What about her studies?'

'There's no reason why she can't study. I'm here to help. Between us, we can sort it out.'

'You know what? Tuesday would love to help,' said Rosalind. 'She's already said as much. I think you contacting her has given her the chance of a new life. She was lonely, you know. I think here, she feels needed.'

'Good,' said Heidi, with a sigh. 'And now I just need to help William get sorted out. Johnny wanted that; I know he did.'

'What about what you want?' Rosalind asked. 'Be careful of your heart. Johnny was a bit impulsive finding William like that.'

'I hardly think waiting thirty-six years to find your son is impulsive,' Heidi replied. 'I'm trying to do the right thing, that's all.'

'I know, love,' Rosalind replied. 'I know you are. I just don't want to see you hurting any more than you already are.'

They watched as Max got out of the sea with ease – unlike Heidi, who found getting out of the water almost more difficult than getting in. Dizzy from the cold, she usually fell over in the shallows as the waves swept her towards the shore, tripped up by the current and stumbling on the uneven, sharp shingle, yelping in pain. Max strode up the beach, pushing his goggles onto the top of his head and grinned at Heidi, who raised her hand in salute.

'Here's Neptune,' Rosalind muttered under her breath as he approached them. Heidi gently slapped Rosalind's knee in reprimand.

'Good swim?' she asked Max when he reached them and dug into his bag for a towel. He slung it over his back, drying his face with one corner.

'Fantastic,' he said. 'Are you both alright? Were you plotting something?'

Rosalind stood up and moved inside the beach hut, where she busied herself with pouring Max a cup of tea.

'No, not at all,' Heidi said, straightening her back. 'We were just talking about the party for Zoe. You'll be there, Max, won't you? Tuesday will be very pleased about that. She never stops talking about you.'

She said the last sentence too loudly and deliberately, so that Rosalind would prick up her ears.

'Oh?' said Rosalind. 'What's this? I can't keep up with this family! Is that why Tuesday is so keen to move here? I thought I was the attraction!'

'It's nothing,' said Max. 'I don't know what Heidi's referring to.'

Heidi gave a small laugh but stopped abruptly when she saw the stony expression on Max's face.

'Sorry, Max. I didn't mean anything—' she started, but he interrupted her.

'I better get back to the workshop,' he said, pulling on his fur-lined waterproof cape – popular with sea swimmers and surfers – and slinging his bag on his back. He left his tea untouched.

'Okay,' said Heidi, picking up her bag. 'I'll give you a lift. Mum, I'll call you later. Sorry to leave so quickly. Will you make one of your pavlovas for Zoe's party? A really big one?'

'Yes,' said Rosalind quietly. 'Yes, I'll make one of my bloody pavlovas.'

They shared a smile.

'Thank you. I'd better go,' said Heidi, running to catch up with Max, who had walked off and was halfway down the beach.

'Max!' she cried. 'Wait up!'

But Max didn't stop. He walked up the cliff path and straight past the Morris. Half running, she stopped at the car and called after him.

'Don't you want a lift?'

But he raised his hand to silence her.

'I'll walk!' he shouted back. 'I want to walk.'

Heidi stood still, confused, watching him march into the distance, before she threw her wet things into the back seat and started up the engine. Pulling up alongside Max and driving extremely slowly, she wound down the window.

'Max, please let me give you a lift,' she said quietly. 'You'll get cold. Please.'

Max stopped walking, threw back his head and exhaled, before climbing into the passenger seat, bringing half a ton of sand with him.

'Sorry about what I said on the beach,' she said, pulling off. 'It was thoughtless. I know Jane was your whole life and that you miss her terribly. It was a flippant comment and stupid. Please accept my apology.'

'Forgiven,' Max mumbled. 'But it's not really about Jane. It's… well, it's something I've been carrying around for a long time.'

Heidi tensed. 'Do you want to talk about it?' she asked carefully, driving towards the traffic lights.

'No,' he said. 'Look, let's just forget about the whole thing.'

A few beats of awkward silence passed between them.

'Okay, so before Johnny died he…' said Max, 'he…'

'He what?' asked Heidi, clenching the steering wheel harder.

'He asked me about what happened between us,' said Max, 'when he went to work in Manchester all those years ago.'

Heidi tensed, her back rigid in the seat.

'We were so young!' she said. 'Did you tell him the truth? Did he know about us?'

Max continued to stare out of the window. Heidi held her breath, waiting for his answer.

'No,' he said. 'I denied the whole thing.'

'Thank you,' said Heidi, relieved.

'But he cracked up laughing and said he knew we'd been an item,' Max said. 'He wasn't angry that you hadn't told him. In fact, he said we made a good couple!'

Heidi blushed. 'Odd thing to say. It was a hundred years ago.'

'I know,' said Max. 'But the thing is, I agree with him. We did make a good couple. I know your heart was always with Johnny, is still with Johnny, but I want you to know that I care about you. A lot.'

Heidi's face was the colour of a box of raspberries. She knew she might be reading between the lines, but she had to spell out the truth.

'Max,' she said, her heart thumping, 'I just want to be entirely honest with you here. You know how much I care about you. You're one of my closest friends. But it will always only be friendship for me. Johnny has only just passed away, but even so, I don't want anything other than friendship. Johnny was the only one for me. I hope you're not offended. I don't want our friendship to be damaged in any way.'

Max grinned. 'Of course not. I knew you'd say that. I just wanted you to know that I care about you. When Johnny had his first heart attack, he asked me to look out for you. Maybe I've been overthinking his request!'

Heidi smiled sadly.

'Sorry if I crossed a line,' said Max. 'I don't know what I was thinking. We're friends – good friends. That's crystal clear. I'm glad that's cleared up.'

Her heart still pounding, at the junction she panicked and stalled the car, annoying the young BMW driver behind.

'Sorry,' she said, raising her hand in the rear-view mirror, but the driver put his foot down on the accelerator and overtook, impatiently and dangerously. As he whizzed by, he gave Heidi an angry V sign shouting, 'Learn to drive, Grandma!' out his window.

Max stuck his hand out the window and returned the gesture, bellowing unrepeatable words to the young driver. The discomfort in Heidi's belly transformed into a bubble of laughter and, all of a sudden, she couldn't stop laughing.

Chapter Thirty-One

Professional help for his gambling problem. That's what Heidi had promised William. And she'd found it in the shape of a group for gambling addicts and friends, who met up in a local church hall. Heidi had offered to go with him but had explained that if he didn't want her to stay, she would leave. Now, waiting in the entrance to the church hall, she checked her watch. The session would soon begin, but there was no sign of William.

When her phone rang, she quickly pulled it from her pocket, expecting it to be him with an excuse for why he wasn't going to make it. But it was Scarlet. Moving her curls out of the way, Heidi pushed the phone to her cheek, alarm shooting up her spine.

'Are you alright?' said Heidi. 'Is Charlie bothering you again?'

'Where are you?' replied Scarlet. 'I'm with Zoe near the pier. We're supposed to be scattering Dad's ashes, aren't we?'

Heidi's hand shot to her mouth and she closed her eyes. She had completely forgotten the arrangement that they'd made weeks before. They'd plucked the date in May from nowhere, she hadn't written it down, and with everything that was going on she had – unbelievable as it might seem – forgotten. She groaned.

'I'm so sorry,' she said. 'I've got completely side-tracked today. Oh, why didn't you remind me? Can we do it tomorrow? I'm so sorry.'

There was a moment's silence on the phone. She imagined Scarlet's face setting into a stony expression, covering up the hurt she no doubt felt.

'I didn't think I'd have to remind you, Mum,' said Scarlet. 'It's Dad's ashes.'

Heidi squeezed her eyes shut.

'I really am sorry, Scarlet,' she said. 'You know I wouldn't simply have forgotten something so important if I wasn't doing something else.'

'Are you with William?' interrupted Scarlet.

'No, I'm—' started Heidi. 'Well yes, I'm waiting for him. I've made him an appointment for him to see… and I… it's important.'

Heidi hadn't breathed a word of William's problems to Scarlet or Zoe. Partly because that was his wish, and partly because she feared Scarlet would hold it against him.

'Clearly,' said Scarlet. 'I've only travelled from Southampton for this and missed a class. Frankie drove me here. Zoe, Mum's not coming. We might as well go.'

She could hear Zoe murmuring on the other side of the phone. She felt suddenly homesick for her daughters, a flicker of resentment towards William blooming inside her. Where the hell was he?

'I'm so sorry,' said Heidi. 'I could come later instead.'

'It's okay,' sighed Scarlet. 'We'll do it another day.'

'Don't worry, Mum,' she heard Zoe's voice pipe up.

Scarlet hung up and Heidi pushed her phone into her bag and covered her face with her hands, silently screaming. Then there was a tap on her shoulder. William. His eyes were red-rimmed, his forehead glittering with light perspiration. She arranged her features into an expression of calm.

'Sorry I'm late,' he said. 'You don't have to come in with me.'

'I'd like to,' she said. 'It might help me to understand better. But I'll go if you prefer.'

Heidi's heart hammered as they went inside, thoughts of her dejected girls swirling around in her head. And what of Johnny's ashes? Left on the shelf in the workshop in that green pot. It wasn't good enough. *She* wasn't good enough.

'I think this is the chap I spoke to,' she said to William, when the group leader, a tall, thin man called Andy, with a lanyard swinging around his neck, approached them. He invited them to take a seat and they sat next to each other, close to a young couple in their twenties on one side and a father and son on the other. Everyone looked nervous, grateful for the handout that Andy was distributing. When the papers arrived in her own clutch – a leaflet about gambling addiction – the words swam around in front of Heidi's eyes. She was acutely aware of William's leg jogging up and down, his heel tapping out a frenzied rhythm on the parquet floor.

'As we all know,' began Andy, 'for every person affected by gambling, at least another five people are also affected. Today, you've all brought along people who are involved in your journey and I thought we could start with you telling us a bit about yourselves. William, shall we begin with you? Please remember this is a non-judgemental space to say whatever you like. Everything you say will remain in these four walls. Please, tell us your story, in whatever order it comes out.'

All eyes turned towards William and Heidi. She held her breath, wondering how William would react in this situation. In their relationship so far he had been reluctant to share very much at all. She gave him a small, encouraging smile.

'Honestly,' said Andy, 'just go for it. This is what this session is for. No one will judge you.'

William sighed and checked his palms, which were shiny with sweat. He chewed the inside of his cheek, then he looked up, sat back in his chair.

'I'm adopted and my adopted dad died when I was a toddler,' he said. 'He fell off a ladder and my mum was heartbroken. She got together with another bloke, my stepdad, who didn't like me much. He had a son, and of course the sun shone out of him. I found out I was adopted when I was thirteen during an argument. My stepdad blurted it out to me and said it was a miracle my mum could put up with me, since I was a reject, that kind of thing. My mum stood up for me and defended me, and I loved her so much, but I spent a lot of years thinking that perhaps I really was a reject. There must have been a reason my birth parents didn't want me. My stepdad then went off with another woman, and when I was eighteen my mum took her own life. I guess she couldn't stand all the loss. I was out somewhere, in a nightclub with some friends, when she jumped off a bridge into a river. A passer-by tried to rescue her, but it was dark and—'

He let out a bark of mournful laughter. The room was completely silent, and Heidi felt sure everyone in there could hear her heartbeat. She remembered standing on Trent Bridge in Nottingham, staring down at the black water. Her throat ached painfully with the need to cry – to scream at the top of her lungs – but she remained motionless.

'I found myself alone in the world,' continued William. 'I finished college, where I was doing a photography course, and tried to put the past behind me. I got a job as a photographer's assistant in this tiny studio with this lovely old guy. I managed to lock my feelings into a box and padlock it shut. I tried to omit the past. I didn't visit my mother's grave. I felt empty. Then, ten years later, I found out that I was born in Dorset. I moved to Poole and I got together with a woman, and we had a child. I loved them so much, I could barely breathe with the fear I might mess it up. And I did. I just couldn't get things right. I had some savings and tried to make a go of being a freelance photographer, but it was tough. I fell into debt. I wanted, so badly, to be a good father and husband, but I felt kind of paralysed.'

William took a deep breath. The room remained silent.

'There was one day I went into a casino with a mate,' he said. 'I got lucky and went straight home and gave the winnings to my wife and said I'd had a photography commission and that I thought things were on the up. Her happiness and relief – it drove me onwards and it went from there. I started using online gambling sites and couldn't stop. I'd nip into the bookies on my lunch break. I felt convinced I'd win big. Someone has to. I just wanted my partner to love me, I guess. I didn't want to disappoint her or lose her. I wanted to prove to everyone that I'm worthwhile, I'm valuable, a provider. Not a reject. Sounds pathetic coming from a grown man, doesn't it?'

Tears flowed down Heidi's cheeks as she listened to William's story. She wiped at her nose and eyes with her cuff but was crying so hard, she had to leave the room.

'Please excuse me for a minute,' she said, pushing back her chair and running to the door. Outside, she leaned against the wall and took deep breaths, gulping in the fresh air. A while later Andy popped his head out of the door.

'Was that news to you?' he asked gently.

Heidi nodded. 'We've only just become acquainted. I'm his birth mother. I'd hoped he was having a happy life. While he was going through all that, I was just going along, enjoying my life.'

Andy shook his head. 'You're not to blame,' he said. 'This process will hopefully make him aware of that. Do you want to come back inside?'

Heidi knew that she should. She tried to channel her strong, resilient core, but it had dissolved with William's story. She shook her head and asked Andy to tell William that she needed air.

'It would be great if you came back inside,' he urged. 'If you can. It would show support. We talk about fight or flight in this group. And it would be helpful to fight in this situation.'

Heidi shook her head sadly. She didn't have the strength.

'Sorry,' she said, before folding her arms around her middle and walking off towards the Morris. The seagull perched on the roof soared through the sky above her as she moved away. Taking flight.

Chapter Thirty-Two

Heidi watched Tuesday furiously chop up a bunch of spring onions, sprinkle them over a potato salad and place the knife down on the chopping board. The kitchen table had bowls and plates of party food on it, and the worktops were scattered with bags of crisps, nuts and salad. Heidi had got carried away in the supermarket, determined to make the party for Zoe and Leo as lovely as possible.

'Are you okay?' said Heidi to Tuesday. 'Have those spring onions offended you?'

Tuesday turned to give Heidi a tight, tense smile.

'I'm fine,' she said. 'How about you? How are you doing? Why do you keep humming that tune? Is it from *Dallas*? I used to watch that show.'

Heidi exhaled. How could she explain how she felt? She had so many different feelings raging inside, she couldn't hold on to one of them for long enough to describe her state of mind.

'When were you going to tell me that you and Max have history?' said Tuesday, before Heidi had time to formulate a reply.

'Sorry?' said Heidi, covering the bowl of potato salad with cling film.

'Rosalind told me about you and Max,' said Tuesday, 'and I wondered if you were going to tell me?'

'That was a million years ago,' said Heidi. 'Sorry, Tuesday, I've had other things to think about, like William and Zoe's pregnancy and this party. I want this to go well; I need Zoe to feel treasured, supported and loved.'

'He still holds a candle for you,' said Tuesday. 'That's what I think. Rosalind says the same.'

Heidi rolled her eyes. Tuesday and Rosalind had developed a close bond in a short time. They seemed to tell each other everything. It was beginning to irritate her – especially if they were going to discuss her.

'Max and I go back a long way, but that's all,' she said. 'I've been married to Johnny for the last thirty years. He was the love of my life.'

The thought of Johnny and how much she wished he was there socked her in the stomach. She thought of the ashes in the workshop and felt compelled to go outside and chat to him.

'Still,' said Tuesday. 'You could have told me. Rosalind said you were happy together at the time.'

Heidi sighed. 'Forget about it, will you? He's a friend. Full stop.'

'Don't you think that he's around a lot for someone who's a friend?' Tuesday asked.

'No, I don't!' Heidi retorted, slamming shut a cupboard door. 'We work together. He was Johnny's friend. And is my friend. He's been a great support since Johnny died, but nothing more. Do stop going on about it. I don't want to be discussing this right now. Can you pass me those tomatoes?'

Tuesday tossed her the packet of tomatoes, much too hard, before angrily placing a bunch of sweet williams into a green glass vase and taking it out into the garden. Heidi shook her head and took a deep breath. Who did Tuesday think she was? Waltzing into the family like she had and claiming Heidi had feelings for Max when Johnny had only just died?

She told herself to calm down, but she felt as though the world was against her. She couldn't seem to get anything right with anyone! Scarlet was still annoyed with her about her missing the day to scatter Johnny's ashes. Tuesday was in a storm about Max. The gambling group session with William had been disastrous. Well not the session itself, but afterwards. She should have been brave enough to go back inside, to support William, but something had stopped her. Fear? Guilt?

There was no doubt she felt guilty and sad that William's experience had been so bad, but there was another confusing thought that kept popping into her head. Why hadn't he told her those things before? By telling his stories in front of a bunch of strangers it was as if… as if he was punishing her. When all she'd tried to do from the moment they'd met was to be kind, offer him shelter, food, support.

She had since tried to talk to him, apologised for not going back into the meeting and suggested they return to another meeting together, but he wouldn't commit to anything. It was as if she'd blown her chance. He'd closed up, locked her out.

In the workshop, during the mornings that he helped Max, he wore earphones, listening to music while he worked. He'd converse with Max, but not say more than a few words to Heidi. And his visits to Freddy were taking twice as long as usual. Even buying a pint of milk took two hours. She worried that he was gambling but couldn't confront him. With him unwilling to communicate, she was unable to do anything other than search Google for as much helpful information as she possibly could. She'd printed out sheets of helpful information and slipped them under his bedroom door for him to read, along with a note that read: *Can we have a proper talk?* But it went unacknowledged.

Heidi thought she needed to take a step back. She needed to concentrate on her girls – in particular Zoe, who was now in her eighth month of pregnancy. She would just have to hope that William opened up again. The only thing that was important right now was this party.

She opened the freezer and collected a handful of ice cubes for a water jug when Zoe came in and kissed Heidi on the cheek.

'Thank you for doing this, Mum,' she said. 'What can I do to help?'

Heidi put the ice in a jug and filled it up with water, smiling at Zoe in her black maternity dress, hair piled up on top of her head and face and neck flushed pink. Zoe picked up a newspaper and waved it like a fan in front of her face, while Heidi poured a glass of iced water for her.

'It's a pleasure,' said Heidi. 'If we'd had a wedding for you, it would have been a bigger party.'

'I don't want anything big,' said Zoe. 'This is perfect.'

She was smiling, but her brow was furrowed.

'What's wrong?' said Heidi. 'Tell me.'

'I hope today will go alright,' she said quietly. 'Leo's parents are quite straight. I think our mismatched crockery will send them into a tailspin.'

Heidi laughed and hugged her daughter.

'I'll make sure it goes well,' said Heidi. 'Leo's parents will have a lovely time. They've been fairly understanding so far, haven't they? And I'm sure they'll understand that the crockery is deliberately mismatched. Look at it – it looks gorgeous out there. Tuesday has done a fantastic job. She's worked so hard. I must thank her.'

They stared out of the kitchen window into the garden, which really did look beautiful. Tuesday had hung strings of paper pom-poms from tree to tree, fairy lights in preparation for the evening, and there were cushions, deckchairs and blankets on the lawn, so people could sit down.

Rosalind was sitting in a deckchair, a straw sun hat shielding her eyes. Tuesday was talking to her and Heidi felt a twinge of envy.

'Have you accepted her yet?' said Zoe. 'I can't tell if you have or not.'

'Of course I accept her!' Heidi said. 'Does it not seem that way?'

Zoe shrugged. 'Just something Grandma said,' she said. 'You're only half-sisters, I guess.'

'What did Grandma say?' asked Heidi, frowning.

'Oh, just that you'd been a bit cagey about Tuesday. Whatever that means.'

Heidi put her head in her hands and did a quiet scream.

'Everything I do is judged or commented upon!' she said. 'I think Tuesday is great. She's so colourful and full of energy, and Grandma loves having her around. I need to tell her that. I just… I suppose I didn't know, when I sent her that first message, that she would become a permanent fixture. Just takes a bit of getting used to. And Grandma seems so close to her already! What about you, Zoe? How do you feel about having a brother?'

Zoe turned away from Heidi and refilled her glass of water.

'He's nice when he's not drinking,' she said. 'Alcohol makes him harsh. Is he coming today or is he out with Freddy?'

Heidi bit the inside of her lower lip. She had tried to shield Zoe from William's binges and dark moods, but her daughter wasn't stupid.

'He said he would come, but I'm not sure he will,' she replied. 'Anyway, we'll see if he turns up. Meanwhile, shall we take these plates out? Guests will be here any minute. Oh, there's the doorbell.'

'I'll get it,' said Zoe, handing her pile of plates to Heidi, who rushed outside with them and placed them on the table that was covered in lace tablecloths, with vases of sweet williams.

'People are arriving,' she said to Tuesday and Rosalind. 'Leo's parents, probably. Be good.'

By early afternoon, the garden was brimming with guests. Scarlet and Frankie talked to Leo and Zoe's friends, while Tuesday and Rosalind chatted to Alice and Katherine, Heidi's neighbours. Heidi's voice was hoarse from talking to Leo and his parents so much. Zoe watched her hopefully, and she kept giving her the thumbs up, to indicate all was going well and that they didn't seem to mind the mismatched crockery. Max looked after the music and kept everyone's drinks topped up.

'Should I bring the pavlova out?' Heidi asked Rosalind towards the end of the afternoon.

'Tuesday's got it covered,' she replied, gesturing towards her other daughter, who was walking out from the kitchen holding the pavlova out in front of her.

'Course she has,' Heidi muttered.

Rosalind grabbed Heidi's hand and squeezed. 'Darling,' she said. 'I love you. Tuesday is trying hard. She will calm down.'

Heidi swallowed and gave Rosalind a small smile but felt tears pricking her eyes. Excusing herself, she popped into the workshop and sat down next to the green pot to take a moment.

'He's not here,' she told Johnny's ashes. 'William hasn't come, but I thought he wouldn't. Ever since that day, the therapy session, he's given me the silent treatment. Anyway, this is Zoe's day. Wish me luck – I'm going to do a speech now. This is your area really, Johnny. I wish you were here.'

Heidi kissed the pot and left the workshop. Although she was gutted that William hadn't arrived, she also felt a confusing slight sense of relief. Whenever she was in his company at the moment, she felt that he was angry with her and pushing her away. Today, she needed to be positive and upbeat for Zoe.

She returned to the garden and took the speech she'd written from her pocket. Banging a spoon on the side of a glass, she cleared her throat and climbed onto a small step. Expectant faces turned towards her.

'I'd just like to say a few words about Zoe and Leo,' she said, her heart banging with nerves.

At that moment, the kitchen door opened, and William walked out into the garden, holding a can of beer. His eyes were red, and as he raised his can shouting, 'Hello,' he swayed.

Heidi's heart both plummeted and rose at the same time and she smiled in his direction, gave him a small wave, before she cleared her throat and continued.

'I won't keep you long,' she said. 'I'm sure you'll join me in wishing Zoe and Leo all the love in the world for the adventure they're about to embark on. They've done things their own way and long may that continue. I want you both to know that you have the support of your whole family, and I personally will do everything I can to help. It can of course be challenging, but having a child is an incredibly precious time and—'

'Bollocks!' interrupted William, staggering across the garden towards her. 'What a load of tosh.'

Leo's father spun round to challenge William. 'I beg your pardon?' he said. 'Who are you?'

William glared at him. 'I said,' he repeated. 'Bollocks!'

A hush descended on the group.

'Oh, William, why don't you go inside?' said Heidi. 'Please, just don't.'

'Don't what?' he said. 'Why should I go inside? Am I not good enough for this family?'

'William,' interrupted Zoe, 'this isn't about you.'

'Your baby is lucky,' he said. 'It's wanted.'

'Please don't do this,' said Zoe, her face crumpling into tears.

Leo put his arms protectively around Zoe and glared at William. 'Shut up, you idiot!'

'It's alright for you,' he said. 'You and Scarlet had everything you wanted growing up! What about me? Out of the three of us, why was I the one that got tossed out on his ass? I didn't fit in, did I? Didn't fit into your rosy future.'

Heidi felt winded. 'It wasn't like that. This is Zoe's day,' she said coolly. 'Can't you put the past behind you?'

William lurched forward and knocked into a table of glasses. The table was unsteady and several cascaded over the edge and smashed on the ground. There was a communal gasp.

'No,' slurred William. 'I can't put the past behind me, because the past has made me who I am.'

Scarlet crossed the garden and stood in front of William's face.

'Go home,' she said to him. 'You're drunk, you're rude and you're ruining everything.'

William laughed. 'I don't have a home. Can you imagine what that's like, Scarlet? You're so entitled I don't suppose you can. You're all so smug.'

'Smug?' said Scarlet. 'We've all bent over backwards trying to include you in our lives.'

'Hardly,' he said. 'You've made it clear you resent me from the moment I met you. Johnny told me all about you, and I thought maybe we'd get on. I didn't expect you to treat me like something you found on your shoe. How do you think that feels, eh? Do you think your dad would be proud of you?'

William's face was contorted with fury, and he opened his mouth to continue, but he'd crossed a line and Scarlet had heard enough. Heidi stepped towards them, but before she could act, Scarlet raised her right hand and slapped William hard around the face.

'Go to hell,' she said, while he held his cheek and staggered backwards.

'Scarlet!' said Zoe, grabbing her arm and pulling her away from William.

Suddenly, Zoe bent forward, with her hands on her bump and groaned, obviously in pain.

'Oh my God, Zoe,' said Heidi, rushing towards her. 'Are you okay? Sit down. Please sit down. Someone get her some cold water.'

With Heidi on one side and Leo on the other, they helped Zoe over to the bench. Scarlet gave her a glass of water. She took a sip and closed her eyes.

'Happy now?' Scarlet spat at William, who looked terrified.

'Are you alright?' he asked in concern, ignoring Scarlet. 'Zoe, are you okay? You need to breathe. When Freddy was born, he came really quickly.'

'The baby's not coming,' said Zoe. 'I think he or she kicked me in a strange way, or it's a Braxton Hicks contraction.'

'You should come with me,' said Max to William, grabbing him by the elbow and steering him towards the workshop and slamming the door shut.

'Just rest there for a moment,' said Heidi, her heart in her mouth, gently stroking Zoe's back. 'Perhaps we should take you to the hospital?'

'It's okay,' Zoe said. 'It's passing. I definitely don't need to go to the hospital. I learned about these in my antenatal group. I just need to have a lie-down.'

'Do you want to go up to your room?' said Heidi.

'Maybe Zoe could come home with us for a bit?' said Shelley, Leo's mum. 'Just while you're sorting things out here? We have a lovely spare room where she can quietly rest. Leo will look after her, and we'll call if there's any change.'

'I-I'm so sorry about all this,' Heidi stuttered. 'We have a few family things going on… What do you think, Zoe? I just want you to be okay.'

'I think I'll go to Leo's for a bit,' she said. 'Sorry, Mum. Thank you.'

Heidi held in her tears and nodded, watching helplessly while the guests politely gathered their things. William and Max's raised voices emanated from the workshop. They were having one hell of an argument. Scarlet emptied her glass and shook her head at Heidi.

'Why didn't you tell William to go?' said Scarlet, gesturing at the workshop. 'Why are you letting Zoe leave, when it's a party for her? Why don't you tell William to just… fuck off out of our lives? He's just caused a massive scene!'

'Scarlet,' said Frankie. 'Calm down.'

Heidi sat down heavily on a chair.

'Scarlet,' Heidi said. 'You slapped William round the face. Why did you do that? How can that ever be the answer?'

Scarlet shook her head and grabbed Frankie's hand. 'I've had enough of you being so weak,' she said to Heidi. 'While William is still here, I'm going and I'm not coming back.'

'Scarlet, he needs our support,' said Heidi. 'This was your dad's wish. What don't you understand about that? I'm doing this for your dad! In his memory! This is about Johnny as much as it's about William! He wanted him to be a part of our lives. I'm trying to make that happen, for God's sake! Didn't you see that photo that William took of your dad when they met up? He was elated! He'd met his son! I'm trying to do the right thing.'

Scarlet looked taken aback but was already picking up her bag and leaving with Frankie, who made a quiet apology.

Heidi watched in dismay as her daughters left, followed by their friends and the neighbours.

'I think I'll take Rosalind home,' said Tuesday.

'Go ahead,' Heidi muttered.

Rosalind raised her hand in the air with a bemused 'bye' as Tuesday shepherded her out to the car.

The only people remaining were William and Max, their argument now less heated. She opened the workshop door and saw William sitting with his head in his hands. Max was leaning against the table, arms folded.

'I'll take it from here, Max, thank you,' said Heidi quietly. 'You can get off home.'

'I can wait,' he said, but Heidi shook her head.

'No!' she snapped. 'Just leave us alone, Max! Just get out! This is my business!'

Max looked hurt, and Heidi immediately regretted her anger but didn't have the energy to apologise.

'I'm on my phone if you need me,' he said quietly, collecting his coat and leaving by the back gate.

'I don't know what to say to you, William,' she said to the top of William's head. 'You've ruined Zoe's day. I wanted this day to be special. I desperately wanted Zoe to feel supported and loved. You've taken that away from her.'

'You ruined my life,' he slurred into his hands.

Heidi clenched her teeth and made her hands into fists. 'Don't be ridiculous. I didn't know what course your life would take, did I? How could I? I'm desperately sorry about all the bad things that have happened, but I've invited you into my life and welcomed you into my family. Why are you so intent on rejecting it?'

William shrugged. 'Well I'm sorry to have disturbed your cosy little life,' he said.

Heidi threw her head back and laughed maniacally. She felt unhinged.

'It's hardly cosy,' she said. 'My husband has just died after his second heart attack. My daughters have walked out. I've been desperately worried about you. Are you happy now?'

'I know you're disappointed in me,' he said. 'I don't need to listen to this.'

He stood and lurched towards her, shoving her out of the way. She stumbled backwards, watching him move to the windowsill. He picked up the musical trinket box and pulled out the drawer so the clown did its little dance while the music played.

'You kept this pathetic thing all these years,' he said. 'Why?'

'To keep you near me,' she said, her voice cracking. 'A memory of your birth.'

'That's rubbish,' he said. 'You didn't even want to find me! It was Johnny who found me. He told me that when you fell pregnant, he wanted to keep me, but you weren't having any of it.'

'You don't know what you're talking about, William,' she said through gritted teeth. 'Seriously, you have no idea. Johnny and I were very young. We had no idea we'd get married years later. I believe that we did the right thing.'

William glared at her then threw the box on the floor: the wood cracked, and the glass shattered. 'This is meaningless,' he said. 'And you're fake. Pretending to want to help me, when all you want to do is mould me into the right shape to fit into your life. Johnny met me alone because he knew that when you got involved, you'd try to change me. Isn't that right?'

She watched him step on the box and crush a piece of glass. Her heart cracked.

'Just get out of here!' she yelled. 'I wish Johnny had never found you!' Her hand shot to her mouth.

'I'm sorry,' she said, immediately regretting her outburst. 'William, I'm sorry; I didn't mean that.'

But the words had been said – and they couldn't be unsaid.

He pushed past her, knocked over a chair and stormed out of the workshop, leaving the back gate swinging open. Heidi followed him as he ran towards the clifftop, where he scrambled over the low cliff barrier fence, trampling over sea pinks and yellow gorse to stand much too close to the edge of the cliff.

'William,' she said, climbing over the fence to join him. 'Please come away from there.'

He sat down, his legs dangling over the edge. Her head swam with vertigo. All it would take was a slight movement. Gingerly, she sat down next to him.

'You don't understand,' he said. 'You don't understand what it's like to be rejected by so many people. It makes you feel worthless. And I keep on making mistake after mistake.'

'William, you're not worthless,' she said, taking hold of his hand. 'Please, I beg you, let's talk this all through. Life isn't straightforward. My life hasn't been straightforward either. There are things in your life that you're not happy with, but you can't go on blaming people for them your whole life. That's self-indulgent. Self-pity is your worst enemy.'

He clenched his jaw. 'Self-pitying. And you wished Johnny hadn't found me,' he said. 'Home truths, eh?'

Heidi bit into her lip until she tasted blood. 'Sorry, but I think you…' she started. Rain began to fall. And in the blink of an eye, his hand was no longer in hers.

Chapter Thirty-Three

Heidi lay on the bed, grief pinning her to the mattress like a stone. Night had thrown a dark blanket over the garden, which was exactly as she'd left it earlier – the potato salad crusting over, the crisps soggy, pavlova shrunken, deserted drinks.

She hadn't even swept up the broken glass. Apart from the sound of her breathing, the house was silent. In her mind, she played out the afternoon's events. One moment William's hand had been in hers. The next, he'd jumped up and climbed back over the barrier fence, shouting at her to leave him alone. Beneath the cliff edge, the dark water had swirled, and for a split second, she imagined leaping off and plunging into the water. Instead, she had followed William. Climbed over the barrier fence and moved to safety, watching him walk off into the distance, before she returned home feeling wounded and drained. Ignoring the detritus in the garden, she had grabbed a bottle of wine and a glass and floated upstairs to bed.

Hours later, a large full moon shone directly into her bedroom – a beautiful sight – but she couldn't move under the weight of all the mistakes she'd made. Her life as she had previously known it had slipped through her fingers. Evaporated. Seeds blown from a dandelion. And it was all her own doing. Her own stupid fault. Why had she said that awful thing to William? It wasn't true. She didn't wish she hadn't found him. But she felt angry with him. Why had he ruined Zoe's party? Why had he got so drunk and smashed her precious box? He was locked into a negative headspace, like a walnut in a hard shell. And what about the way she'd spoken to Scarlet? She hadn't meant to be so hard on her – Scarlet was in pain too. She'd lost her dad and was trying to protect their grieving family. Tuesday and Max had received the sharp end of her tongue too – she'd really blown it with everyone.

Sighing, she turned onto her side, picked up her mobile and scrolled through her photos, pausing at one of Johnny. She longed to talk to him. Craved his reassurance, his smile, his warm touch. She squeezed her eyes tightly shut, trying to figure out what to do. Was her family broken beyond repair?

Moments later, her phone pinged with a message – a reply from Zoe.

'I'm fine, Mum,' it said. 'I feel perfectly fine. I'm going to stay here for a few days as I'm being waited on hand and foot!'

Heidi fell into a pit of despair. She should be waiting on her daughter hand and foot. She should be preparing the bedroom ready for the baby's arrival. She so wanted to find a suitable chair, similar to the rose chair she'd so loved, for in front of the window, so Zoe could sit there with her baby in her arms. Instead, she was in the middle of a mess.

Tapping out an upbeat reply, she also messaged Scarlet, apologising for her tough words. Scarlet replied with a couple of kisses, but no words. That was no surprise – she was angry and hurting. There was nothing from William.

Heidi felt desolate and closed her eyes, waiting for sleep to come, hoping to dream of nothing.

She spent the next few days worrying so much, she was incapable of doing anything useful, and the days and nights merged into one. She made calls to Zoe, to check up on how she was doing – and was pleased to hear she was feeling fine. Scarlet and Rosalind called her, but she didn't pick up. Instead, she sent a text after they'd left a voicemail, saying she'd call them tomorrow and that she was busy trying to catch up on things, and that there was nothing to worry about. 'Let's move on,' she tapped out, though she hadn't moved anywhere in days.

Almost a week passed by and she still hadn't cleaned up the garden. Lying in bed late one morning, she bolted upright when she heard Walter calling her from outside. Clients weren't supposed to come to the house – only the workshop – but he banged on the kitchen door for so long and called out her name at the top of his voice that she worried something awful had happened to Rosalind. She ran downstairs and opened the door, still wearing her dressing gown, her hair sticking up like a hedge on her head.

'What's going on?' he said, gesturing behind him at the remains of the party, then noticing the mess in the kitchen. 'Are you sick? Does your mother know?'

The look of concern on Walter's face squeezed Heidi's heart. She forced herself to smile.

'I'm not sick,' she said. 'Can I help you? Is my mother okay?'

'She's perfectly well,' he said. 'Are *you* okay?'

She nodded. 'I will be. I've just lost track of time. I need to get on with… I'll be fine.'

'Mrs Eagle,' he said again. 'I really do need that chair looking at – the one I talked to you about. Perhaps you could spare the time? As I said, I need it quite urgently.'

He looked at her with such kindness and gentleness, a tear dripped down her cheek. She swiped it away.

'My dear girl,' he said. 'I don't know what's gone on here, but here's my penny's worth. My generation never talked about their feelings, but I always found that keeping busy helped me. When Lily, my wife, was younger, she was always there, ready to catch me when I fell. And I did fall, several times over. Now she's poorly, you know, with dementia, I'm there for her. Everyone needs that really, don't they? Someone to catch them, should they fall. Do you have that?'

She thought of William and that he felt nobody was there for him. Heidi's throat was thick with the need to cry. She managed to nod and offer Walter a small smile.

'So,' he said, straightening up. 'When you have time to pick up my chair, that would be very helpful. I'd love to take it next time I visit Lily.'

'Visit?' said Heidi. 'Has she… where is she?'

'I couldn't carry on looking after her at home,' he said. 'She's gone into a care home, overlooking the sea. It's very nice, but she needs her chair… that's why I asked for your help.'

Heidi pulled the band from her wrist and tied back her hair.

'Of course,' she said. 'I'll pop in tomorrow.'

Walter raised his hand and staggered out of the garden, crunching on the glass as he went.

'Thank you,' he said.

'Careful,' she called after him as he slipped out of the gate. 'Thank you.'

She surveyed the rotting mess in the garden, the state of the kitchen, and though she felt completely overwhelmed by it, Walter's presence and seeing the place through his eyes shocked her into action. She pulled on an apron and a pair of rubber gloves and started to tackle it. There were unopened bottles of wine on the side that guests had brought. Cards for Zoe and Leo. Two bunches of flowers that had wilted. Heidi blushed at the waste.

Taking bin bags out into the garden, she picked up the pieces of broken glass and plates of moulded food and cleared up the remains of the party. As she worked, she thought of the broken musical trinket box on the workshop floor – and tears flooded her eyes.

'I can never throw it away,' she whispered. 'I'll fix it.'

Slipping into the workshop, she carefully picked up the pieces. The hand-painted wood case was cracked, the glass shattered, but the clown was still intact – and, pulling out the drawer, the music still played.

Laying out the pieces on the worktop, she located the tools she needed, the wood glue and measured the glass she would need to replace. Fully concentrating on the box, she didn't hear the back gate open and jumped when Tuesday stuck her head around the workshop door.

'Thought you'd be in here!' she said. She was dressed in a sundress covered in red apples. It was impossible not to smile at the sight of her.

'I've been calling you,' she said, walking straight over to Heidi and hugging her. 'What's going on?'

Heidi hugged her back. 'I'm sorry. I just needed a few days to lick my wounds. I've made a bit of a mess of things. I'm sorry about how I was the other day.'

'That's okay,' said Tuesday. 'I was pretty short with you too. But I think we need to talk. Do you?'

Heidi nodded. 'Come inside,' she said. 'But I warn you, it's not pretty.'

Tuesday made a pot of tea while Heidi cleared away the last of the dirty dishes and they moved into the living room, taking a seat on the Chesterfield sofa. Tuesday poured the tea.

'This is so presumptuous of me,' she said, putting the teapot down. 'I think that's the problem here, isn't it? I've just barged my way into your life, and you haven't really had a say in the matter, have you?'

Heidi opened her mouth and closed it again. Then she leaned her head back and sighed.

'Tuesday, you've been an absolute delight,' she said. 'My mother – our mother – is clearly enamoured by you, which is wonderful.'

Tuesday stayed quiet for a moment and took a sip of her tea. Then she said, 'If we're to be real sisters, I think we need to be really honest with each other. Go on – tell me how you really feel.'

Heidi smiled and nodded. 'I think you're great,' she said. 'I really do. Everyone does. I suppose I just feel that my mother has opened up to you in a way she hasn't with me. You seem to have got so close in such a short space of time.'

Heidi gave Tuesday a wobbly smile. Tuesday reached for her hand and gave it a squeeze.

'I don't think she treats me like a daughter,' said Tuesday. 'I think she treats me more like a younger sister – and perhaps that's where the confusion is. She spends most of the time talking about you and your girls. I don't have any intention of taking your place, Heidi. Don't forget I have my own parents, who I love very much.'

'Oh, Tuesday, I know that – of course I do. I guess I've been feeling a bit jealous. When you first came into my life, I thought you and I could become close, but then you and Mum got close first. It's childish, I know. I was excited about us being sisters.'

Tuesday inched along the Chesterfield and gave Heidi a hug.

'I'd love to spend more time with you,' she said. 'But you have so much going on. I didn't want to get in the way. I'm sorry how I spoke to you about Max too. It's your business. You're the one with the history and the friendship. It's nothing to do with me.'

Heidi laughed gently and shook her head. 'Max is my friend and will never be any more than that,' she said. 'I think you should ask him out. Go on a date. You might have fun together. Honestly, you have my blessing. Johnny has only just gone and I could never imagine having a relationship with anyone else. I just need to concentrate on the girls and on William, but I've wrecked everything.'

'You haven't wrecked anything,' said Tuesday.

'I told William I wished I'd never found him,' Heidi said. 'He'll never speak to me again.'

Tuesday twirled the ring on her finger round and round.

'Rosalind wrote to me years ago telling me not to get in touch ever again,' she said. 'It broke my heart. I thought that was it – over, dreams smashed. But look at us now. Never say never. Try again, if that's what you want to do. We all need to give each other second chances. Second. Third. Possibly fourth.'

Heidi nodded. 'That's not what Scarlet would say. She's more of a "one strike and you're out" type of person.'

'I think she'll surprise you,' said Tuesday. 'I think she needed to hear what you said at the party too. You've done all of this for Johnny. She knows that underneath. She's just being protective of you.'

Heidi nodded, feeling suddenly utterly exhausted. She yawned and stretched her arms above her head.

'You look like you haven't got out of that dressing gown in a week,' said Tuesday. 'Why don't you go and get showered while I finish off in the kitchen with those last few bits and pieces?'

Tuesday picked up the teapot and carried it into the kitchen. In the shower, Heidi could hear her singing along to the radio outside and a little ray of sunshine shone into her heart. Letting the hot water run over her face, she knew what she had to do. She had to ask William for a second chance.

Chapter Thirty-Four

'No, he's moved on,' said Ian, William's old 'flatmate'. 'He hasn't been here for ages. Left a pair of socks here. But no sign of the man himself. You could ask Martha.'

Heidi sighed. 'I rang her,' she said. 'She hasn't seen him either, or heard from him, which is strange. I'm worried. Do you think he'd... he'd... do something stupid?'

Ian shook his head. 'No,' he said. 'His mum, she... He wouldn't do that to Freddy. No way.'

Heidi's shoulders sagged with relief. 'You're probably right,' she said. 'Thank you. If you hear from him, please tell him to call Heidi. Tell him I've been trying to contact him – and that it's urgent.'

Ian's flat had been Heidi's second port of call. She'd tried Martha, who spoke to her in whispers, because she was on holiday in Greece with Freddy and her new boyfriend. When Heidi asked if Martha had told William about the holiday or the new boyfriend, Martha had said, 'I'm not as bad as you like to think,' and put the phone down.

Heidi didn't know where else to look. She didn't know his other friends, though he was often talking to people on his mobile. Finding someone without having a clue where they might be was like finding a needle in a haystack. It made her realise how little she knew about him.

Driving through Poole, she slowed down at every doorway where someone was sleeping rough. There were so many. Far too many. She went to the One Stop shop she'd seen William at before and lurked outside for an hour, wondering if he might come in. She tried the Blackbird Café and asked one of the waitresses. Then, she went into several betting shops, scanning the people inside, seething with anger and sorrow at the advertising, the lures, the pointless 'when it's no longer fun, stop' messaging all over the walls. She rang around the hospitals. But he was nowhere. And he was still not picking up his phone.

'Just leave it for a while,' she instructed herself, deciding to return to the workshop.

In an attempt to distract herself from all her worries and woes, Heidi focused on her work. She hadn't spoken to Max since she'd been so rude to him at the party – and couldn't face calling him in to help out with the outstanding jobs. She would get on top of things herself.

Switching on the radio and tidying up the workshop, she finished the dancing-clown trinket box first, placing it on the windowsill where it had stood before William had smashed it. She wanted him to have it. Johnny would want him to have it. Perhaps on his birthday, if he ever came back. 'Please come back,' she said over and over in her head.

When Annie came to collect the 'Barry' chair, Heidi was transported back to the day that Johnny had died. She tried not to convey the heart-breaking memory of that day on her face as Annie talked about the cruise she'd been on.

'I've had the best few weeks of my life,' she told Heidi. 'How about you?'

Heidi almost laughed – it was better than crying. Not knowing where to start, she sidestepped the question and showed Annie the cocktail chair. Annie gave her a quick hug.

'My husband will be delighted,' she said. 'Our memory of Barry will live on! Thank you.'

When Heidi visited Walter, he was tending his balcony garden. He seemed genuinely overjoyed to see her, inviting her inside his small flat, which was decorated with a lifetime of photos of himself and his wife Lily. His flat was underneath Rosalind's but couldn't be more different. Where hers was spartan, Walter's was packed with possessions; ornaments, pictures, books, things. It reminded her of the workshop and made her feel instantly at home.

He showed her the chair he wanted her to reupholster – an armchair covered in brown wool fabric – and which was one of two positioned in front of the window overlooking the sea. On the windowsill was a family of pottery Siamese cat ornaments, all with piercing blue eyes. The sight of the two armchairs pulled at Heidi's heartstrings. Those chairs were at the heart of so many conversations.

'I talk to that chair as if she's in it!' Walter said. 'Those cats must think I'm crazy! Your mum tells me I am.'

He smiled at his own joke and Heidi laughed gently, warmly.

'As I said before, I think I should have the chair with her, and to be honest I'm concerned there's not that much time left,' he said, with sadness in his eyes. 'She loved sitting in this chair, and I'd love to make it more comfortable for her. Sounds silly, but you have to hold on to these small things, threads from the past. When the big things get taken away, the small things mean a lot.'

'I'll do it straight away,' said Heidi. 'Of course.'

'Thank you, my love,' he said. 'Are you visiting your mother today? I see she has someone staying with her. A lady with pink hair!'

Heidi nodded and smiled. 'That's Tuesday,' she said. 'My half-sister.'

'Which half?' said Walter with a gentle laugh. 'Left or right?'

'I suppose I should just say "my sister",' she said, 'shouldn't I?'

'Why "suppose"?' he asked.

Heidi sat down and sighed. 'No reason. She's only recently come into my life and it's taken some getting used to, that's all. She's a lovely person. Mum loves her.'

'The more love there is floating around, the better, in my opinion,' Walter said. 'You can never have too much of the stuff. I'm close to the end of my life now and I wish I'd loved more loudly, more expansively, just *more*. Because before you know it, you've run out of opportunities.'

Heidi nodded and gave Walter a little smile.

'Okay, I'd better get upstairs,' she said. 'I'll collect your chair on my way out and reupholster it for you. I have some almost identical fabric.'

'That's marvellous,' he said, opening the door. 'Thank you.'

Upstairs, Rosalind and Tuesday were sitting on the balcony, surrounded by galvanised metal buckets of red and pink geraniums. Rosalind had got rid of the sunlounger she normally made use of and installed two deckchairs instead – so the two of them could sit there together.

'Don't worry,' said Rosalind, before Heidi could say a word. 'There's one for you too. I know you like red, so I've reserved this one for you.'

She set up a third deckchair, a red-and-white-striped one, and the three of them sat on the balcony overlooking the sea, which was dead calm. Paddleboarders and kayakers were enjoying the flat conditions, and several families were camped out under colourful umbrellas and sun tents. Tuesday offered to make tea and biscuits, while Rosalind and Heidi caught up about William.

'It's hard to hear, but maybe he just doesn't want to see you at the moment,' said Rosalind. 'Things don't always work out how you want them to. People often aren't who you want them to be.'

Rosalind's words grated on Heidi. 'I know that,' she said. 'Christ, of course I know that! Okay, so he doesn't want me in his life. I'm just supposed to accept that and never contact him again? What sort of person would I be if I did that?'

Her nose and throat burned with tears.

'Give it some time,' advised Rosalind gently, patting Heidi's knee. 'I didn't mean to upset you. I just want you to look after your heart. Things can change. Look how things have changed for me. I've got you to thank for that, Heidi.'

They both glanced towards the kitchen, where Tuesday was laying out cups and saucers on a tray.

'I'm glad you're happy,' said Heidi. 'You didn't even want to meet Tuesday at first.'

'I know,' said Rosalind softly. 'But I was just so scared of the prospect. You persuaded me to because you're a wonderful daughter and you have a big heart. It turned out really well. I'm lucky; I know that. I feel like I've got a new lease of life.'

Heidi smiled.

'I love you,' said Rosalind quietly. 'You know that, don't you?'

'I love you too,' said Heidi.

Tuesday walked towards them and set the tray down on the table before settling herself into a deckchair. She started to tell them both about where her parents lived in France and that she was planning to go out to visit them next month to fill them in about everything.

'If you ever want to come with me for a break,' she said to Heidi. 'I'd love that. My parents would love to meet you.'

Tuesday was looking at Heidi with such hope in her eyes, Heidi's heart contracted. She reached over to Tuesday and gave her a brief hug.

'Thank you,' she said. 'I'd love that.'

From inside her bag, Heidi's phone rang and, seeing Scarlet was calling, she quickly answered.

'Mum?' said Scarlet. 'Can you come to the hospital? Zoe's gone into labour.'

'Oh my God,' said Heidi. 'Is she doing okay?'

'Yes,' said Scarlet. 'But it's coming quite quickly. Leo's not here yet.'

Heidi stood up from the deckchair, knocking into the tray, the phone still pressed to her ear.

'What is it?' Rosalind asked, her face full of concern.

'The baby's coming,' Heidi said to Rosalind and Tuesday, then addressed Scarlet. 'I'm on my way.'

Chapter Thirty-Five

Scarlet waited at the entrance of the hospital and waved enthusiastically at Heidi as she rushed towards her. Quickly, they embraced before Scarlet filled her in on the details.

'How is she?' Heidi asked, her heart pounding in her chest, gripping the strap of her bag over her shoulder. 'Is she okay?'

'She's fine,' said Scarlet calmly. 'There's nothing to worry about; it's all happening as it should. She's just a little bit early, but not too early. Leo arrived about five minutes ago and is with her now. She's quite advanced and is in active labour. Shall we sit in the café for a while? Leo said he'd call the moment the baby is born.'

Heidi exhaled with relief, so grateful that Zoe's labour was progressing normally. There was no reason to think it wouldn't, but it was still a worry. She thought about Johnny and how he'd feel if he was here. Swallowing back the tears, she knew he'd be nervous as hell.

Heidi and Scarlet walked arm in arm through the hospital reception area towards the café, where Scarlet ordered them both coffees. They took a seat by the window, which overlooked the car park. Heidi stared out at the people rushing to and fro, their lives loaded with good and bad news, shocks and relief. Only months before, she'd been here and seen Johnny's lifeless body, and now she was waiting for her grandchild to be born – how quickly life changes. She sipped her coffee and smiled at Scarlet, regretting that their last exchanges had been so angry.

'So, what happened?' Heidi asked. 'If Leo wasn't around, did you bring Zoe in?'

Scarlet looked down at the table for a moment, before looking back up to meet Heidi's gaze. A pink bloom coloured her cheeks and she suddenly looked twelve years old again.

'William brought her in,' Scarlet said. 'Me and William brought her into the hospital.'

'William?' said Heidi, utterly confused. 'How? What? Why was William…?'

She let her words trail off, frowning at Scarlet while she waited for an explanation. Scarlet sighed and put her palms flat on the table.

'Don't be mad at me for not telling you,' Scarlet said quietly, 'but after the party, after what you said about finding William being Dad's wish, that you were doing all this for Dad, I went to see William to talk to him. I haven't been fair to him right from the start. I don't know why. I think I felt protective of you – of us.'

'You went to see him?' asked Heidi. 'How did you know where to find him?'

'I went to his son's school,' said Scarlet. 'And waited for him there.' She took a sip of her coffee. 'I suddenly realised that him and me weren't that different,' she continued. 'I've been so angry about Dad dying, and he's so angry about lots of things. I thought we should talk. I thought I should give William a second chance.'

'Scarlet, I'm… I'm…' Heidi stuttered, 'shocked.'

'He was going to crash at a friend's house and I thought that if he did that his situation would never change but also that our situation would never change,' she said. 'I've had to face up to reality. You would be worrying about him, he would never get out of the hopeless situation he's in and Dad's wish would never be fulfilled. I thought he could do with some help, but one step removed. So I organised for him to stay with Max.'

'Max?' said Heidi, surprised that he hadn't told her about it, though of course she hadn't see him since the party.

'Yes. Max has put all these rules in place, and William agreed to stick to them. We were together, me, Zoe and William, when

Zoe's contractions started. We were trying to sort things out a bit between us before getting you involved again. We wanted to give you some breathing space. Anyway, then Zoe went into labour and so William drove us here in Max's van. He's put William on his insurance, you see.'

'Is he here?' asked Heidi, stunned by the news.

'No,' she said. 'He said he didn't want to intrude. He told me he'd come if we needed him and that he'd do whatever we needed and to tell him the news when the baby was born. He got quite emotional. I think it brought back memories of Freddy being born.'

'Wow,' said Heidi. 'I don't know what to say.'

'You don't need to say anything,' said Scarlet. 'Frankie made me see things in a different way. I've been so unfair to you, while you've been grieving and trying to do the right thing. I'm so sorry.'

Heidi leaned over the table to hug Scarlet. 'You've nothing to apologise for,' she said. 'I should be apologising to you for everything that's happened. And I should also be thanking you for being so grown up about this and going to see William. I'm proud of you, Scarlet. So, has William had a change of heart? He seemed so full of resentment at the party.'

Scarlet leaned back in her chair. 'I think he was full of beer. He's stopped drinking. He says he's never going to touch the stuff again. When we talked he got really upset and told Zoe and I that you and our family mean a lot to him, but that he has a self-destruct button that he presses when someone appears to be precious. Don't get me wrong, he's got a long way to go. We all have, but I think this is better than how it was. I just wanted to make something better, rather than ripping everything up for once. You know what I'm like.'

Heidi wiped at a tear that was dripping down her cheek and hugged Scarlet once more, her heart swelling with pride. This must have all been so hard for Scarlet, but she'd overcome her anger and her suspicion and had found space in her heart to give William another chance.

Heidi glanced at the clock. They'd been sitting there for over an hour. Suddenly, an ash-faced Leo appeared at the table, his hands clearly trembling.

'What?' said Heidi, shooting up from her seat. 'Is she okay?'

Leo smiled and nodded as tears leaked from his eyes.

'She's done it,' he said, blinking in wonder. 'We've had a boy. We have a son. We've called him Johnny. Johnny William.'

Heidi couldn't hold in the tears now. Throwing her arms around Leo, she wept with joy.

Chapter Thirty-Six

It was Heidi's birthday – and William's too. Max had phoned early, when Heidi was only just out of bed and drinking tea with Zoe and Leo at the kitchen table. Leo held baby Johnny in his arms while Zoe gave Heidi a beautiful vintage photograph frame decorated with tiny hand-painted flowers and a bunch of fragrant cream roses for her birthday. This was her first birthday for as long as she could remember without Johnny, and quietly, she missed him terribly.

'It's a big day,' Max said on the phone. 'Would you like to come over for coffee? I know Johnny had a birthday surprise planned for today for you – and it hasn't quite worked out how he wanted it to, but William would like to see you. *I'd* like to see you. We thought we could go for a swim together. We've been doing a lot of swimming. It's been going well actually, Heidi. You'll be proud of William.'

It would be the first time she'd seen William since the awful day on the cliff, though she'd heard more stories about him and how delighted he seemed to be an uncle from both her daughters since she and Scarlet had spoken in the hospital.

She had also spoken to Max, who had explained how he'd given William an ultimatum and that William had accepted.

'Remember I gave you one of those years ago?' he'd said, the sound of a smile in his voice. 'Didn't quite go as I'd hoped.'

'I remember,' Heidi had said gently.

Max had offered William a room if he promised to attend the sessions with Andy and persuaded him to change his mobile to one of the old-fashioned ones without internet access, so he wouldn't be tempted by gambling apps. He wasn't to touch alcohol and he had to swim in the sea, with Max, every day, for at least an hour, whatever the weather. If he slipped up, even once, he was out on his ear.

Heidi didn't know how she felt about all of this. She was grateful to Max, but also disappointed that she hadn't been able to do the same thing – that what she had offered William wasn't enough. 'It's not that your help wasn't enough,' Max had told her gently, reading her mind. 'I think it was too much. There was so much riding on it, Heidi, for you both. Think about it. You're both suffering in different ways, with grief, loss and, in William's case, addiction. You need time to heal before taking each other on – that's how I see it. As someone looking in.'

Heidi dressed carefully. Choosing her button earrings and a grey linen dress, she thought of Johnny and the years that they'd been married, but also when they'd first met in Johnny's family's shop; when they were innocent young things. She smiled at the thought.

'Do you want me to come with you?' asked Zoe when Heidi said goodbye, the clown trinket box wrapped in tissue paper in her bag.

'No,' she said, giving baby Johnny a kiss on his cheek. 'I'll be fine. You've got your hands full here.'

Max must have been waiting by the front door he opened it so promptly.

'Come in, Heidi,' he said. 'William's out in the garden. Happy birthday to you.'

'Thanks, Max,' she said, patting his arm. 'Thank you for everything.'

Trembling, Heidi walked through Max's hallway, through the kitchen and out towards the garden. A wall of photographs caught her eye and she stopped briefly to admire them. He didn't have Johnny's talent, but Max had captured some wonderful images of Jane and their son, Ben. There was one of Heidi and Johnny, too, at a party on the beach, taken years ago. They were both holding glasses and laughing at something. They looked so happy it brought tears to Heidi's eyes. Quickly, she blinked them away.

'Hi,' said William when Heidi walked into the garden, her legs jelly. Briefly, they embraced. 'Happy birthday.'

'Happy birthday to you,' she said, smiling as she took a seat. They both gave a little laugh. William sat down opposite her while Max crashed around in the kitchen making coffee. Just the sight of William made Heidi feel emotional. Tears threatened to fall.

'I'm sorry for what I said about wishing Johnny hadn't found you,' Heidi began. 'It wasn't true. Not at all true. I was angry. I guess I've felt pretty angry since Johnny died. Probably since he had his first heart attack actually.'

William's knee jogged up and down nervously. He gave her a small smile and nodded in understanding.

'I was angry too,' he said quietly. 'I have been angry for so long. I was angry when I found out I was adopted. Angry that I didn't get on with my stepdad. Angry that my mum took her own life. Angry that my marriage failed. Angry that I couldn't stop gambling. Angry that my photography career fell flat. Angry that Johnny died. Angry that I couldn't give my son the things he wanted. Angry that I couldn't accept your kindness. Angry with myself most of the time. Just so bloody angry!'

He half laughed and pushed his hand through his hair. Heidi reached over to him and gently touched his hand.

'I know,' she said. 'You've had a lot to be angry about.'

'It was easier to be furious with the world,' he replied. 'When I met you, I wanted to find a reason to be angry because I knew I'd lose you anyway, in the end. It was better to push you away, keep you at a distance. And then, when you said you wished Johnny hadn't found me, I felt validated. I knew I'd lost you. I'd been proven right, so I could go on feeling furious with the world.'

'You haven't lost me,' said Heidi, through tears. 'I've been desperate to talk to you, desperate to see you, but I gathered you needed some space and thought I should respect that.'

William nodded. 'I wanted the next time we saw each other to be different,' he said. 'I wanted to be stronger and know that I'm not going to let you down again. Will you give me a second chance?'

'You haven't let me down,' said Heidi. 'And yes, of course I will. Will you give *me* a second chance?'

'Yes, of course,' he said, with a smile. 'Not that you need to ask for one. Heidi, I want you to know that I understand why I was adopted and that I loved my mum more than anything. She was a wonderful person and loved me very much. I think her death floored me and I guess I felt rejected, in a way. I thought if she couldn't stay alive for me, there must be something seriously wrong with me.'

'There's nothing wrong with you,' said Heidi. 'Your poor mother. I'd love to hear more about her. I've always wondered about her. I don't intend to try to replace her, William. I would just like to know you. To love you.'

William smiled and wiped his eyes. After a few moments, he jumped up from his chair.

'I've got something for your birthday,' he said. 'It's to show you that I too would like us to get to know each other properly. And to apologise for how I've been.'

He disappeared inside Max's house and came out carrying something big, hidden under a decorating sheet. He gestured that she could take the sheet off – and when she did, she saw a spoon-back chair with a seat embroidered with roses, recently restored and reupholstered. It was almost the same as the one at Joanna's house – the beautiful chair where she'd nursed William. She gasped.

'It's fantastic,' she said. 'I've been looking for one like this forever!'

'Max helped me bring it back to life,' he said. 'It might not be perfect, but I found it on eBay. It's pretty similar, isn't it? What do you think?'

Heidi traced one of the embroidered roses with a finger.

'It's beautiful,' she said. 'Thank you so much. I'm really touched by this. And I've had a great idea. I can put this in Zoe's room, so she can sit with baby Johnny there, in the sunshine.'

She swallowed, knowing that she couldn't keep the tears in for much longer.

'I've got something for you,' she said, handing William the musical trinket box. 'I know, when you were angry, you said it didn't mean anything, but this box has always meant so much to me. It marked the day you were born and Johnny sent it to me at Joanna's house where I had you. I've kept it all these years, tucked away. I've repaired it, because I want you to have it.'

William's eyes misted over. He swallowed and gently opened the box, pulling out the drawer and looking at the Polaroid inside.

'Thank you,' he said. 'Really, thank you for this.'

Heidi moved towards William and they embraced, holding on to each other for a long few moments, half crying, half laughing.

'You'll start me off in a minute,' Max said from the kitchen doorway, holding a couple of cups of coffee. 'Anyone fancy a swim instead of coffee? It's a perfect day for it.'

The beach was almost empty. There was no breeze, and the sea was flat and silvery, warmth coming from the sunshine that broke through the clouds. Seagulls hovered in the sky above, keeping a beady eye on the nanny goats munching the shrubs on the cliffs.

Max and William changed and went straight into the water, while Heidi sat on a towel and thought about Johnny and the birthday present he would have revealed had he still been alive.

She admired him, for taking such a huge step to find William on his own – and she missed him, beyond words.

'Thank you for my gift,' she whispered. 'Thank you for our son.'

Standing, she pulled off her dress to reveal her swimming costume. Leaving her clothes in a small pile on her towel, she grabbed her goggles and ran towards the sea and into the cold water, letting out a yelp when she submerged her shoulders. Then she put her face into the water and opened her eyes, looking at the wavy patterns in the sand on the seabed.

Lifting her head back up, she spotted Max and William, a little further out from the shore. They waved at her, and she waved back, smiling with abandon, before swimming to join them, full of hope and light.

Epilogue

'Is everyone ready for this?' Heidi said, standing at the water's edge, holding the green frog pot of Johnny's ashes out in front of her. 'I think he's ready to leap in.'

The family had come to the beach before sunrise. Rosalind was wrapped in a thick cardigan and had her arm linked through Tuesday's; Scarlet and Frankie held hands; Leo stood tall, a new father with his hand on Zoe's shoulder as she cradled baby Johnny in her arms; William clutched several stems of roses and Max busied himself setting up a chair for Rosalind to sit on. Now, at just after 5 a.m., the sky was staggering. The rising sun painted brushstrokes of orange and gold and pink across the sky. Gentle waves lapped rhythmically on the sand while Heidi pulled off her sandals, wading a little way into the water. The sea was cool and clear, inviting. Tiny fish darted about her ankles. Heidi opened the pot and cleared her throat.

'We all miss you, Johnny,' she said, her voice cracking slightly. 'And we all love you, have loved you, will keep on loving you, but I can't keep you trapped in this pot any longer on the workshop shelf. It's time for you to be free; out here on your favourite beach, in the sea, in the wind, part of nature. Goodbye, Johnny – and thank you.'

When she said 'thank you', she glanced at William and he gave her a smile, before she lifted the pot into the air and released the ashes. Max started the applause and then they all joined in – Scarlet and Frankie cheering through tears.

As the ashes scattered across the water, a seagull called out, and a small wave swept them further out to sea, like a hand reaching out to gather him up, accepting him. Heidi stood there for a moment, looking out to sea, feeling calm and peaceful, before wading back towards the beach.

'Would you like me to take a photograph?' asked William. 'I've got the camera.'

'Yes,' said Heidi. 'Yes please. But can you do it on a timer, so you can be in it too?'

They arranged themselves into a group, with Zoe at the heart, baby Johnny on her lap.

'Huddle in,' Heidi said, bringing the family in closer, tighter.

They all stood still, waiting for the shutter to go off, and Heidi was struck by a memory of the Polaroid of herself and William – how alone she'd seemed in that photograph. It wouldn't be like that for Zoe – she'd make sure of that.

She reached for William's hand and squeezed. Baby Johnny would never be alone. His family were all around him – a big safety net of love, ready to catch him should he ever fall. And wasn't that what everybody needed? Anyone, whatever their story, whatever mistakes they'd made or decisions they lived to regret. Someone to be there offering a second chance. A hand to hold, no matter what.

The Bournemouth *Gazette*

Birth Notice

HANSON, Johnny William, born on 10 June, to Zoe (née Eagle) and Leo, weighing 7lbs 3oz. A treasured grandson to Heidi, great-grandson to Rosalind, nephew to Scarlet and William, and great-nephew to Tuesday. A new chapter begins.

A Letter from Amy

Dear Reader,

I want to say a huge thank you for choosing to read *The Day My Husband Left*. If you did enjoy it and want to keep up to date with all my latest releases, just sign up at the following link. Your email address will never be shared and you can unsubscribe at any time.

www.bookouture.com/amy-miller

I am a firm believer in second chances. I think if we were all more understanding and honest with one another, people would suffer less. If there's one thing I'd like this book to be about it's the importance of giving people a second chance. Many families have secrets or issues they never speak of because it's too painful, or they're worried about what people will think – and adoption can in some circumstances be one of those difficult issues. Adoption is something that has historically affected close members of my own family, and its conversations around this subject that helped inspire this book. I hope to show that, even when things don't turn out how you hoped, with understanding and patience, problems can be overcome. Also, I think when people suffer from serious illness such as heart disease, as Johnny does in the book, life is brought into sharp focus – the past, the present and the future. It's at these times when people think 'now or never' and take brave steps they've perhaps previously avoided.

A note on upholstery: I am not an upholsterer and though I've spoken to experts in the field, I hope you can forgive any inaccuracies in terminology or practice! I chose to make Heidi an upholsterer because she gives pieces of furniture a second chance and doesn't give up on them. This is her approach to William when she is reunited with him and vice versa – everyone deserves a second chance.

Finally, I've set the story in Southbourne-on-Sea, Bournemouth, which is close to where I live and where I, like Heidi, enjoy swimming in the sea to clear my head. Though various locations do exist, I've changed names and street names.

Amy Miller

 AmyMillerBooks

 @AmyBratley1

Acknowledgements

I would like to thank the amazing team at Bookouture, including Helen Jenner and Kim Nash, as well as my agent Veronique Baxter. I'm hugely thankful to family and friends for sharing their life experiences and whose stories around adoption have helped inspire this book. I also read many moving stories online and found information on websites including bemyparent.org.uk, first4adoption.org. uk, adoptionuk.org, adoption.com, www.adoptionsearchreunion. org.uk, movementforanadoptionapology.org, helpwithadoption. com and on newspaper websites including *The Irish Times* and the *Guardian*.

To better understand the grief a person feels after losing their partner I found cruse.org.uk helpful, and a friend recommended Megan Devine's podcasts and website refugeingrief.com, which is incredibly insightful and moving. I researched people's experiences of heart disease online and read many people's moving stories about recovery. What struck me was how many partners of someone who'd had a heart attack felt so fearful about the future and whether it would happen again. That sense of living in fear and alongside anxiety helped form Heidi's character.

Websites on the subject I found particularly helpful include bhf. org.uk, lifeaftercardiacarrest.org and sca-aware.org, among others.

Finally, though the book doesn't delve deeply into gambling addiction, I found case studies and information on gamcare.org. uk and gamblingtherapy.org a useful source of research, as well as a heart-wrenching programme on BBC Radio 4, *My husband the gambling addict* which happened to come onto the radio when I was parking one day – and I stayed in the car to listen to.

Thanks to my upholsterer friend Vicky Grubb, of theupholstery-cabin.co.uk. She has a beautiful studio space in her garden which helped inform my idea, plus I loved reading her book, *Beginner's Guide to Upholstery*. Vicky kindly helped with some of my questions. I was also inspired by the work of Simion Hawtin-Smith of relovedupholstery.co.uk, who breathes new life into vintage chairs.

Finally, I very much enjoyed the lovely stories told in the BBC's *Repair Shop* and hoped to inject into *The Day My Husband Left* some of that warmth and hope in the fact that old, tired things can be rescued and brought back to life. Inspiration and ideas always come from so many places and people – I do hope I haven't forgotten to mention anyone.

Thanks finally to my lovely family, friends, swimming pals and to my husband Jimmy and children, Sonny and Audrey.

Made in the USA
Monee, IL
18 June 2021

71693115R00144